Edited by Jack Dann & Gardner Dozois

D1287957

FUTURE CRIMES

EDITED BY
JACK DANN & GARDNER DOZOIS

2003
50TH
ANNIVERSARY
ACE BOOKS, NEW YORK

FUTURE CRIMES

An Ace Book / published by arrangement with
the editors

PRINTING HISTORY
Ace mass-market edition / December 2003

Copyright © 2003 by Jack Dann and Gardner Dozois.
Cover art by Getty Images.
"Woman Surrounded by Network of Grids and Lines (Digital Composite)" © 2003 by Zap Art.
Cover design by Rita Frangie.

For information address: The Berkley Publishing Group, a division of Penguin Group (USA) Inc., 375 Hudson Street, New York, New York 10014.

ISBN: 0-441-01118-7

ACE®
Ace Books are published by The Berkley Publishing Group, a division of Penguin Group (USA) Inc., 375 Hudson Street, New York, New York 10014. ACE and the "A" design are trademarks belonging to Penguin Group (USA) Inc.

PRINTED IN THE UNITED STATES OF AMERICA

10 9 8 7 6 5 4 3 2 1

CONTENTS

PREFACE

For thousands of years, an evolutionary arms-race has been going on between the guardians of the Law and those who want to break it. Usually, the criminals are a step or two ahead, thinking of clever new ways to Get Away With It—until the Law catches up with them, quite literally, and closes the clever new loopholes they've opened with new methods and techniques.

In the last hundred years, this arms-race has dramatically escalated, as new technologies have given surprising new weapons to those on either side of the Law—cars and airplanes on one hand, making it easier for criminals to get away, fingerprinting and DNA testing and instant world-wide communications, on the other hand, making it harder for them to avoid capture or identification.

Some of the battlefields didn't even exist only a few decades back. Forty years ago, there was no such thing as computer crime (because there was no such thing as *com-puters*, at least in the forms we know them today)—but there was *also* no such thing as the use of computers to *in-vestigate* crime, either, a task at which they have proved awesomely effective.

So you win some, and you lose some. Take two steps forward, and then a step back.

And you ain't seen *nothing* yet!

As technology continues to increase in sophistication and power, so the opportunities to *use* that technology for crime will increase. In the high-speed future just ahead, we're likely to see crimes that don't even exist yet, as high-tech criminals come up with whole new categories of crime that nobody has even *thought* of yet, here in the opening days of the twenty-first century—and the evolu-tionary arms-race will continue to escalate as well, at a faster pace than ever before, as the Law scrambles to come up with new ways to frustrate those bizarre new crimes and bring even the most technologically sophisticated criminals to justice.

So open the pages of this book, and let some of the world's most expert dreamers show you what the ancient game of Cops and Robbers is going to look like in the future, when high-tech identity theft, mutant con men, cyborg Mafia dons, murderous inventions, sinister Group Minds, people who kill for apartment space, sophisticated art thieves operating on the blazing surface of Mercury, and many other now-unknown crimes (including futures where you could be breaking the law by *urinating* . . . or by being late for work!) are the things that must be combated by the equally high-tech *detectives* of the future. So break out your spacesuit and your Virtual Reality set, your time-shuttle, your laser gun, and your faithful robot Watson, and get ready to solve some science fiction mysteries that are literally out of this world—sometimes *way* out.

The game is afoot! Enjoy!

(For more speculations about future crime of one sort or another, check out our Ace anthologies *Hackers, Clones, Nanotech,* and *Genometry*.)

THE DOG SAID
BOW-WOW

Michael Swanwick

Michael Swanwick made his debut in 1980, and in the twenty-three years that have followed has established himself as one of SF's most prolific and consistently excellent writers at short lengths, as well as one of the premier novelists of his generation. He has several times been a finalist for the Nebula Award, as well as for the World Fantasy Award and for the John W. Campbell Award, and has won the Theodore Sturgeon Award and the Asimov's Science Fiction Readers Award poll. In 1991 his novel Stations of the Tide won him a Nebula Award as well, and in 1995 he won the World Fantasy Award for his story "Radio Waves." In the last few years he's been busy winning Hugo Awards—he won the Hugo in 1999 for his story "The Very Pulse of the Machine," another Hugo in 2000 for "Scherzo with Tyrannosaur," and his third Hugo in 2002 for the story that follows. His other books include his first novel, In the Drift, which was published in 1985, a novella-length book, Griffin's Egg, 1987's popular novel Vacuum Flowers, a critically acclaimed fantasy novel, The Iron Dragon's Daughter, which was a finalist for the World Fantasy Award and the Arthur C. Clarke Award (a rare distinction!), and Jack Faust, a sly reworking of the Faust legend that explores the unexpected impact of technology on society. His short fiction has been assembled in Gravity's Angels, A Geography of Unknown Lands, Slow Dancing through Time (a collection of his collaborative short work with other writers), Moon Dogs, Puck Aleshire's Abecedary, and Tales of Old Earth. He's also published a collection of critical articles, The Postmodern Archipelago, *and a book-length interview,* Being Gardner Dozois. *His most recent book is a major new novel,* Bones of the Earth. *Swanwick lives in Philadelphia with his wife, Marianne Porter (son Sean left for college). He has a website at www.michaelswanwick.com.*

Here he takes us to a colorful, curious, and eccentric future to spin a swashbuckling, slyly entertaining adventure that shows us that certain kinds of con games will probably go on forever, and that con men will probably always be with us—no matter what they look like.

T*he dog looked* as if he had just stepped out of a children's book. There must have been a hundred physical adaptations required to allow him to walk upright. The pelvis, of course, had been entirely reshaped. The feet alone would have needed dozens of changes. He had knees, and knees were tricky.

To say nothing of the neurological enhancements.

But what Darger found himself most fascinated by was the creature's costume. His suit fit him perfectly, with a slit in the back for the tail, and—again—a hundred invisible adaptations that caused it to hang on his body in a way that looked perfectly natural.

"You must have an extraordinary tailor," Darger said. The dog shifted his cane from one paw to the other, so they could shake, and in the least affected manner imaginable replied, "That is a common observation, sir."

"You're from the States?" It was a safe assumption, given where they stood—on the docks—and that the schooner *Yankee Dreamer* had sailed up the Thames with the morning tide. Darger had seen its bubble sails over the rooftops, like so many rainbows. "Have you found lodgings yet?"

"Indeed I am, and no I have not. If you could recommend a tavern of the cleaner sort?"

''No need for that. I would be only too happy to put you up for a few days in my own rooms.'' And, lowering his voice, Darger said, ''I have a business proposition to put to you.''

''Then lead on, sir, and I shall follow you with a right good will.''

The dog's name was Sir Blackthorpe Ravenscairn de Plus Precieux, but ''Call me Sir Plus,'' he said with a self-denigrating smile, and ''Surplus'' he was ever after.

Surplus was, as Darger had at first glance suspected and by conversation confirmed, a bit of a rogue—something more than mischievous and less than a cut-throat. A dog, in fine, after Darger's own heart.

Over drinks in a public house, Darger displayed his box and explained his intentions for it. Surplus warily touched the intricately carved teak housing, and then drew away from it. ''You outline an intriguing scheme, Master Darger—''

''Please. Call me Aubrey.''

''Aubrey, then. Yet here we have a delicate point. How shall we divide up the . . . ah, *spoils* of this enterprise? I hesitate to mention this, but many a promising partnership has foundered on precisely such shoals.''

Darger unscrewed the salt cellar and poured its contents onto the table. With his dagger, he drew a fine line down the middle of the heap. ''I divide—you choose. Or the other way around, if you please. From self-interest, you'll not find a grain's difference between the two.''

''Excellent!'' cried Surplus and, dropping a pinch of salt in his beer, drank to the bargain.

It was raining when they left for Buckingham Labyrinth. Darger stared out the carriage window at the drear streets and worn buildings gliding by and sighed. ''Poor, weary old London! History is a grinding-wheel that has been ap-plied too many a time to thy face."

"It is also," Surplus reminded him, "to be the making of our fortunes. Raise your eyes to the Labyrinth, sir, with its soaring towers and bright surfaces rising above these shops and flats like a crystal mountain rearing up out of a ramshackle wooden sea, and be comforted."

"That is fine advice," Darger agreed. "But it cannot comfort a lover of cities, nor one of a melancholic turn of mind."

"Pah!" cried Surplus, and said no more until they ar-rived at their destination.

At the portal into Buckingham, the sergeant-interface strode forward as they stepped down from the carriage. He blinked at the sight of Surplus, but said only, "Papers?"

Surplus presented the man with his passport and the credentials Darger had spent the morning forging, then added with a negligent wave of his paw, "And this is my autistic."

The sergeant-interface glanced once at Darger, and for-got about him completely. Darger had the gift, priceless to one in his profession, of a face so nondescript that once someone looked away, it disappeared from that person's consciousness forever. "This way, sir. The officer of proto-col will want to examine these himself."

A dwarf savant was produced to lead them through the outer circle of the Labyrinth. They passed by ladies in bio-luminescent gowns and gentlemen with boots and gloves cut from leathers cloned from their own skin. Both women and men were extravagantly bejeweled—for the ostenta-tious display of wealth was yet again in fashion—and the halls were lushly clad and pillared in marble, porphyry, and jasper. Yet Darger could not help noticing how worn the carpets were, how chipped and sooted the oil lamps. His sharp eye espied the remains of an antique electrical system, and traces as well of telephone lines and fiber optic cables from an age when those technologies were yet workable.

These last he viewed with particular pleasure.

The dwarf savant stopped before a heavy black door carved over with gilt griffins, locomotives, and fleurs-de-lis. "This is a door," he said. "The wood is ebony. Its binomial is *Diospyros ebenum*. It was harvested in Serendip. The gilding is of gold. Gold has an atomic weight of 197.2."

He knocked on the door and opened it.

The officer of protocol was a dark-browed man of imposing mass. He did not stand for them. "I am Lord Coherence-Hamilton, and this—" he indicated the slender, clear-eyed woman who stood beside him—"is my sister, Pamela."

Surplus bowed deeply to the Lady, who dimpled and dipped a slight curtsey in return.

The protocol officer quickly scanned the credentials. "Explain these fraudulent papers, sirrah. The Demesne of Western Vermont! Damn me if I have ever heard of such a place."

"Then you have missed much," Surplus said haughtily. "It is true we are a young nation, created only seventy-five years ago during the Partition of New England. But there is much of note to commend our fair land. The glorious beauty of Lake Champlain. The gene-mills of Winooski, that ancient seat of learning the *Universitas Vridis Montis* of Burlington, the Technarchaeological Institute of—" He stopped. "We have much to be proud of, sir, and nothing of which to be ashamed."

The beautiful official glared suspiciously at him, then said. "What brings you to London? Why do you desire an audience with the queen?"

"My mission and destination lie in Russia. However, England being on my itinerary and I a diplomat, I was charged to extend the compliments of my nation to your monarch." Surplus did not quite shrug. "There is no more to it than that. In three days I shall be in France, and you will have forgotten about me completely.''

Scornfully the officer tossed his credentials to the savant, who glanced at and politely returned them to Surplus. The small fellow sat down at a little desk scaled to his own size and swiftly made out a copy. ''Your papers will be taken to Whitechapel and examined there. If everything goes well—which I doubt—and there's an opening—not likely—you'll be presented to the queen sometime between a week and ten days hence.''

''Ten days! Sir, I am on a very strict schedule!''

''Then you wish to withdraw your petition?''

Surplus hesitated. ''I . . . I shall have to think on't, sir.''

Lady Pamela watched coolly as the dwarf savant led them away.

The room they were shown to had massively framed mirrors and oil paintings dark with age upon the walls, and a generous log fire in the hearth. When their small guide had gone, Darger carefully locked and bolted the door. Then he tossed the box onto the bed, and bounced down alongside it. Lying flat on his back, staring up at the ceiling, he said, ''The Lady Pamela is a strikingly beautiful woman. I'll be damned if she's not.''

Ignoring him, Surplus locked paws behind his back, and proceeded to pace up and down the room. He was full of nervous energy. At last, he expostulated, ''This is a deep game you have gotten me into, Darger! Lord Coherence-Hamilton suspects us of all manner of blackguardry.''

''Well, and what of that?''

''I repeat myself: We have not even begun our play yet, and he suspects us already! I trust neither him nor his genetically remade dwarf.''

''You are in no position to be displaying such vulgar prejudice.''

''I am not *bigoted* about the creature, Darger, I *fear* him!

Once you let suspicion of us into that macroencephalic head of his, and he will worry at it until he has found out our every secret."

"Get a grip on yourself, Surplus! Be a man! We are in this too deep already to back out. Questions would be asked, and investigations made."

"I am anything but a man, thank God," Surplus replied. "Still, you are right. In for a penny, in for a pound. For now, I might as well sleep. Get off the bed. You can have the hearth-rug."

"I! The rug!"

"I am groggy of mornings. Were someone to knock, and I to unthinkingly open the door, it would hardly do to have you found sharing a bed with your master."

The next day, Surplus returned to the Office of Protocol to declare that he was authorized to wait as long as two weeks for an audience with the queen, though not a day more.

"You have received new orders from your government?" Lord Coherence-Hamilton asked suspiciously. "I hardly see how."

"I have searched my conscience, and reflected on certain subtleties of phrasing in my original instructions," Surplus said. "That is all."

He emerged from the office to discover Lady Pamela waiting outside. When she offered to show him the Labyrinth, he agreed happily to her plan. Followed by Darger, they strolled inward, first to witness the changing of the guard in the forecourt vestibule, before the great pillared wall that was the front of Buckingham Palace before it was swallowed up in the expansion of architecture during the mad, glorious years of Utopia. Following which, they proceeded toward the viewers' gallery above the chamber of state.

"I see from your repeated glances that you are interested in my diamonds. 'Sieur Plus Precieux!" Lady

Pamela said. "Well, you might you be. They are a family trea-
sure, centuries old and manufactured to order, each stone
flawless and perfectly matched. The indentures of a hundred autistics would not buy the like."

Surplus smiled down again at the necklace, draped
about her lovely throat and above her perfect breasts. "I assure you, madame, it was not your necklace that held me
so enthralled."

She colored delicately, pleased. Lightly, she said, "And
that box your man carries with him wherever you go?
What is in it?"

"That? A trifle. A gift for the Duke of Muscovy, who is
the ultimate object of my journey," Surplus said. "I assure
you, it is of no interest whatsoever."

"You were talking to someone last night," Lady Pamela
said. "In your room."

"You were listening at my door? I am astonished and
flattered."

She blushed. "No, no, my brother . . . it is his job, you
see, surveillance."

"Possibly I was talking in my sleep. I have been told I
do that occasionally."

"In accents? My brother said he heard two voices."

"In that, he was mistaken." Surplus looked away.

England's queen was a sight to rival any in that ancient
land. She was as large as the lorry of ancient legend, and
surrounded by attendants who hurried back and forth,
fetching food and advice and carrying away dirty plates
and signed legislation. From the gallery, she reminded
Darger of a queen bee, but unlike the bee, this queen did
not copulate, but remained proudly virgin.

Her name was Gloriana the First, and she was a hundred
years old and still growing.

Lord Campbell-Supercollider, a friend of Lady
Pamela's met by chance, who had insisted on accompany-

ing them to the gallery leaned close to Surplus and murmured, "You are impressed, of course, by our queen's magnificence." The warning in his voice was impossible to miss. "Foreigners invariably are."

"I am dazzled," Surplus said.

"Well might you be. For scattered through her majesty's great body are thirty-six brains, connected with thick ropes of ganglia in a hypercube configuration. Her processing capacity is the equal of many of the great computers from Utopian times."

Lady Pamela stifled a yawn. "Darling Rory," she said, touching the Lord Campbell-Supercollider's sleeve. "Duty calls me. Would you be so kind as to show my American friend the way back to the outer circle?"

"Or course, my dear." He and Surplus stood (Darger was, of course, already standing) and paid their compliments. Then, when Lady Pamela was gone and Surplus started to turn toward the exit, "Not that way. Those stairs are for commoners. You and I may leave by the gentlemen's staircase."

The narrow stairs twisted downward beneath clouds of gilt cherubs-and-airships, and debouched into a marble-floored hallway. Surplus and Darger stepped out of the stairway and found their arms abruptly seized by baboons.

There were five baboons all told, with red uniforms and matching choke collars with leashes that gathered in the hand of an ornately mustached officer whose gold piping identified him as a master of apes. The fifth baboon bared his teeth and hissed savagely.

Instantly, the master of apes yanked back on his leash and said, "There, Hercules! There, sirrah! What do you do? What do you say?"

The baboon drew himself up and bowed curtly. "Please come with us," he said with difficulty. The master of apes cleared his throat. Sullenly, the baboon added, "Sir."

"This is outrageous!" Surplus cried. "I am a diplomat, and under international law immune to arrest."

"Ordinarily, sir, this is true," said the master of apes courteously. "However, you have entered the inner circle without her majesty's invitation and are thus subject to stricter standards of security."

"I had no idea these stairs went inward. I was led here by—" Surplus looked about helplessly. Lord Campbell-Supercollider was nowhere to be seen.

So, once again, Surplus and Darger found themselves escorted to the Office of Protocol.

"The wood is teak. Its binomial is Tectonia grandis. Teak is native to Burma, Hind, and Siam. The box is carved elaborately but without refinement." The dwarf savant opened it. "Within the casing is an archaic device for electronic intercommunication. The instrument chip is a gallium-arsenide ceramic. The chip weighs six ounces. The device is a product of the Utopian end-times."

"A modem!" The protocol officer's eyes bugged out. "You dared bring a *modem* into the inner circle and almost into the presence of the queen?" His chair stood and walked around the table. Its six insectile legs looked too slender to carry his great, legless mass. Yet it moved nimbly and well.

"It is harmless, sir. Merely something our technarchaeologists unearthed and thought would amuse the Duke of Muscovy, who is well-known for his love of all things antiquarian. It is, apparently, of some cultural or historical significance, though without re-reading my instructions, I would be hard pressed to tell you what."

Lord Coherence-Hamilton raised his chair so that he loomed over Surplus, looking dangerous and domineering. "*Here* is the historic significance of your modem: The Utopians filled the world with their computer webs and nets, burying cables and nodes so deeply and plentifully that they shall never be entirely rooted out. They then released into that virtual universe demons and mad gods.

These intelligences destroyed Utopia and almost destroyed humanity as well. Only the valiant worldwide destruction of all modes of interface saved us from annihilation!" He glared.

"Oh, you lackwit! Have you no history? These creatures hate us because our ancestors created them. They are still alive, though confined to their electronic netherworld, and want only a modem to extend themselves into the physical realm. Can you wonder, then, that the penalty for possessing such a device is—" he smiled menacingly—"death?"

"No, sir, it is not. Possession of a *working* modem is a mortal crime. This device is harmless. Ask your savant."

"Well?" the big man growled at his dwarf. "Is it functional?"

"No. It—"

"Silence." Lord Coherence-Hamilton turned back to Surplus. "You are a fortunate cur. You will not be charged with any crimes. However, while you are here, I will keep this filthy device locked away and under my control. Is that understood, Sir Bow-Wow?"

Surplus sighed. "Very well," he said. "It is only for a week, after all."

That night, the Lady Pamela Coherence-Hamilton came by Surplus's room to apologize for the indignity of his arrest, of which, she assured him, she had just now learned. He invited her in. In short order they somehow found themselves kneeling face-to-face on the bed, unbuttoning each other's clothing.

Lady Pamela's breasts had just spilled delightfully from her dress when she drew back, clutching the bodice closed again, and said, "Your man is watching us."

"And what concern is that to us?" Surplus said jovially. "The poor fellow's an autistic. Nothing he sees or hears matters to him. You might as well be embarrassed by the presence of a chair."

"Even were he a wooden carving, I would his eyes were not on me."

"As you wish " Surplus clapped his paws. "Sirrah! Turn around."

Obediently, Darger turned his back. This was his first experience with his friend's astonishing success with women. How many sexual adventuresses, he wondered, might one tumble, if one's form were unique? On reflection, the question answered itself.

Behind him, he heard the Lady Pamela giggle. Then, in a voice low with passion, Surplus said, "No, leave the diamonds on."

With a silent sigh, Darger resigned himself to a long night. Since he was bored and yet could not turn to watch the pair cavorting on the bed without giving himself away, he was perforce required to settle for watching them in the mirror.

They began, of course, by doing it doggy-style.

The next day, Surplus fell sick. Hearing of his indisposition, Lady Pamela sent one of her autistics with a bowl of broth and then followed herself in a surgical mask.

Surplus smiled weakly to see her. "You have no need of that mask," he said. "By my life, I swear that what ails me is not communicable. As you doubtless know, we who have been remade are prone to endocrinological imbalance."

"Is that all?" Lady Pamela spooned some broth into his mouth, then dabbed at a speck of it with a napkin. "Then fix it. You have been very wicked to frighten me over such a trifle."

"Alas," Surplus said sadly, "I am a unique creation, and my table of endocrine balances was lost in an accident at sea. There are copies in Vermont, of course. But by the time even the swiftest schooner can cross the Atlantic twice, I fear me I shall be gone."

"Oh, dearest Surplus!" The Lady caught up his paws in her hands. "Surely there is some measure, however desperate, to be taken?"

"Well . . ." Surplus turned to the wall in thought. After a very long time, he turned back and said, "I have a confession to make. The modem your brother holds for me? It is functional."

"Sir!" Lady Pamela stood, gathering her skirts, and stepped away from the bed in horror. "Surely not!"

"My darling and delight, you must listen to me." Surplus glanced weakly toward the door, then lowered his voice. "Come close and I shall whisper."

She obeyed.

"In the waning days of Utopia, during the war between men and their electronic creations, scientists and engineers bent their efforts toward the creation of a modem that could be safely employed by humans. One immune from the attack of demons. One that could, indeed, compel their obedience. Perhaps you have heard of this project."

"There are rumors, but . . . no such device was ever built."

"Say rather that no such device was built *in time*. It had just barely been perfected when the mobs came rampaging through the laboratories, and the Age of the Machine was over. Some few, however, were hidden away before the last technicians were killed. Centuries later, brave researchers at the Technarchaeological Institute of Shelburne recovered six such devices and mastered the art of their use. One device was destroyed in the process. Two are kept in Burlington. The others were given to trusted couriers and sent to the three most powerful allies of the Demesne—one of which is, of course, Russia."

"This is hard to believe," Lady Pamela said wonderingly. "Can such marvels be?"

"Madame, I employed it two nights ago in this very room! Those voices your brother heard? I was speaking with my principals in Vermont. They gave me permission to extend my stay here to a fortnight."

He gazed imploringly at her. "If you were to bring me the device, I could then employ it to save my life."

Lady Coherence-Hamilton resolutely stood. "Fear nothing, then. I swear by my soul, the modem shall be yours tonight."

The room was lit by a single lamp that cast wild shadows whenever anyone moved, as if of illicit spirits at a witch's Sabbath.

It was an eerie sight. Darger, motionless, held the modem in his hands. Lady Pamela, who had a sense of occasion, had changed to a low-cut gown of clinging silks, dark-red as human blood. It swirled about her as she hunted through the wainscoting for a jack left unused for centuries. Surplus sat up weakly in bed, eyes half-closed, directing her. It might have been, Darger thought, an allegorical tableau of the human body being directed by its sick animal passions, while the intellect stood by, paralyzed by lack of will.

"There!" Lady Pamela triumphantly straightened, her necklace scattering tiny rainbows in the dim light.

Darger stiffened. He stood perfectly still for the length of three long breaths, then shook and shivered like one undergoing seizure. His eyes rolled back in his head.

In hollow, unworldly tones, he said, "What man calls me up from the vasty deep?" It was a voice totally unlike his own, one harsh and savage and eager for unholy sport. "Who dares risk my wrath?"

"You must convey my words to the autistic's ears," Surplus murmured. "For he is become an integral part of the modem—not merely its operator, but its voice."

"I stand ready," Lady Pamela replied.

"Good girl. Tell it who I am."

"It is Sir Blackthorpe Ravenscairn de Plus Precieux who speaks, and who wishes to talk to . . ." She paused.

"To his most august and socialist honor, the mayor of Burlington."

"His most august and socialist honor," Lady Pamela began. She turned toward the bed and said quizzically, "The mayor of Burlington?"

"'Tis but an official title, much like your brother's, for he who is in fact the spy-master for the Demesne of Western Vermont," Surplus said weakly. "Now repeat to it: I compel thee on threat of dissolution to carry my message. Use those exact words."

Lady Pamela repeated the words into Darger's ear.

He screamed. It was a wild and unholy sound that sent the Lady skittering away from him in a momentary panic. Then, in mid-cry, he ceased.

"Who is this?" Darger said in an entirely new voice, this one human. "You have the voice of a woman. Is one of my agents in trouble?"

"Speak to him now, as you would to any man: forthrightly, directly, and without evasion." Surplus sank his head back on his pillow and closed his eyes.

So (as it seemed to her) the Lady Coherence-Hamilton explained Surplus's plight to his distant master, and from him received both condolences and the needed information to return Surplus's endocrine levels to a functioning harmony. After proper courtesies, then, she thanked the American spy-master and unjacked the modem. Darger returned to passivity.

The leather-cased endocrine kit lay open on a small table by the bed. At Lady Pamela's direction, Darger began applying the proper patches to various places on Surplus's body. It was not long before Surplus opened his eyes.

"Am I to be well?" he asked and, when the Lady nodded, "Then I fear I must be gone in the morning. Your brother has spies everywhere. If he gets the least whiff of what this device can do, he'll want it for himself."

Smiling, Lady Pamela hoisted the box in her hand. "Indeed, who can blame him? With such a toy, great things could be accomplished."

"So he will assuredly think. I pray you, return it to me."

She did not. "This is more than just a communication device, sir," she said. "Though in that mode it is of incalculable value. You have shown that it can enforce obedience on the creatures that dwell in the forgotten nerves of the ancient world. Ergo, they can be compelled to do our calculations for us."

"Indeed, so our technarchaeologists tell us. You must . . ."

"We have created monstrosities to perform the duties that were once done by machines. But with *this,* there would be no necessity to do so. We have allowed ourselves to be ruled by an icosahexadexal-brained freak. Now we have no need for Gloriana the Gross, Gloriana the Fat and Grotesque, Gloriana the Maggot Queen!"

"Madame!"

"It is time, I believe, that England had a new queen. A human queen."

"Think of my honor!"

Lady Pamela paused in the doorway. "You are a very pretty fellow indeed. But with this, I can have the monarchy and keep such a harem as will reduce your memory to that of a passing and trivial fancy."

With a rustle of skirts, she spun away.

"Then I am undone!" Surplus cried, and fainted onto the bed.

Quietly, Darger closed the door. Surplus raised himself from the pillows, began removing the patches from his body, and said, "Now what?"

"Now we get some sleep," Darger said. "Tomorrow will be a busy day."

•   •   •

The master of apes came for them after breakfast, and marched them to their usual destination. By now, Darger was beginning to lose track of exactly how many times he had been in the Office of Protocol. They entered to find Lord Coherence-Hamilton in a towering rage, and his sister, calm and knowing, standing in a corner with her arms crossed, watching. Looking at them both now, Darger wondered how he could ever have imagined that the brother outranked his sister.

The modem lay opened on the dwarf savant's desk. The little fellow leaned over the device, studying it minutely.

Nobody said anything until the master of apes and his baboons had left. Then Lord Coherence-Hamilton roared, "Your modem refuses to work for us!"

"As I told you, sir," Surplus said coolly, "it is inoperative."

"That's a bold-arsed fraud and a goat-buggering lie!" In his wrath, the Lord's chair rose up on its spindly legs so high that his head almost bumped against the ceiling. "I know of your activities—" he nodded toward his sister—"and demand that you show us how this whoreson device works!"

"Never!" Surplus cried stoutly. "I have my honor, sir."

"Your honor, too scrupulously insisted upon, may well lead to your death, sir."

Surplus threw back his head. "Then I die for Vermont!"

At this moment of impasse, Lady Hamilton stepped forward between the two antagonists to restore peace. "I know what might change your mind." With a knowing smile, she raised a hand to her throat and denuded herself of her diamonds. "I saw how you rubbed them against your face the other night. How you licked and fondled them. How ecstatically you took them into your mouth."

She closed his paws about them. "They are yours, sweet 'Sieur Precieux, for a word."

"You would give them up?" Surplus said, as if amazed at the very idea. In fact, the necklace had been his and Darger's target from the moment they'd seen it. The only

barrier that now stood between them and the merchants of
Amsterdam was the problem of freeing themselves from
the Labyrinth before their marks finally realized that the
modem was indeed a cheat. And to this end they had the
invaluable tool of a thinking man whom all believed to be
an autistic, and a plan that would give them almost twenty
hours in which to escape.

"Only think, dear Surplus." Lady Pamela stroked his
head and then scratched him behind one ear, while he
stared down at the precious stones. "Imagine the life of
wealth and ease you could lead, the women, the power. It
all lies in your hands. All you need do is close them."

Surplus took a deep breath. "Very well," he said. "The
secret lies in the condenser, which takes a full day to re-
charge. Wait but—"

"Here's the problem," the savant said unexpectedly. He
poked at the interior of the modem. "There was a wire
loose."

He jacked the device into the wall.

"Oh, dear God," Darger said.

A savage look of raw delight filled the dwarf savant's
face, and he seemed to swell before them.

"*I am free!*" he cried in a voice so loud it seemed impossible that it could arise from such a slight source. He
shook as if an enormous electrical current were surging
through him. The stench of ozone filled the room.

He burst into flames and advanced on the English spy-
master and her brother.

While all stood aghast and paralyzed, Darger seized
Surplus by the collar and hauled him out into the hallway,
slamming the door shut as he did.

They had not run twenty paces down the hall when the
door to the Office of Protocol exploded outward, sending
flaming splinters of wood down the hallway.

Satanic laughter boomed behind them.

Glancing over his shoulder, Darger saw the burning dwarf, now blackened to a cinder, emerge from a room engulfed in flames, capering and dancing. The modem, though disconnected, was now tucked under one arm, as if it were exceedingly valuable to him. His eyes were round and white and lidless. Seeing them, he gave chase.

"Aubrey!" Surplus cried. "We are headed the *wrong way!*"

It was true. They were running deeper into the Labyrinth, toward its heart, rather than outward. But it was impossible to turn back now. They plunged through scattering crowds of nobles and servitors, trailing fire and supernatural terror in their wake.

The scampering grotesque set fire to the carpets with every footfall. A wave of flame tracked him down the hall, incinerating tapestries and wallpaper and wood trim. No matter how they dodged, it ran straight toward them. Clearly, in the programmatic literalness of its kind, the demon from the web had determined that having early seen them, it must early kill them as well.

Darger and Surplus raced through dining rooms and salons, along balconies and down servants' passages. To no avail. Dogged by their hyper-natural nemesis, they found themselves running down a passage, straight toward two massive bronze doors, one of which had been left just barely ajar. So fearful were they that they hardly noticed the guards.

"Hold, sirs!"

The mustachioed master of apes stood before the doorway, his baboons straining against their leashes. His eyes widened with recognition. "By gad, it's you!" he cried in astonishment.

"Lemme kill 'em!" one of the baboons cried. "The lousy bastards!" The others growled agreement.

Surplus would have tried to reason with them, but when he started to slow his pace, Darger put a broad hand on his back and shoved. "Dive!" he commanded. So of necessity the dog of rationality had to bow to the man of action. He tobaggoned wildly across the polished marble floor between two baboons, straight at the master of apes, and then between his legs.

The man stumbled, dropping the leashes as he did.

The baboons screamed and attacked.

For an instant, all five apes were upon Darger, seizing his limbs, snapping at his face and neck. Then the burning dwarf arrived, and, finding his target obstructed, seized the nearest baboon. The animal shrieked as its uniform burst into flames.

As one, the other baboons abandoned their original quarry to fight this newcomer who had dared attack one of their own.

In a trice, Darger leaped over the fallen master of apes, and was through the door. He and Surplus threw their shoulders against its metal surface and pushed. He had one brief glimpse of the fight, with the baboons aflame, and their master's body flying through the air. Then the door slammed shut. Internal bars and bolts, operated by smoothly oiled mechanisms, automatically latched themselves.

For the moment, they were safe.

Surplus slumped against the smooth bronze, and wearily asked, "Where did you *get* that modem?"

"From a dealer of antiquities." Darger wiped his brow with his kerchief. "It was transparently worthless. Whoever would dream it could be repaired?"

Outside, the screaming ceased. There was a very brief silence. Then the creature flung itself against one of the metal doors. It rang with the impact.

A delicate girlish voice wearily said, "What is this noise?"

They turned in surprise and found themselves looking up at the enormous corpus of Queen Gloriana. She lay upon her pallet, swaddled in satin and lace, and abandoned by all, save her valiant (though doomed) guardian apes. A pervasive yeasty smell emanated from her flesh. Within the tremendous folds of chins by the dozens and scores was a small human face. Its mouth moved delicately and asked, "What is trying to get in?"

The door rang again. One of its great hinges gave.

Darger bowed. "I fear, madame, it is your death."

"Indeed?" Blue eyes opened wide and, unexpectedly, Gloriana laughed. "If so, that is excellent good news. I have been praying for death an extremely long time."

"Can any of God's creations truly pray for death and mean it?" asked Darger, who had his philosophical side. "I have known unhappiness myself, yet even so life is precious to me."

"Look at me!" Far up to one side of the body, a tiny arm—though truly no tinier than any woman's arm— waved feebly. "I am not God's creation, but Man's. Who would trade ten minutes of their own life for a century of mine? Who, having mine, would not trade it all for death?"

A second hinge popped. The doors began to shiver. Their metal surfaces radiated heat.

"Darger, we must leave!" Surplus cried. "There is a time for learned conversation, but it is not now."

"Your friend is right," Gloriana said. "There is a small archway hidden behind yon tapestry. Go through it. Place your hand on the left wall and run. If you turn whichever way you must to keep from letting go of the wall, it will lead you outside. You are both rogues, I see, and doubtless deserve punishment, yet I can find nothing in my heart for you but friendship."

"Madame . . ." Darger began, deeply moved.

"Go! My bridegroom enters."

The door began to fall inward. With a final cry of "Farewell!" from Darger and "Come on!" from Surplus, they sped away.

By the time they had found their way out side, all of Buckingham Labyrinth was in flames. The demon, however, did not emerge from the flames, encouraging them to believe that when the modem it carried finally melted down, it had been forced to return to that unholy realm from whence it came.

•   •   •

The sky was red with flames as the sloop set sail for Calais. Leaning against the rail, watching, Surplus shook his head. "What a terrible sight! I cannot help feeling, in part, responsible."

"Come! Come!" Darger said. "This dyspepsia ill becomes you. We are both rich fellows, now! The Lady Pamela's diamonds will maintain us lavishly for years to come. As for London, this is far from the first fire it has had to endure. Nor will it be the last. Life is short, and so, while we live, let us be jolly!"

"These are strange words for a melancholiac," Surplus said wonderingly.

"In triumph, my mind turns its face to the sun. Dwell not on the past, dear friend, but on the future that lies glittering before us."

"The necklace is worthless," Surplus said. "Now that I have the leisure to examine it, free of the distracting flesh of Lady Pamela, I see that these are not diamonds, but mere imitations." He made to cast the necklace into the Thames.

Before he could, though, Darger snatched away the stones from him and studied them closely. Then he threw back his head and laughed. "The biters bit! Well, it may be paste, but it looks valuable still. We shall find good use for it in Paris."

"We are going to Paris?"

"We are partners, are we not? Remember that antique wisdom that whenever a door closes, another opens? For every city that burns, another beckons. To France, then, and adventure! After which, Italy, the Vatican Empire, Austro-Hungary, perhaps even Russia! Never forget that you have yet to present your credentials to the Duke of Muscovy."

"Very well," Surplus said. "But when we do, *I'll* pick out the modem."

A SCRAPING AT
THE BONES

Algis Budrys

As the icy and elegant shocker that follows ably demonstrates, the nature of crime changes as society changes, with new social conditions calling forth new crimes, as well as new and strange motivations for committing some very old ones. . . .

Algis Budrys published his first SF story in 1952, and quickly established himself as one of the finest writers of his generation. His most famous novel is probably Rogue Moon, *one of the classic SF novels of the sixties. His other books include* Who?, The Falling Torch, *and* Some Will Not Die, *as well as the critically acclaimed* Michaelmas— *one of the best SF novels of the seventies—and the collection* Blood and Burning. *Budrys is also one of SF's most astute critics—his reviews and columns of writing advice appeared for years in* Galaxy, The Magazine of Fantasy and Science Fiction, *and* Locus; *his* Galaxy *review columns were collected in* Benchmarks: Galaxy Bookshelf. *His most recent books are the novel* Hard Landing *and, as editor, the* Writers of the Future *anthologies.*

The wastes processing foreman was doughy and soft: looking at his greenish pallor and watching the convulsed workings at the corners of his mouth, Ned Brosmer wondered what would happen if the man lost hold of himself and began puking. Would it all come up—first the stomach, and then the very nearly similar material of the limbs, and then the pelvis and torso and ears, until finally the

empty royal blue slick-finish coverall would be lying at his
feet under a heap of something like oatmeal? "It's in there,
Officer," the foreman was saying with a relinquishing gesture toward the open inspection plate, the wave of his arm
ending with his hand in front of his mouth.

"All right," Brosmer said. "I'll look.

Down here, many levels below the dwelling units that
clambered skyward in the complex shape of Panorama
Tower, it was all pumps and tubing and worklights. The
particular duct from which the smell came was four feet in
diameter, and was painted an ivory white. Coded red decal
symbols identified it as the north tower branch feed to the
central waste macerator.

The hatch was a three-by-two plate, swung back and
up; an extension light dangled over it, swaying from the
cord as the constant air currents within the duct came gust-
ing out. "Are we going to get flooded?" Brosmer asked,
and the foreman shook his head violently.

"Hell, no!" he said. "We got this branch shut off back
there, where the tube comes straight down from upstairs
and makes that bend, see? There's this surge tank there,
like you got to have, and you can use that big valve to
block everything between it and here."

"Got you," Brosmer said. "Would a body pass through
that valve?"

"No way. Jam it, maybe. But most likely it would just
stay in the tank until the next time we cleaned it out."

"So it probably went into the duct right through this
hatch."

"That would figure, yeah. Somebody came down here
and put it in."

"Or it's suicide."

"You're kidding! Who would want to drown himself
in—"

"I was kidding," Brosmer said. He had taken a respirator from his kit bag and was putting it on. His voice

sounded remote in his ears, as if he were on dope. He sighed and looked into the duct.

The air flow was backing up from the hydrolizing tanks beyond the macerator, whistling against the torn edges of the thin metal blade that terminated the duct. The blade was designed to rotate at high rpm; it had shattered against something in the body, which had been passing feet-first through it without incident up to that point. Brosmer clenched his teeth, grasped one of the shoulders, and turned it over. A white male, middle-aged, hair gray, eyes brown, several post-mortem abrasions and superficial lacerations, and the apparently fatal puncture wound in the upper right-hand quadrant of the thorax. Made with a thin, long, sharp weapon, Brosmer decided, for he had seen the exit wound below the left shoulder blade. It wouldn't have bled very much; whatever rags had mopped up the spill had probably preceded the corpse down the duct, and were on their way to the farmers by now. And—Brosmer looked more closely. Right. A stainless steel replacement ball and Teflon socket for the original left hip joint. That was what had stopped the blade.

Brosmer drew his head and shoulders back out of the inspection hatchway. "Recognize him, Mr. Johnson?" he said to the foreman. "Take a good look. Sorry." He kept himself out of the way and put a hand on Johnson's elbow to urge him forward.

Johnson craned briefly, then stepped back. "No—I don't know him."

"He's just about got to live in this unit," Brosmer said.

"I don't see none of them. They're up there and I'm down here. There's thousands of them and three guys in my crew and me. That's the way they want it, and that's the way I want it. This is a different kind of place down here."

"OK," Brosmer said. No matter what, the longest delay in making an identification would be a routine four-hour turnaround time for the Social Security print files in Omaha; sooner if anybody wanted to rush it. He stripped off his examining gloves and dropped them in a waste can. "Somebody'll be along to pick it up."

"Is this all?" the foreman asked.

Brosmer looked at him with the appearance of great wisdom. "You mean, where's the sergeant and the lieutenant and the Chief Medical Examiner of New York City? Well, the sergeant's tied up collating officers' reports, and the lieutenant's in a conference with some sergeants. There'll be a photographer with the meat wagon crew. You see," he explained patiently, "this isn't a stage set; this is real. We don't need a lot of mouths full of dialogue to establish the plot."

"You're all the cop we're going to get on this case?"

"I'm 3-D and in color, Mr. Johnson. You can even feel me, if you don't get personal. That's good enough for an unidentified male found in a sewer."

"Well, you sure as hell look young to me, to be handling something like this all by yourself."

"That's right, I do," Brosmer said, packing away his respirator. "You've got my card. Call me if anybody starts asking you questions about the plumbing. I'm getting out of here. I hate dismal places." He turned back once: "Don't tell anybody about this, or I'll bust your ass to someplace where they use buckets."

At the lobby level, Brosmer walked through one Kasuba environment after another, eschewing their invitations to energy or lassitude, until he had reached the lobby area. He rang Building Management.

"Please state your business," the hologram said, and then caught itself. "Oh, it's you, Officer." Her lips took on fullness, but her eyes widened with something other than love. "I'll put you through to Mr. Vermeil." She faded, to be replaced by a naively interesting sculpture that rotated gently under lights, and with the sound of Japanese wind chimes, which in turn yielded to a representation of a man in body-fitting burgundy crushed velvet. It seemed to Brosmer it was a little soon in the evening for that, but perhaps the manager was an early riser.

"Yes, Officer?" Vermeil said busily, not having bothered to put down his frappe.

"There'll be a mortuary truck to get the body, so you'll want to alert your perimeter security people," Brosmer said. "A police photographer will take ID shots; you'll be expected to look at them, in case you can identify the victim. It's almost a sure thing he's one of your residents."

"Good heavens, Officer, *I* don't know every Tom, Dick and Harry who lives here! Why on Earth should I?"

"Nobody ever calls you up about anything? You know, there was a time when tenants hammered on pipes for more heat, or had their dripping faucets fixed by the super. And the manager came around every month to collect the rent. They've got to be in touch with you now and then."

"I *don't* remember them, Officer. The bank evicts them if their credit goes, and Central Services has the building maintenance contract. They can hammer all they want to on their . . . *pipes,* did you say? Why, yes, Officer, there *was* a time when pipes brought on the heat, wasn't there?" He smirked.

"Vermeil, when the photographer calls you up and shows you the pictures, look at them. And remember it's a sworn admissible communication, whatever you tell him. I'll be in touch when I need you." Brosmer rang off. He went to the lobby doors and flashed his buzzer at the sensing devices. The inner doors opened, and he stepped into the lock. "NYPD shield number 062-26-8729," he said perfunctorily. "One man going out."

There was a pause, and the intervening sound of wind chimes. Then the outer doors opened. He stepped into the raw air, grimacing, and walked toward the transit station, keeping clear of low walls and shrubbery. Above him, the brownish precast concrete settings clambered heavenward to frame waterfalls of reflectorized glass. As he walked, he

rang a police channel and talked to his sergeant, telling
him the story.

"What do you think, Ned?" the sergeant asked when he
had all the data.

"I think somebody knows in his heart he got away with
it. Thinks our victim's a bag of nutrient for the rutabaga.
I'm going to get that sucker."

"Why do you suppose he wanted to obliterate the body?
How'd he know how plumbing works?"

"What are you, Sarge—an old fire horse? Those are *my*
questions."

"All right. You gonna be home?"

"Ten minutes transit time first. Thereafter."

"Good. I'll call you on a landline as soon as we have a
working collation."

"I'll be there when I'm needed."

"Say hello to Dorrie for me."

"Should I give any particular name?"

Once on the train, he punched his destination on the coder
in his armrest. When the straps went around him, the back
of his mind thought of Dorrie. The train took off as soon as
his interlock was made, and the front of his mind busied itself reviewing the people in the other seats. There were
two or three persons with lunchbucket faces: technicians.
The rest were pimps and whores. All of us personal servants make up the subway-riding public, he thought.

In the middle of his mind, he pondered an individual
who could stuff a stripped corpse into the Jakes, but was
too overwhelmed by his or her accomplishment to cut
down through an old orthopedic scar and just check to see
what might lie behind it. An amateur. But then, professionals just left 'em lying. There weren't any more feckless
people. Everyone was numbered. When they died, there
was a hole in the credit banks, the dwelling occupancy
budget, the place where ongoing supermarket billings

might be. There were no unmarked graves: IBM's tomb-
stone punches represented more substance than the inci-
dental flesh could ever show.

Please note, he told the place where he stored his experience: With the lower limbs absent, the free-floating position is face down.

He lived in Riverscene Heights. In the lobby lock, he said,
"City civil servant," which put him in the system's admissible tenant class, and then gave his Society Security number. "One man coming in," he said for the voiceprint. In
the motionless elevator, he gave his apartment number.
In this building, the systems played music during intervals.
When he had been properly scanned, the elevator unlocked
and took him to his floor. He got out and walked down
Hall 114, which also recognized him, and came to Door
11489, which let him in. Dorrie moved toward him out of
the forefront of a crowd of dancers.

She was slight and dark, wearing black openwork hip-
huggers and bronze jewelry; her long ashy hair fell over
one eye; the apartment lights reflected from the amber lens
over the other.

"Hello," he said.

She touched her upper lip with her tongue. "Welcome
home," she said softly. They touched each other.

He couldn't get enough of her. Wincing, he pulled his
shirt open so more of them would be touching. "Can't stay
long," he said. "Working." She had put perfume on the top
of her head. Her hands passed gently over his deltoid
musculature.

"Home tonight?" she asked softly.

"Don't know. Probably not."

"I'll go down the hall, then, Iris Ruthven asked me to
join her Bezant class with her."

He grimaced into her hair.

"You know," she said quickly, "that's not something

you can do by phone." She leaned back in his arms, took off her glasses, and looked directly into his eyes. "I mean, when you all get around the table, you actually have to *touch* hands, or it doesn't work."

"Does it work if you do?"

"Oh, don't be so *rational!*" She tapped his bicep mock-pettishly with her glasses.

And don't be such a liar, he thought. Another thing worked better in the flesh, too. Why she thought she had to be so convincing and yet so transparent, he couldn't imagine. Husbands weren't supposed to be selfish, were they? But he was; he was, and he was pretty sure she lied to reproach him subtly, come to think of it.

"Rational is as rational does," he said. "There's one fresh soul I'd sure like to contact. I'll bet he's got a story he'd love to tell."

She danced away from him a little, replacing her glasses. "Are you on a murder?" she asked, her lips parting.

"Over at Panorama." He moved toward a chair.

"Where the *artists* live? Did you go inside? What are the units like? I'll bet they're *fabulous!*"

"They don't get any more cubic feet per body than we do," he said, dropping into the chair. "Besides, I wasn't up on the dwelling levels." He put his feet up on the edge of the daybed and sighed. He reached out and touched Dorrie's thigh as she moved about him. "Listen, I hate to cut off the party, but I want to watch the news."

She nodded. "'S OK." He switched off the hi-fi and the dancers winked out. Moving toward the bar, Dorrie rummaged, keeping one hip cocked so as not to break the contact between his hand and her leg. "Stick?" she asked.

Dialing the phone for Laurent Michaelmas, he shook his head. "Working," he reminded her.

"You're funny," she murmured fondly as the Michaelmas hologram formed a few paces to her left. "You wouldn't even be back downstairs before your head was all straight again."

"Working *now*," he said, evading the central issue.

"Good evening," Michaelmas said. He was, as usual, in a plain black suit. Looking at him, Brosmer thought that the self-contained, square-bodied man, with his economical gestures and his lively, intelligent face, might understand him. He hoped that someday an assignment would let them meet. But it seemed hardly likely; Brosmer wasn't even sure whether Michaelmas lived in Manhattan, and he worked all over the world.

"I just want *local crime*," Brosmer said to him, uttering the last two words distinctly.

Michaelmas nodded. There was a slight flicker. "Local crime," he said. He began a series of expositions, some of which involved Brosmer in the chase of a stolen boat, hunting over the riparian complexes like a midge among the stock shelves of a glass shoe store, sweeping down over the Hudson with a flurry of vanes and surging rpm changes in the turbines, whirling skyward again among the glittering windows as the thieves throttled down and circled disconsolately in the bay. In another sequence, ambulances ran mugging victims toward resuscitation centers, whistling among the pylons and freight ramps of the streets. Michaelmas's voice was crisp and measured, his data succinct. Dorrie, the broken end of a stick trailing between her enameled nails, smiled roguishly toward Brosmer and intertwined her limbs with Michaelmas, running her hands over the shoulders of the suit, miming with such casual skill that Brosmer had to laugh as Michaelmas continued to speak and move obliviously. Only a few of his gestures surpassed her anticipation; at one point, his left arm protruded between her shoulder blades, but in the next she had recovered and was mock-biting gently with her white teeth along his forearm.

There was nothing about Panorama.

"All right," Brosmer said to himself, and to Michaelmas by way of good-bye as he dialed him off. The hologram disappeared from Dorrie's caresses. She turned and faced

Brosmer slump-shouldered, dangling her glasses in one hand against her thigh and looking at him through her lashes. Her lower lip was tentatively between her teeth. She moved her feet. She reached behind her to fully opaque the window wall.

Grinning awkwardly, Brosmer shook his head. "You know we're on an open police landline. George Holmeir could be calling any time now."

Well, what would he see that he didn't know first-hand? Brosmer thought as Dorrie smiled at him sadly. But her expression did change slightly at the mention of the sergeant's name. What would he see? Brosmer finished the thought. He'd see me. He might feel it was inappropriate.

And in fact Holmeir formed without preliminaries, between Dorrie and Brosmer. "OK, Ned," he said. "Here's what there is."

Brosmer shifted in his chair so the pickup would give Holmeir eye-contact with him. "Go ahead."

"Your DOA is Charles Castelvecchio. Resident at 25609 Panorama North, accompanied by Nola Furness Castelvecchio and one infant son. Castelvecchio was a writer on the *Warbirds of Time* series. Here's the stats on them; want to take it?" Holmer held up the sheet. Brosmer nodded and activated his camera.

"Got it."

Holmier put the sheet down on his desk. "OK. Now that's a positive ID. Positive. Fingerprints, dental charts, surgical records, every way we could do it.

Brosmer raised his eyebrows. "Thorough."

"Had to be. He's still doing business; we reviewed his phone calls. He was part of a story conference half an hour ago. Seemed a little jumpy, but did his fair share."

"While he was down in that duct all the time."

"Dead twelve hours, Forensics says, and soaking in that thing for an hour before he was found."

"Killed in the building."

"Had to be. He didn't just materialize." Holmeir looked at Brosmer expectantly.

"How do you mean?"

"He never went in or out through any door. But the elevator wasn't used once all day. That's what the building tapes say."

"It's a glitch. You're getting a false memory readout."

Holmeir nodded. "Sure. Something screwed up in the building system. It happens. Of course, maybe nobody *did* use the elevator. That happens, too. So maybe somebody's found a way to make a hologram you can feel. Only which one is it—the dead one or the one that suggested sending a squadron of Spads to strafe Charlemagne?"

"Come off it, Sarge."

"Well, I'll be damned if I can explain it. But I don't have to. Sergeants sit and officers walk."

"How about the widow? Did you talk to her?"

"Come off it, Ned. How would I know she didn't do it? It's all yours. He's not even officially dead."

Brosmer nodded. "It's a sweetheart of a case."

Holmeir grinned. "Yeah. I never heard of an MO like this. You're gonna be breaking new ground. They'll give it your name at the Academy—every time it ever comes up again, they'll call it a Brosmer. It'll be good for you when you're tired enough to apply for sergeant."

"And I'll apply for green feathers and fly to the Moon," Brosmer said, trying to picture himself as Holmeir, and wincing.

"OK," he said. "I'll call in when I've got something."

"Right. I'm going off-shift in about an hour. But I'll leave a cue in my phone for you."

"OK."

Dorrie had moved around to where the pickup could find her. "Hello, George," she said.

"Hello, Dorrie."

"See you, Sarge," Brosmer said.

As soon as he was gone, Dorrie turned to Brosmer with

her glasses off and her eyes full of stick. Hearing himself gasp, he knew there was nothing he could do to prevent it, or wanted to. Afterward, soft in his arms, blurred with lassitude, full of confidentiality, she murmured: "You silly, don't you know I don't see George any more; I've even mostly forgotten where he lives in this building. And besides, it's *you* I want to live with. You're so gentle with me," and he wished she didn't try so hard to teach a coherent understanding of the world to him.

It was funny how it all fell together. He had decided to call on the widow and see if there was any sense to be made of it. Appropriately dressed, his pockets full of supporting data, he walked up to her door as if it hadn't been his buzzer that had gotten him in, but when he rang at the door, nothing happened for a while. Brosmer stood plumped-out in the hall, thinking now about calling in for a warrant unlock, but instead the next door opened, and a man was standing there. "May I help you?" he said from under unceasingly restless eyes.

Brosmer shifted his feet in awkwardness and scratched the back of his neck. "Well, I don't know . . ." he said.

The man was tall and fleshy, dressed in a floor-length robe of figured iridescent orange. The flesh under one eye was jumping regularly, and his upper lip was wet. "It's all right. It's all right. I often come out," he said reassuringly. "The Castlevecchios aren't home; were they expecting you?"

"Well, yeah, Charlie left a cue in the system for me, and . . ."

"Strange. Yet he's not here. I'm Timothy Fortnum."

"Lou Marchant," Brosmer said. "I'm his cousin."

"Of this city?"

"Chicago," Brosmer said, having been there on a fugitive pickup once. Originally, he had been a young writer from the Bronx, for the widow's benefit, and he was shifting things around inside, watching Fortnum, looking non-plussed, wondering how a man could look so guilty and still keep talking.

Fortnum was calming down. "I knew he had no relatives in New York," he said, "Well, come in—let me offer you some hospitality while we straighten this thing out." He took Brosmer by the upper arm to urge him inside. Brosmer had to relax his muscles instantly to come off the pressure plates in the police undersuit beneath his garments, but his arm was only humanly resistant when Fortnum's hand closed on it.

Fortnum was much bolder now. His hip swung to bump Brosmer past him. Most of his attention was concentrated on closing and locking the door with swift, complex motions of his fingers.

"Sit down . . . sit down!" Fortnum said heartily, moving up behind him. "This is my wife, Martita. Darling, this is Mr. Marchant, Charles Castelvecchio's Chicago cousin, come to us unexpectedly."

Brosmer found himself having to look up. Martita Fortnum was leaning over the railing of an area to his left whose floor began at normal ceiling height. She was a slim, blonde woman in a red veil khaftan, her limbs long and straight, but aging as she descended a circular staircase. The elevated area, he saw, occupied the unit's worth of space above the Castelvecchio unit. Over his head, the ceiling, two ceilings high, supported a crystalline chandelier with soft lights playing upon it. Hanging gardens of opaque silky fabric draped the wall where three window frames ought to have been visible.

"I've never seen a place like this!" Brosmer said.

"Yes. I'm an architect. It's amazing what you can do. *Sit* down, Mr. Marchant. Tell us about yourself." His hand pressed Brosmer's shoulder. "Martita—bring our guest something, will you?"

The wall in the far corner was for shelves of books; a swing-down drawing board, and a prose encoder. Beside

the encoder was a roughly similar machine—if he had not
seen one in a documentary on popular music, he would not
have known it was for editing tune material. All that space
was occupied. These people had no visible food prepara-
tion area.

Fortnum's hand was still pressing. Brosmer let himself
fall into the chair beside the wall between the Fortnum and
Castelvecchio units.

Martita Fortnum had reached this floor. She turned with a
fluidity strongly reminiscent of youth and passed through
an opening behind the staircase. Its edges were fresh: un-
finished. There were wallboard fragments on a dropcloth
laid in the opening, and it led into the next unit. Martita
Fortnum threw Brosmer a fleeting smile as she moved out
of sight.

"What are you *doing?*" Brosmer asked, turning his face
up to Fortnum.

"Why, we're entertaining you," Fortnum said heartily.
"There's so much I want to know about you. Any visitor of
Charlie's is bound to be such a surprise to me. He was saying to me just yesterday that he never received any
callers." Fortnum put one buttock on the arm of another
chair, which stood where the daybed ought to have been,
and eyed Brosmer's face intently. A pair of huge antique
geometrician's dividers, massive in bronze, each slender
two-foot arm ending in a glistening steel point, hung on the
wall near his right shoulder.

"It's an old cue," Brosmer said. "I called him weeks ago
and said I'd be in town on business, and he put it into the
building system for me right then."

"What business are you in, Mr. Marchant?"

"I'm a writer," Brosmer answered, slapping his pocket so
Fortnum could hear the impact on the cassette he'd put there
when he still thought Castelvecchio had any survivors.

"Like Charles. Talent runs in families. Ah, here's Martita with some refreshment. Do you have any gifted children, Mr. Marchant? But you're so young—are you even married?"

"I'm a bachelor," Brosmer said. "In fact, I'm an orphan. Charlie's my only relative." He watched Fortnum's eyes widen in satisfaction. It was always so easy to believe what you hoped for. Brosmer reached out and took the goblet Martita Fortnum handed him silently, her broad mouth pursed quizzically, her eyes peering pale blue through dark cosmetics.

"Have a drink," she said in a husky whisper when he held the rim to his lips. "Both of us have just had some, or we'd join you."

Ah, Jesus, he thought as he inhaled. It was a thing they called Swindle on the street; none of the successful pimps would use it, but the whores all did. It made things so easy. And she hadn't lied; you could see it in both their eyes— they were drifting and dreaming of tense cleverness, lazily riding the hurtling nightmare.

"A harmless relaxant," Fortnum was saying.

Oh, yes, yes, yes, Brosmer thought. In a little while, you can play music and I can dance, I can toss up my hair and be one with the wind, and when you speak to me, I shall answer in tongues that I learned as a child and forgot that I knew.

He pressed his arm against his side, firing Dexedrine into his body, and took a long draught. Amateur animals, he thought, gazing amiably, his nostrils tingling with fumes.

"Isn't that better?" Martita Fortnum whispered.

"Mm-hmm." He smiled at Fortnum. "Do you know where Charlie is? He must have taken his whole family with him."

"Oh, as a matter of fact, they went slightly ahead of him," Fortnum said, and Martita Fortnum giggled.

He could feel it working on him; not just the Swindle gradually winning over the clumsily saurian rages of the

Dexedrine, but the rightness, the inevitability of these monsters and what had been swimming in their systems long before entertainment chemistry had come along with snappily saleable products to validate it. What the hell am I doing here? he thought. I fly a Spad and these people are propelled by turbines.

He lolled his head back in his chair and looked up. There were brass placards in bronze frames hanging over where the door to 25709 could still be faintly made out in mid-air. Over the door to 25711, and over a bed, he imagined, was a nearly wall-width painting which, he deduced from what he could see of it, was of the ocean as one might glimpse it from a bower in a sea cave. The brass placards over the (permanently locked) door to 25709 were bas-reliefs of people in coveralls tearing patches off their clothing, baring buttocks and breasts.

"You killed them for their space," he whispered. "You chewed away their walls, and you stuffed them in the duct for their dwelling allocations."

Fortnum sprang to his feet. Martita recoiled. Fortnum stared at him goggle-eyed: "You're a cop!"

Brosmer lolled in his chair. He gestured idly with his goblet. "Cousin Fuzz." He keyed his phone to the DA's channels. "NYPD shield number 062-26-8729 arresting Timothy and Martita Fortnum, 25609 North Panorama, charge Murder I three counts with additional pending. Attempted Murder of Police Officer, one count. Stand by and monitor. Sit down, Fortnum," he said.

Martita Fortnum sat down at the foot of the circular stairs, one hand over her eyes, the other wandering idly, clambering unconsciously up the bannister to its fullest extension, then trailing swiftly back down to the newel post and clambering again.

Brosmer smiled from very far away. He held out his goblet to Fortnum. "Drink me," he said. "That's an order. You are being questioned."

Breathing sharply through white nostrils, Fortnum complied.

"How do you do it?" Brosmer said after the proper interval.

Fortnum sprawled. "Do what? Get through the walls? That's no trick—you just scrape away the material without nicking the sensors; you know, they're just all elementary. Thermocouples and manometers and things; standard hardware. After you get the wall structure cleared out, you swing all the wiring up so the sensors are reading each other; all the damn building systems care about is whether things are burning or flooding, or if the windows are broken. Then you hang drapes over it."

"Do architects know about plumbing?"

Fortnum raised his head and snorted. "What the hell do you think architecture is, these days? Everybody's got the same space allocation, and the building code's uniform, isn't it? What the hell makes a difference between units except the efficiency of the services? The hell, man, *you* could do it—dial up the library. It's all in there. Plumbing, phone systems . . . everything." A spasm crossed his face. "But *you* never thought of that. You're going home to your place, wherever it is, and dial up *Warbirds,* or do you watch cop shows?"

"I get along," Brosmer said. "Is that how you got to the elevator memory? Do you know about that from the library?"

"*You'd* have to. I *learned* it." It was amazing how much scorn and pride were getting through the Swindle. Brosmer took it in through the buzzing in his ears.

"The story conference," he said. "I can see how you might have learned to intercut tapes of Castelvecchio, but how did you fake being a writer?"

Fortnum giggled shockingly. He wiped his open lips. "Fake being a writer." He grinned. "Fake. Writers." He stood up suddenly and pulled the covering off the chair. Underneath was a metal cabinet. "There she is," he said fondly, running his hands over the home-joined crackled panels. He peered over his shoulder at Brosmer. "This is what it takes," he said, "you know. It's just an assembly of standard logic switchboard. You give it a lot of tapes of Charlie Castelvecchio sitting in a chair and babbling his life away, and when you speak into it, it puts his face on the phone and talks in his voice. Every time it can't match a lip-movement, it shows him turning his face away from the point of view or putting his hand in front of his mouth. It makes him look like he's got the jerks, but who's gonna notice that?"

"And it does the writing for you?"

"Writing? You simple boob, all you need is a hero the audience can identify with, and you give him an immediate serious problem. Then you introduce complications that get him in deeper and deeper, but in the end he does something characteristic on his own hook, and gets out of it. The rest is just atmosphere. You think that stuff in your living room is *art*? Listen—" He waved his arm and dialed. Music swelled up in the room. It thrummed and shook in the air. "That's art," Fortnum said, bracing himself against the wall with one hand. "That's a little ditty called *Jesu, Joy of Man's Desiring,* by Johann Sebastian Bach, the mightiest voice in the Public Domain." He dialed it off hastily. "You know what you can do with that? You can give it an up-tempo, write a set of words that make sounds like screwing but don't use the word, and you're rich. That's how that *momser* upstairs makes his living," Fortnum gasped, waving at the chandelier. "And over *there,*" he panted, pointing into the emptiness above his head, "is the woman who sculpts by dipping paper strands in epoxy and throwing them into the air just before they harden. I can be any of them. I can be all three of them and me, too, all at the same time. And what do you think of that, cop?" He turned, and for a moment his hand rested on the antique scriber. He looked over his shoulder guiltily at Brosmer. Brosmer shook his forefinger at him.

It was the woman who moved—who sprang from her place and flew to the wall, and so it developed that it was

for her—for the To Be Widow Fortnum—that Brosmer had
worn his suit. She gaped at him unbelievingly as his servos
operated the auxiliary mesh skin over his body and gave
him the speed and strength of ten, so that though she flew
as a gannet, he struck as a hawk. And then it was over; she
and her husband sat comforting each other with justifica-
tions, a police lock on their open phone and police locks on
their door(s) as Brosmer made his way home.

Dorrie greeted him. Her eyes did not meet his. "You—
you're home very soon," she said. "I haven't left yet. Do
you want me to stay?"

He went over to his chair, walking around her as best he
could, thinking. He thought of what would happen. Perhaps already, the libraries were being restricted in access.
Only those with certain credentials, such as police buzzers,
would be able to obtain certain classes of data.

"Ned?"

"What? Oh—no, no, you go ahead and do what you've
promised. I've been thinking," he said. "Panorama owes
me the standard rate on about seven Murder I's, and even
after I give George his 25-percent commission, and pay the
bill from Forensic, that's pretty good. I think maybe we
should get mirrors put in. On the walls . . . maybe on the
ceiling."

Dorrie put her fingertip to her mouth. "It'll make it so
much sexier in here," she murmured.

"Bigger," he said. "For a while."

THE RETRIEVAL ARTIST

Kristine Kathryn Rusch

Kristine Kathryn Rusch started out the decade of the 1990s as one of the fastest-rising and most prolific young authors on the scene, took a few years out of mid-decade for a very successful turn as editor of The Magazine of Fantasy and Science Fiction, *and, since stepping down from that position, has returned to her old standards of production here in the twenty-first century, publishing a slew of novels in four genres, writing fantasy, mystery, and romance novels under various pseudonyms as well as science fiction. She has published more than fifteen novels under her own name, including* The White Mists of Power, *the four-volume Fey series, the Black Throne series,* Alien Influences, *and several* Star Wars *books written with husband Dean Wesley Smith. Her most recent book is a major new SF novel,* The Disappeared. *In 1999 she won Readers Award polls from the readerships of both* Asimov's Science Fiction *and* Ellery Queen's Mystery Magazine, *an unprecedented double honor! As an editor, she was honored with the Hugo Award for her work on* The Magazine of Fantasy and Science Fiction *and shared the World Fantasy Award with Dean Wesley Smith for her work as editor of the original hardcover anthology version of* Pulphouse. *As a writer, she has also won the John W. Campbell Award and been a finalist for the Arthur C. Clarke Award, and she took home a Hugo Award in 2000 for her story "Millennium Babies," making her one of the few people in genre history to win Hugos for both editing* and *writing.*

Here she takes us to a domed city on the Moon to introduce us to a detective who specializes in finding things that are lost—whether they want to be found or not.

I

I had just come off a difficult case, and the last thing I wanted was another client. To be honest, not wanting another client is a constant state for me. Miles Flint, the reluctant Retrieval Artist. I work harder than anyone else in the business at discouraging my clients from seeking out the Disappeared. Sometimes the discouragement fails and I get paid a lot of money for putting a lot of lives in danger, and maybe, just maybe, bringing someone home who wants to come. Those are the moments I live for, the moments when it becomes clear to a Disappeared that home is a safe place once more.

Usually, though, my clients and their lost ones are more trouble than they're worth. Usually, I won't take their cases for any price, no matter how high.

I do everything I can to prevent client contact from the start. The clients who approach me are the courageous ones or the really desperate ones or the ones who want to use me to further their own ends.

I try not to take my cases personally. My clients and their lost ones depend on my objectivity. But every once in a while, a case slips under my defenses—and never in the way I expect.

This was one of those cases. And it haunts me still.

II

My office is one of the ugliest dives on the Moon. I found an original building still made of colonial permaplastic in the oldest section of Armstrong, the Moon's oldest colony. The dome here is also made of permaplastic, the clear kind, although time and wear have turned it opaque. Dirt covers the dome near the street level. The filtration system tries to clean as best it can, but ever since some well-meaning dome governor pulled the permaplastic flooring and forgot to replace it, this part of Armstrong Dome has had a dust problem. The filtration systems have been upgraded twice in my lifetime, and rebuilt at least three times since the original settlement, but they still function at one-tenth the level of the state-of-the-art systems in colonies like Gagarin Dome and Glenn Station. Terrans newly off the shuttle rarely come to this part of Armstrong; the high-speed trains don't run here, and the unpaved streets strike most Terrans as unsanitary, which they probably are.

The building that houses my office had been the original retail center of Armstrong, or so says the bronze plaque that someone had attached to the plastic between my door and the rent-a-lawyer's beside me. We are a historic building, not that anyone seems to care, and rent-a-lawyer once talked to me about getting the designation changed so that we could upgrade the facilities.

I didn't tell him that if the designation changed, I would move.

You see, I like the seedy look, the way my door hangs slightly crooked in its frame. It's deceptive. A careless Tracker would think I'm broke, or equally careless. Most folks don't guess that the security in my little eight-by-eight cube is state-of-the-art. They walk in, and they see permaplastic, and a desk that cants slightly to the right, and only one chair behind it. They don't see the recessed doors that hide my storage in the wall between the rent-a-lawyer's cube and my own, and they don't see the electronics because they aren't looking for them.

I like to keep the office empty. I own an apartment in one of Armstrong's better neighborhoods. There I keep all the things I don't care about. Things I do care about stay in my ship, a customized space yacht named *The Emmeline*. She's my only friend and I treat her like a lover. She's saved my life more times than I care to think about, and for that (and a few other things), she deserves only the best.

I can afford to give her the best, and I don't need any

more work, although, as I said, I sometimes take it. The cases that catch me are usually the ones that catch me in my Sir Galahad fantasy—the one where I see myself as a rescuer of all things worthy of rescue—although I've been known to take cases for other reasons.

But, as I'd said, I'd just come off a difficult case, and the last thing I needed was another client. Especially one as young and innocent as this one appeared to be.

She showed up at my door wearing a dress, which no one wears in this part of Armstrong anymore, and regular shoes, which had to have been painful to walk in. She also had a personal items bag around her wrist, which, in this part of town, was like wearing a giant *Mug Me!* sign. The bags were issued on shuttles and only to passengers who had no idea about the luggage limitations.

She was tall and raw-boned, but slender, as if diet and exercise had reduced her natural tendency toward lushness. Her dress, an open and inexpensive weave, accented her figure in an almost unconscious way. Her features were strong and bold, her eyes dark, and her hair even darker.

My alarm system warned me she was outside, staring at the door or the plaque or both. A small screen popped up on my desk revealing her and the street beyond. I shut off the door alarm and waited until she knocked. Her clutched fist, adorned with computer and security enhancements that winked like diamonds in the dome's fake daylight, rapped softly on the permaplastic. The daintiness of the movement startled me. I wouldn't have thought her a dainty woman.

I had been cleaning up the final reports, notations, and billings from the last case. I closed the file and the keyboard (I never use voice commands for work in my office—too easily overheard) folded itself into the desk. Then I leaned back in the chair, and waited.

She knocked three times before she tried the door. It opened, just like it had been programmed to do in instances like this.

"Mr. Flint?" Her voice was soft, her English tinted with a faintly Northern European accent.

I still didn't say anything. She had the right building and the right name. I would wait to see if she was the right kind of client.

She squinted at me. I was never what clients expected. They expected a man as seedy as the office, maybe one or two unrepaired scars, a face toughened by a hard life and space travel. Even though I was thirty-five, I still had a look some cultures called angelic: blond curls, blue eyes, a round and cherubic face. A client once told me I looked like the pre-Raphaelite paintings of Cupid. I had smiled at him and said, *Only when I want to.*

"Are you Mr. Flint?" The girl stepped inside, then slapped her left hand over the enhancements on her right. She looked faintly startled, as if someone had shouted in her ear.

Actually, my security system had cut in. Those enhancements linked her to someone or something outside herself, and my system automatically severed such links, even if they had been billed as unseverable.

"You want to stay in here," I said, "you stay in here alone. No recording, no viewing, and no off-site monitoring."

She swallowed, and took another step inside. She was playing at being timid. The real timid ones, severed from their security blankets, bolt.

"What do you want?" I asked.

She flinched, and took another step forward. "I understand that you . . . find . . . people."

"Where did you hear that?"

"I was told in New York." One more step and she was standing in front of my desk. She smelled faintly of lavender soap mixed with nervous sweat. She must have come here directly from the shuttle. A woman with a mission, then.

"New York?" I asked as if I'd never heard of it.

"New York City."

I had several contacts in New York, and a handful of former clients. Anyone could have told her, although none were supposed to. They always did though; they always saw their own desperation in another's eyes, figured it was time to help, time to give back whatever it was they felt they had gained.

I sighed. "Close the door."

She licked her lips—the dye on them was either water-proof or permanent—and then walked back to the door. She looked into the street as if she would find help there, then gently pushed the door closed.

I felt a faint hum through my wrist as my computer notified me that it had turned the door security back on.

"What do you want?" I asked before she turned around.

"My mother," she said. "She's—"

"That's enough." I kept my tone harsh, and I didn't stand. I didn't want this girl/woman to be too comfortable. It was always best to keep potential clients off balance.

Children, young adults, and the elderly were the obvious choices of someone trying to use my system for the wrong purposes, and yet they were the ones most likely to contact me. They never seemed to understand the hostility I had to show clients, the insistence I put on identity checks, and they always balked at the cost. *It feels as if I'm on trial, Mr. Flint,* they would say, and I wouldn't respond. They were. They had to be. I always had to be sure they were only acting on their own interests. It was too easy for a tracker to hire someone to play off a Retrieval Artist's sympathies, and initiate a search that would get the Disappeared killed—or worse.

The girl turned. Her body was so rigid that it looked as if I could break her in half.

"I don't find people," I said. "I uncover them. There's a vast difference. If you don't understand that, then you don't belong here."

That line usually caused half my potential clients to

exit. The next line usually made most of the remaining fifty percent excuse themselves, never to darken my door again.

"I charge a minimum of two million credits. Moon issue, not Earth issue—" which meant that they were worth triple what she was used to paying "—and I can charge as much as ten million or more. There is no upper limit on my costs nor is there one on my charges. I charge by the day, with expenses added in. Some investigations take a week, some take five years. You would be my exclusive employer for the period of time it takes to find your—mother—or whomever I'd be looking for. I have a contract. Several of my former clients have tried to have the courts nullify it. It holds up beautifully. I do not take charity cases, no matter what your sob story is, and I do not allow anyone to defer payment. The minute the money stops, so do I."

She threaded her fingers together. Her personal items bag bumped against her hip as she did so. "I'd heard about your financial requirements." Which meant that one of my former clients had recommended me to her. Dammit. "I have limited funds, but I can afford a minor investigation."

I stood. "We're done talking. Sorry I can't help you." I walked past her and pulled open the door. Security didn't mind if I did that. It would have minded if she had.

"Can't you do a limited search, Mr. Flint?" Her eyes were wide and brown. If she was twenty, she was older than I thought. I checked for tears. There were none. She could be legit, and for that I was sorry.

I closed the door so hard the plastic office shook. "Here's what you're asking me," I said. "If the money runs out, I quit searching, which is no skin off my nose. But I'll have dug a trail up to that particular point, and your mother—or whomever I'm looking for—

She flinched again as I said that. A tender one. Or a good actress.

"—would be at more of a risk than she is now. Right

now, she's simply disappeared. And since you've come to me, you've done enough research to know that one of six government programs—or one of fifteen private corporations—has gone to considerable expense to give her a new life somewhere else. If the cover on that existence gets blown, your mother dies. It's that simple. And maybe, just maybe, the people who helped her will die too, or the people who are now important to her, or the people who were hidden with her, for whatever reason. Half an investigation is a death sentence. Hell, sometimes a full investigation is a death sentence. So I don't do this work on whim, and I certainly don't do it in a limited fashion. Are we clear?"

She nodded, just once, a rabbit-like movement that let me know I'd connected.

"Good," I said and pulled the door back open. "Now get out."

She scurried past me as if she thought I might physically assault her, and then she hurried down the street. The moon dust rose around her, clinging to her legs and her impractical dress, leaving a trail behind her that was so visible, it looked as if someone were marking her as a future target.

I closed the door, had the security system take her prints and DNA sample off the jamb just in case I needed to identify her someday, and then tried not to think of her again.

It wouldn't be easy. Clients were rare, and if they were legit, they always had an agenda. By the time they found me, they were desperate, and there was still a part of me that was human enough to feel sympathy for that.

Sympathy is rare among Retrieval Artists. Most Retrieval Artists got into this line of work because they owed a favor to the Disty, a group of aliens who'd more or less taken over Mars. Others got into it because they had discovered, by accident, that they were good at it, usually making that discovery in their jobs for human corporations or human crime syndicates.

I got in through a different kind of accident. Once I'd

been a space cop assigned to Moon Sector. A lot of the Disappeared come through here on their way to new lives, and over time, I found myself working against the clock, trying to save people I'd never met from the people they were hiding from. The space police frowned on the work—the Disappeared are often reformed criminals and not worth the time, at least according to the Moon Sector—and so, after one of the most horrible incidents of my life, I went into business on my own.

I'm at the top of my profession, rich beyond all measure, and usually content with that. I chose not to have a spouse or children, and my family is long dead, which I actually consider to be a good thing. Families in this business are a liability. So are close friends. Anyone who can be broken to force you to talk. I don't mind being alone.

But I do hate being manipulated, and I hate even more taking revenge, mine or anyone else's. I vigilantly protect myself against both of those things.

And this was the first time I failed.

III

After the girl left, I stayed away from the office for two days. Sometimes snubbed clients come back. They tell me their stories, the reasons they're searching for their parent/child/spouse, and they expect me to understand. Sometimes they claim they've found more money. Sometimes they simply try to cry on my shoulder, believing I will sympathize.

Once upon a time maybe I would have. But Sir Galahad has calluses growing on his heart, I am beginning to hate the individuals. They always take a level of judgment that drains me. The lawyers trying to find a long-lost soul to meet the terms of a will; the insurance agents, required by law to find the beneficiaries, forced by the government to search "as far as humanly possible without spending the benefits"; the detective, using government funds to find the one person who could put a career criminal, serial killer, or child molester away for life; these people are the clients I like the most. Almost all are repeat customers. I still have to do background checks, but I have my gut to rely on as well. With individuals, I can never go by gut, and even armed with information, I've been burned.

I've gotten to the point where coldness is the way of the game for me, at least at first. Once I sign on, I become the most intense defender of the Disappeared. The object of my search also becomes the person I protect and care about the most. It takes a lot of effort to maintain that caring, and even more to manage the protection.

Sometimes I'll go to extremes.

Sometimes I have no other choice.

On the third day, I went back to my office, and of course, the girl was waiting. This time she was dressed appropriately, a pair of boots, cargo pants that cinched at the ankles, and a shirt the color of sand. Her personal items bag was gone—obviously someone, probably the maître d' at the exclusive hotel she was most likely staying at, had told her it made her a mark for pickpockets and other thieves. Thin mesh gloves covered her enhancements. Only her long hair marked her as a newcomer. If she stayed longer than a month, she'd cut it off just like the rest of us rather than worry about keeping it clean.

She was leaning against my locked door, her booted feet sticking into the street. In that outfit, she looked strong and healthy, as if she were hiring me to take her on one of those expeditions outside the dome. The rent-a-lawyer next door, newly out of Armstrong Law, was eyeing her out of his scarred plastic window, a sour expression on his thin face. He probably thought she was scaring away business.

I stopped in the middle of the street. It was hot and airless as usual. There was no wind in the dome, of course, and the recycled air got stale real fast. Half the equipment in this part of town had been on the fritz for the last week, and the air here wasn't just stale, it was thin and damn near rancid. I hated breathing bad air. The shallow breaths and the increased heartbeat made me feel as if there was danger around when there probably wasn't. If the air got any thinner, I'd have to start worrying about my clarity of thought.

She saw me when I was still several meters from the place. She stood, brushed the dust off her pants, and watched me. I pretended as if I were undecided about my next move, even though I knew I'd have to confront her sooner or later. Her kind only went away when chased.

"I'm sorry," she said as I approached. "I was told that you expected negotiation, so I—"

"Lied about the money, did you?" I asked, knowing she was lying now too. If she knew enough to find me, she also knew that I didn't negotiate. All the lie proved was that she had an ego big enough to believe that the rules were different for her.

I shoved past her to use my palm scan when someone else was present. It let us in, but initiated a higher level of security monitor.

She started to follow me, but I slammed the door in her face. Then I went to my desk, and switched on my own automatic air. It was illegal, and it wouldn't be enough, but I wasn't planning to stay long. I would finish the reports from the last case, get the final fees, and then maybe I'd take a vacation. I had never taken one before. It was past time.

I wish, now, that I had listened to my gut and gone. But there was just enough of Sir Galahad left in me to make me watch the door. And of course, it opened just like I expected it to.

She came inside, a little downtrodden but not defeated. Her kind seldom were. "My name is Anetka Sobol," she said as if I should know it. I didn't. "I really do need your help."

"You should have thought of that before," I said. "This isn't a game."

"I'm not trying to play one."

"So what was that attempt at negotiation?"

She shook her head. "My source—"

"Who is your source?"

"He said I wasn't—"

"Who is it?"

Again she licked that lower lip just like she had the day before, a movement that was too unconscious to be planned. The nervousness, then, wasn't feigned. "Norris Gonnot."

Gonnot. Sobol was the third client he'd sent to me in the last year. The other two checked out, and both cases had been easy to solve. But he was making himself too visible, and I would have to deal with that, even though I hated to do so. He was extremely grateful that I had found his daughter and granddaughter alive (although they hadn't appreciated it), and he'd been even more grateful when I was able to prove that the Disty were no longer looking for them.

"And how did you find him?"

She frowned. "Does it matter?"

I leaned back in my chair. It squeaked and the sound made her jump ever so slightly. "Either you're up front with me now or the conversation ends."

The frown grew deeper, and she clutched her left wrist with her right hand, holding the whole mess against her stomach. The gesture looked calculated. "Do you treat everyone like this?"

"Nope. Some people I treat worse."

"Then how do you get any work?"

I shrugged. "Just lucky."

She stared at me for a moment. Then she glanced at the door. Was she letting her thoughts be that visible on purpose or was she again acting for my benefit? I wasn't sure.

"A cop told me about him. Norris, that is." She sounded reluctant. "I wasn't supposed to tell you."

"Of course not. Gonnot wasn't supposed to talk to anyone. This cop, was he a rent-a-cop, a real cop, a Federal cop, or with the Earth Force?"

"She," she said.

"Okay," I said. "Was she a—"

"She was a New York City police officer who had her own detective agency."

"That's illegal in New York."

She shrugged. "So?"

I closed my eyes. Ethics had disappeared everywhere. "You hired her?"

"She was my fifth private detective. Most would work for a week and then quit when they realized that searching for an interstellar Disappeared is a lot harder than finding a missing person."

I waited. I'd heard that sob story before. Most detectives kept the case and simply came to someone like me.

"Of course," she said, "my father's looming presence doesn't help either."

"Your father?"

She was staring at me as if I had just asked her what God was.

"I'm Anetka Sobol," she said as if that clarified everything.

"And I'm Miles Flint. My name doesn't tell you a damn thing about my father."

"My father is the founding partner of the Third Dynasty."

I had to work to hide my surprise. I knew what the Third Dynasty was, but I didn't know the names of its founders. The Dynasty itself was a formidable presence all over the galaxy. It was a megacorp with its fingers in a lot of pies, mostly to do with space exploration, establishing colonies in mineral-rich areas, and exploitation of new resources. My contacts with the Third Dynasty weren't on the exploration level, but within its narrow interior holdings. The Third Dynasty was the parent company for Privacy Unlimited, one of the services which helped people disappear.

Privacy Unlimited had been developed, as so many of the corporate disappearance programs had, when humans discovered the Disty, and realized that in some alien cultures, there was no such word as forgiveness. The Disty were the harshest of our allies. The Revs, the Wygnin, and the Fuetrer also targeted certain humans, and our treaties with these groups allowed the targeting if the aliens could show cause.

The balance was a delicate one, allowing them their cultural traditions while protecting our own. Showing cause had to happen before one of eighteen multicultural tribunals, and if one of those tribunals ruled in the aliens' favor, the humans involved were as good as dead. We looked the other way most of the time. Most of the lives involved were, according to our government, trivial ones. But of course, those people whose lives had been deemed trivial didn't feel that way, and that was when the disappearance services cropped up. If a person disappeared and could not be found, most alien groups kept an outstanding warrant, but stopped searching.

The Disty never did.

And since much of the Third Dynasty's business was conducted in Disty territory, its disappearance service, Privacy Unlimited, had to be one of the best in the galaxy.

Something in my face must have given my knowledge away, because she said, "Now do you understand my problem?"

"Frankly, no," I said. "You're the daughter of the big kahuna. Go to Privacy Unlimited and have them help you. It's usually not too hard to retrace steps."

She shook her head. "My mother didn't go to Privacy Unlimited. She used another service."

"You're sure?"

"Yes." She brushed a hand alongside her head, to move the long hair. "It's my father she's running from."

A domestic situation. I never get involved in those. Too messy and too complicated. Never a clear line. "Then she didn't need a service at all. She probably took a shuttle here, then a transport for parts unknown."

Anetka Sobol crossed her arms. "You don't seem to understand, Mr. Flint. My father could have found her with his own service if she had done something like that. It's simple enough. My detectives should have been able to find her. They can't."

"Let me see if I can understand this," I said. "Are you looking for her or is your father?"

"I am."

"As a front for him?"

Color flooded her face. "No."

"Then why?"

"I want to meet her."

I snorted. "You're going to a lot of expense for a 'hello, how are you?' Aren't you afraid Daddy will find out?"

"I have my own money."

"Really? Money daddy doesn't know about? Money Daddy doesn't monitor?"

She straightened. "He doesn't monitor me."

I nodded. "That's why the mesh gloves. Fashion statement?"

She glanced at her enhancements. "I got them. They have nothing to do with my father."

My smile was small. "Your father has incredible resources. You don't think he'd do something as simple as hack into your enhancement files. Believe me, one of those pretty baubles is being used to track you, and if my security weren't as good as it is, another would have been monitoring this conversation."

She put her left hand over her right as if covering the enhancements would make me forget them. All it did was remind me that this time, she didn't react when my security shut down her links. This was one smart girl, and one I didn't entirely understand.

"Go home," I said. "Deal with Daddy. If you want family ties, get married, have children, hire someone to play your mother. If you need genetic information or disease history, see your family doctors. I suspect they'll have all the records you need and probably some you don't. If you want Daddy to leave you alone, I'd ask him first before I go to any more expense. He might just do what you want. And if you're trying to make him angry, I'll bet you've gone far enough. You'll probably be hearing from him very soon."

Her eyes narrowed. "You're so sure of yourself, Mr. Flint."

"It's about the only thing I am sure of," I said, and waited for her to leave.

She didn't. She stared at me for a long moment, and in her eyes, I saw a coldness, a hardness I hadn't expected. It was as if she were evaluating me and finding me lacking.

I let her stare. I didn't care what she thought one way or another. I did wish she would get to the point so that I could kick her out of my office.

Finally she sighed and pursed her lips as if she had eaten something sour. She looked around, probably searching for some place to sit down. She didn't find one. I don't like my clients to sit. I don't want them to be comfortable in my presence.

"All right," she said, and her voice was somehow different. Stronger, a little more powerful. I knew the timidity had been an act. "I came to you because you seem to be the only one who can do this job."

My smile was crooked and insincere. "Flattery."

"Truth," she said.

I shook my head. "There are dozens of people who do this job, and most are cheaper." I let my smile grow colder. "They also have chairs in their offices."

"They value their clients," she said.

"Probably at the expense of the people they're searching out."

"Ethics," she said. "That's why I've come here. You're the only one in your profession who seems to have any."

"You have need of ethics?" Somehow I had trouble believing the woman with that powerful voice had need of anyone with ethics. "Or is this simply another attempt at manipulation?"

To my surprise, she smiled. The expression was stunning. It brought life to her eyes, and somehow seemed to make her even taller than she had been a moment before.

"Manipulation got me to you," she said. "Your Mr. Gonnot seems to have a soft spot for people who are missing family."

"Everyone who's missing is a member of a family," I said, but more to the absent Gonnot than to her. I could see how he could be manipulated, and that made it more important than ever to stop him from sending customers my way.

She shrugged at my comment, then she sat on the edge of my desk. I'd never had anyone do that, not in all my years in the business. "I do have need of ethics," she said. "If you breathe a single word of what I'm going to tell you . . ."

She didn't finish the sentence, on purpose of course, probably figuring that whatever I could imagine would be worse than what she could come up with.

I sighed. This girl—this woman—liked games.

"If you want the sanctity of a confessional," I said, "see a priest. If you want a profession that requires its practitioners to practice confidentiality as a matter of course, see a psychiatrist. I'll keep confidential whatever I deem worthy of confidentiality."

She folded her slender hands on her lap. "You enjoy judging your clients, don't you?"

I stared at her—up at her—which actually put me at a disadvantage. She was good at intimidation skills, even better than she had been as an actress. It made me uncomfortable, but somehow it seemed more logical for the daughter of the man who ran the Third Dynasty.

"I have to," I said. "A lot of lives depend on my judgments."

She shook her head slightly. It was as if my earlier answer stymied her, prevented her from continuing. She had to learn that we would do this on my terms or we wouldn't do it at all.

I waited. I could wait all day if I had to. Most people didn't have that kind of patience no matter what sort of will they had.

She clearly didn't. After a few moments, she brushed her pants, adjusted the flap on one of the pockets, and sighed again. She must have needed me badly.

Finally, she closed her eyes, as if summoning strength. When she opened them, she was looking at me directly. "I am a clone, Mr. Flint."

Whatever I had thought she was going to say, it wasn't that. I worked very hard at keeping the surprise off my face.

"And my father is dying." She paused, as if she were testing me.

I knew the answer, and the problem. When her father died, she couldn't inherit. Clones were barred from familial inheritance by interstellar law. The law had been adapted universally after several cases where clones created by a nonfamily member and raised far from the original (wealthy) family inherited vast estates. The basis of the inheritance was a shared biology that anyone could create. Rather than letting large fortunes get leached off to whoever was smart enough to steal a hair from a hairbrush and use it to create a copy of a human being, legislators finally decided to create the law. The courts upheld it. It was rigid.

"Your father could change his will," I said, knowing that she had probably broached this with him already.

"It's too late," she said. "He's been ill for a while. The change could easily be disputed in court."

"So you're not an only child?" I had to work to keep from asking if she were an only copy.

"I am the only clone," she said. "My father had me made, and he raised me himself. I am, for all intents and purposes, his daughter."

"Then he should have changed his will long ago."

She waved a hand, as if the very idea were a silly one. And it probably was. A clone had to come from somewhere. So either she was the copy of a real child or a copy of the woman she wanted me to find. Perhaps the will was unchanged because the original person was still out there.

"My mother vanished with the real heir," she said.

I waited.

"My father always expected to find them. My sister is the one who inherits."

I hated clone terminology. "Sister" was such an inaccurate term, even though clones saw themselves as twins. They weren't. They weren't raised that way or thought of that way. The Original stood to inherit. The clone before me did not.

"So you, out of the goodness of your heart, are searching for your missing family." I laid the sarcasm on thick. I've handled similar cases before. Where money was involved, people were rarely altruistic.

"No," she said, and her bluntness surprised me. "My father owns 51 percent of the Third Dynasty. When he dies, it goes into the corporation itself, and can be bought by other shareholders. I am not a shareholder, but I have been raised from birth to run the Dynasty. The idea was that I would share my knowledge with my sister, and that we would run the business together."

This made more sense.

"So I need to find her, Mr. Flint, before the shares go back into the corporation. I need to find her so that I can live the kind of life I was raised to live."

I hated cases like this. She was right. I did judge my clients. And if I found them the least bit suspicious, I didn't take on the case. If I believed that what they would do would jeopardize the Disappeared, I wouldn't take the case either. But if the reason for the disappearance was gone, or if the reason for finding the missing person benefited or did not harm the Disappeared, then I would take the case.

I saw benefit here, in the inheritance, and in the fact that the reason for the disappearance was dying.

"Your father willed his entire fortune to his missing child?"

She nodded.

"Then why isn't he searching for her?"

"He figured she would come back when she heard of his death."

Possible, depending on where she had disappeared to, but not entirely probable. The girl might not even know who she was.

"If I find your mother," I said, "then will your father try to harm her?"

"No," she said. "He couldn't if he wanted to. He's too sick. I can forward the medical records to you."

One more thing to check. And check I would. I guess I was taking this case, no matter how messily she started it. I was intrigued, just enough.

"Your father doesn't have to be healthy enough to act on his own," I said. "With his money, he could hire someone."

"I suppose," she said. "But I control almost all of his business dealings right now. The request would have to go through me."

I still didn't like it, but superficially, it sounded fine. I would, of course, check it out. "Where's your clone mark?"

She frowned at me. It was a rude question, but one I needed the answer to before I started.

She pulled her hair back, revealing a small number eight at the spot where her skull met her neck. The fine hairs had grown away from it, and the damage to the skin had been done at the cellular level. If she tried to have the eight removed, it would grow back.

"What happened to the other seven?" I asked.

She let her hair fall. "Failed."

Failed clones were unusual. Anything unusual in a case like this was suspect.

"My mother," she said, as if she could hear my thoughts, "was pregnant when she disappeared. I was cloned from sloughed cells found in the amnio."

"Hers or the baby's?"

"The baby's. They tested. But they used a lot of cells to find one that worked. It took a while before they got me."

Sounded plausible, but I was no expert. More information to check.

"Your father must have wanted you badly."

She nodded.

"Seems strange that he didn't alter his will for you."

Her shoulders slumped. "He was afraid any changes he made wouldn't have been lawyer-proof. He was convinced I'd lose everything because of lawsuits if he did that."

"So he arranged for you to lose everything on his own?"

She shook her head. "He wanted the family together. He wanted me to work with my sister to—"

"So he said."

"So he says." She ran a hand through her hair. "I think he hopes that my sister will cede the company to me. For a percentage, of course."

There it was. The only loophole in the law. A clone could receive an inheritance if it came directly from the person whose genetic material the clone shared, provided that the Original didn't die under suspicious circumstances. Of course, a living person could, in Anetka's words, "cede" that ownership as well, although it was a bit more difficult.

"You're looking for her for money," I said in my last-ditch effort to get out of the case.

"You won't believe love," she said.

She was right. I wouldn't have.

"Besides," she said. "I have my own money. More than enough to keep me comfortable for the rest of my life. Whatever else you may think of my father, he provided that. I'm searching for her for the corporation. I want to keep it in the family. I want to work it like I was trained. And this seems to be the only way."

It wasn't a very pretty reason, and I'd learned over the years, it was usually the ugly reasons that were the truth. Not, of course, that I could go by gut, I wouldn't.

"My retainer is two million credits," I said. "If you're lucky, that's all this investigation will cost you. I have a contract that I'll send to you or your personal representative, but let me give you the short version verbally."

She nodded.

I continued, reciting, as I always did, the essential terms so that no client could ever say I'd lied to her. "I have the right to terminate at any time for any reason. You may not terminate until the Disappeared is found, or I have concluded that the Disappeared is gone for good. You are legally liable for any lawsuits that arise from any crimes committed by third parties as a result of this investigation. I am not. You will pay me my rate plus expenses whenever I bill you. If your money stops, the investigation stops, but if I find you've been withholding funds to prevent me from digging farther, I am entitled to a minimum of ten million credits. I will begin my investigation by investigating you. Should I decide you are unworthy as a client before I begin searching for the Disappeared, I will refund half of your initial retainer. There's more but those are the salient points. Is all of that clear?"

"Perfectly."

"I'll begin as soon as I get the retainer."

"Give me your numbers and I'll have the money placed in your account immediately."

I handed her my single printed card with my escrow account embedded into it. The account was a front for several other accounts, but she didn't need to know that. Even my money went through channels. Someone who is good at finding the Disappeared is also good at making other things disappear.

"Should you need to reach me in an emergency," I said, "place 673 credits into this account."

"Strange number," she said.

I nodded. The number varied from client to client, a random pattern. Sometimes, past clients sent me their old amounts as a way to contact me about something new. I kept the system clear.

"I'll respond to the depositing computer from wherever I am, as soon as I can. This is not something you should do frivolously nor is it something to be done to check up on me. It's only for an emergency. If you want to track the progress of the investigation, you can wait for my weekly updates."

"And if I have questions?"

"Save them for later."

"What if I think I can help?"

"Leave me mail." I stood. She was watching me, that hard edge in her eyes again. "I've got work to do now. I'll contact you when I'm ready to begin my search."

"How long will this investigation of me take?"

"I have no idea," I said. "It depends on how much you're hiding."

IV

Clients never tell the truth. No matter how much I instruct them to, they never do. It seems to be human nature to lie about something, even when it's something small. I had a hunch, given Anetka Sobol's background, she had lied about a lot. The catch was to find out how much of what she had lied about was relevant to the job she had hired me for. Finding out required research.

I do a lot of my research through public accounts, using fake ID. It is precautionary, particularly in the beginning, because so many case don't pan out. If a Disappeared still has a Tracker after her, repeated searches from me will be flagged. Searches from public accounts—especially different public accounts—will not. Often the Disappeared are already famous or become famous when they vanish, and are often the subject of anything from vidspec to school reports.

My favorite search site is a bar not too far from my office. I love the place because it serves some of the best food in Armstrong, in some of the largest quantities. The large quantities are required, given the place's name. The Brownie Bar serves the only marijuana in the area, baked into specially marked goods, particularly the aforementioned brownies. Imbibers get the munchies, and proceed to spend hundreds of credits on food. The place turns quite a profit, and it's also comfortable; marijuana users seem to like their creature comforts more than most other recreational drug types.

Recreational drugs are legal on the Moon, as are most things. The first settlers came in search of something they called "freedom from oppression," which usually meant freedom to pursue an alternative lifestyle. Some of those lifestyles have since become illegal or simply died out, but others remain. The only illegal drugs these days, at least in Armstrong, are those that interfere with the free flow of air. Everything from nicotine to opium is legal—as long as its user doesn't smoke it.

The Brownie Bar caters to the casual user as well as the hard-core and, unlike some drug bars, doesn't mind the non-user customer. The interior is large with several sections. One section, the party wing, favors the bigger groups, the ones who usually arrive in numbers larger than ten, spend hours eating and giggling, and often get quite obnoxiously wacky. In the main section, soft booths with tables shield clients from each other. Usually the people sitting there are couples or groups of four. If one group gets particularly loud, a curtain drops over the open section of the booth, and their riotous laughter fades to nearly nothing.

My section caters to the hard core, who sometimes stop for a quick fix in the middle of the business day, or who like a brownie before dinner to calm the stress of a hectic afternoon. Many of these people have only one, and continue work while they're sitting at their solitary tables. It's quiet as a church in this section, and many of the patrons are plugged into the client ports that allow them access to the Net.

The access ports are free, but the information is not. Particular servers charge by the hour in the public areas, but have the benefit of allowing me to troll using the server or the bar's identicodes, I like that; it usually makes my preliminary searchers impossible to trace.

That afternoon, I took my usual table in the very back. It's small, made of high-grade plastic designed to look like wood—and it fools most people. It never fooled me, partly because I knew the Brownie Bar couldn't afford to import, and partly because I knew they'd never risk something that valuable on a restaurant designed for stoners. I sat cross-legged on the thick pillow on the floor, ordered some turkey stew—made here with real meat—and plugged in.

The screen was tabletop and had a keyboard so that the user could have complete privacy. I'd heard other patrons complain that using the Brownie Bar's system required them to read, but it was one of the features I liked.

I started with Anetka and decided to work my way backwards through the Sobol family. I found her quickly enough; her life was well covered by the tabs, which made no mention of her clone status. She was twenty-seven, ten to twelve years older than she looked. She'd apparently had those youthful looks placed in stasis surgically. She'd look girlish until she died.

Another good fact to know. If there was an Original, she might not look like Anetka. Not anymore.

Anetka had been working in her father's corporation since she was twelve. Her IQ was off the charts—surgically enhanced as well, at least according to most of the vidspec programs—and she breezed through Harvard and then Cambridge. She did postdoc work at the Interstellar Business School in Islamabad, and was out of school by the time she was twenty-five. For the last two years, she'd been on the corporate fast track, starting in lower management and working her way to the top of the corporate ladder.

She was, according to the latest feeds, her father's main assistant.

So I had already found Possible Lie Number One: She wasn't here for herself. She was, as I had suspected, a front for her father. Not to find the wife, but to find the real heir.

I wasn't sure how I'd feel if that were true. I needed to find out if, indeed, the Original was the one who'd inherit. If she wasn't, I wouldn't take the case. There'd be no point.

But I wasn't ready to make judgments yet. I had a long way to go. I looked up Anetka's father and discovered that Carson Sobol had never remarried, although he'd been seen with a bevy of beautiful women over the years. All were close to his age. He never dated women younger than he was. Most had their own fortunes, and many their own companies. He spent several years as the companion to an acclaimed Broadway actress, even funding some of her more famous plays. That relationship, like the others, had ended amicably.

Which led to Possible Lie Number Two: a man who terrorized his wife so badly that she had to run away from him also terrorized his later girlfriends. And while a man could keep something like that quiet for a few years, even-

tually the pattern would become evident. Eventually one of
the women would talk.

There was no evidence of terrorizing in the stuff I
found. Perhaps the incidents weren't reported. Or perhaps
there was nothing to report. I would vote for the latter. It
seemed, from the vidspec I'd read, everyone knew that the
wife had left him because of his cruelty. My experience
with vidspec reporters made me confident that they'd be
on the lookout for more proof of Carson Sobol's nasty
character. And if they found it, they'd report it.

No one had.

I didn't know if that meant Sobol had learned his lesson
when the wife ran off, or perhaps Sobol had learned that
mistreatment of women was bad for business. I couldn't
believe that a man could terrify everyone into silence. If
that were his methodology, there would be a few leaks that
were quickly hushed up, and one or two dead bodies float-
ing around—bodies belonging to folks who hadn't listened. Also, there would be rumors, and there were none.

Granted, I was making assumptions on a very small
amount of information. Most of the reports I found
about Sobol weren't about his family or his love life,
but about the Third Dynasty as it expanded in that period to new worlds, places that human businesses had
never been before.

The Third Dynasty had been the first to do business
with the Fuetrer, the HDs, and the chichers. It opened
plants on Korsve, then closed them when it realized that
the Wygnin, the dominant life-form on Korsve, did not—
and apparently could not—understand the way that humans did business.

I shuddered at the mention of Korsve. If a client approached me because a family member had been taken by
the Wygnin, I refused the case. The Wygnin took individuals to pay off debt, and then those individuals became
part of a particular Wygnin family. For particularly
heinous crimes, the Wygnin took firstborns, but usually,

the Wygnin just took babies—from any place in the family structure—at the time of birth, and then raised them. Occasionally they'd take an older child or an adult. Sometimes they'd take an entire group of adults from offending businesses. The adults were subject to mind control and personality destruction as the Wygnin tried to remake them to fit into Wygnin life.

All of that left me with no good options. Children raised by the Wygnin considered themselves Wygnin and couldn't adapt to human cultures. Adults who were taken by the Wygnin were so broken that they were almost unrecognizable. Humans raised by the Wygnin did not want to return. Adults who were broken always wanted to return, and when they did, they signed a death warrant for their entire family—or worse, doomed an entire new generation to kidnap by the Wygnin.

But Wygnin custom didn't seem relevant here. Despite the plant closings, the Third Dynasty had managed to avoid paying a traditional Wygnin price. Or perhaps someone had paid down the line, and that information was classified.

There were other possibles in the files. The Third Dynasty seemed to have touched every difficult alien race in the galaxy. The corporation had an entire division set aside for dealing with new cultures. Not that the division was infallible. Sometimes there were unavoidable errors.

Sylvy Sobol's disappearance had been one of those. It had caused all sorts of problems for both Sobol and the Third Dynasty. The vidspecs, tabs, and other media had had a field day when she had disappeared. The news led to problems with some of the alien races, particularly the Altaden. The Altaden valued non-violence above all else, and the accusations of domestic violence at the top levels of the Third Dynasty nearly cost the corporation its Altaden holdings.

The thing was, no one expected the disappearance—or the marriage, for that matter. Sylvy Sobol had been a European socialite, better known for her charitable works and her incredible beauty than her interest in business. She belonged to an old family with ties to several still-existing monarchies. It was thought that her marriage would be to someone else from the accepted circle.

It had caused quite a scandal when she had chosen Carson Sobol, not only because of his mixed background and uncertain lineage, but also because some of his business practices had taken large fortunes from the countries she was tied to and spent them in space instead.

He was controversial; the marriage was controversial; and it looked, from the vids I watched, like the two of them had been deeply in love.

I felt a hand on my shoulder. A waitress stood behind me, holding a large ceramic bowl filled with turkey stew. She smiled at me.

"Didn't want to set it on your work."

"It's fine," I said, indicating an empty spot near the screen. She set my utensils down, and then the bowl. The stew smelled rich and fine, black beans and yogurt adding to the aroma. My stomach growled.

The waitress tapped one of the moving images. "I remember that," she said. "I was living in Vienna. The Viennese thought that marriage was an abomination."

I looked up. She was older than I was, without the funds to prevent the natural aging process. Laugh lines crinkled around her eyes, and her lips—unpainted and untouched—were a faint rose. She smiled.

"Guess it turned out that way, huh? The wife running off like that? Leaving that message?"

"Message?" I asked. I hadn't gotten that far.

"I don't remember exactly what it was. Something like, 'The long arm of the Third Dynasty is impossible to fight. I am going where you can't find me. Maybe then I'll have the chance to live out my entire life.' I guess he nearly beat her to death." The waitress laughed, a little embarrassed.

"In those days I had nothing better to do than study the lives of more interesting people."

"And now?" I asked.

She shrugged. "I figured out that everybody's interesting. I mean, you've got to try. You've got to live. And if you do, you've done something fascinating."

I nodded. People like her were one of the reasons I liked this place.

"You want something to drink?" she asked.

"Bottled water."

"Got it," she said as she left.

By the time she brought my bottled water, I had indeed found the note. It had been sent to all the broadcast media, along with a grainy video, taken from a hidden camera, of one of the most brutal domestic beatings I'd ever seen. The images were sometimes blurred and indistinct, but the actions were clear. The man had beat the woman senseless.

There was no mention of the pregnancy in any of this. There was, however, notification of Anetka's birth six months before her mother had disappeared.

Which led me to Possible Lie Number Three: Anetka had said her mother traveled pregnant. Perhaps she hadn't. Or, more chillingly, someone had altered the record either before or after the clones were brought to term. There had to be an explanation of Anetka in the media or she wouldn't be accepted. If that explanation had been planted before, something else was going on. If it were planted afterwards, Sobol's spokespeople could have simply said that reporters had overlooked her in their rush to other stories.

I checked the other media reports and found the same story. It was time to go beneath those stories and see what else I could find. Then I would confront Anetka about the lies before I began the search for her mother.

V

I contacted her and we met, not at my office, but at her hotel. She was staying in Armstrong's newest district, an addition onto the dome that caused a terrible controversy before it was built. Folks in my section believe the reason for the thinner air is that the new addition has stretched resources. I know they aren't right—with the addition came more air and all the other regulation equipment—but it was one of those arguments that made an emotional kind of sense.

I thought of those arguments, though, as I walked among the new buildings, made from a beige material not even conceived of thirty years before, a material that's supposed to be attractive (it isn't) and more resistant to decay than permaplastic. This entire section of Armstrong smelt new, from the recycled air to the buildings rising around me. They were four stories high and had large windows on the dome side, obviously built with a view in mind.

This part of the dome is self-cleaning and see-through. Dust does not slowly creep up the sides as it does in the other parts of Armstrong. The view is barren and stark, just like the rest of the Moon, but there's a beauty in the starkness that I don't see anywhere else in the universe.

The hotel was another large four-story building. Most of its windows were glazed dark, so no one could see in, but the patrons could see out. It was part of a chain whose parent company was, I had learned the day before, the Third Dynasty. Anetka was doing very little to hide her search from her father.

Inside, the lobby was wide, and had an old-fashioned feel. The walls changed images slowly, showing the famous sites from various parts of the galaxy where the hotels were located. I had read before the hotel opened that the constantly changing scenery took eight weeks to repeat an image. I wondered what it was like working in a place where the view shifted constantly, and then decided I didn't want to know.

The lobby furniture was soft and a comforting shade of dove gray. Piano music, equally soft and equally comforting, was piped in from somewhere. Patrons sat in small groups as if they were posing for a brochure. I went up to the main desk and asked for Anetka. The concierge led me to a private conference room down the main hallway.

I expected the room to be monitored. That didn't bother me. At this point, I still had nothing to hide. Anetka did, but this was her company's hotel. She could get the records, shut off the monitors, or have them destroyed. It would all be her choice.

To my surprise, she was waiting for me. She was wearing another dress, a blue diaphanous thing that looked so fragile I wondered how she managed to move from place to place. Her hair was up and pinned, with diamonds glinting from the soft folds. She also had diamonds glued to the ridge beneath her eyebrows, and trailing down her cheeks. The net effect was to accent her strength. Her broad shoulders held the gown as if it were air, and the folds parted to reveal the muscles on her arms and legs. She was like the diamonds she wore; pretty and glittering, but able to cut through all the objects in the room.

"Have you found anything?" she asked without preamble.

I shut the door and helped myself to the carafe of water on the bar against the nearest wall. There was a table in the center of the room—made, it seemed—of real wood, with matching chairs on the side. There was also a workstation, and a one-way mirror with a view of the lobby.

I leaned against the bar, holding my water glass. It was thick and heavy, sturdy like most things on the Moon. "Your father's will has been posted among the Legal Notices on all the nets for the last three years."

She nodded. "It's common for CEOs to do that to allay stockholder fears."

"It's common for CEOs to authorize the release after they've died. Not before."

Her smile was small, almost patronizing. "Smaller corporations, yes. But it's becoming a requirement for major shareholders in megacorps to do this even if they are not dead. Investigate farther, Mr. Flint, and you'll see that all of the Third Dynasty's major shareholders have posted their wills."

I had already checked the other shareholders' wills, and found that Anetka was right. I also looked for evidence that Carson Sobol was dead, and found none.

She took my silence to be disbelief. "It's the same with the other megacorps. Personal dealings are no longer private in the galactic business world."

I had known that the changes were taking place. I had known, for example, that middle managers signed loyalty oaths to corporations, sometimes requiring them to forsake family if the corporation called for it. This, one pundit had said, was the hidden cost of doing business with alien races. You had to be willing to abandon all you knew in the event of a serious mistake. The upshot of the change was becoming obvious. People to whom family was important were staying away from positions of power in the megacorps.

I said, "You're not going to great lengths to hide this search from your father."

She placed a hand on the wooden chair. She was not wearing gloves, and mingled among the enhancements were more diamonds. "You seem obsessed with my father."

"Your mother disappeared because of him. I'm not going to find her only to have him kill her."

"He wouldn't."

"Says you."

"This is your hesitation?"

"Actually, no," I said. "My hesitation is that, according to all public records, you were born six months before your mother disappeared."

I didn't tell her that I knew all the databases had been

tampered with, including the ones about her mother's disappearance. I couldn't tell if the information had been altered to show that the disappearance came later or that the child had been born earlier. The tampering was so old that the original material was lost forever.

"My father wanted me to look like a legitimate child."

"You are a clone. He knew cloning laws."

"But no one else had to know."

"Not even with his will posted?"

"Like you said, it's only been posted for the last three years."

"Is that why you're not mentioned?"

She raised her chin. "I received my inheritance before—already," she said. I found the correction interesting. "The agreement between us about my sister is both confidential and binding."

"'All of my worldly possessions shall go to my eldest child,'" I quoted, "That child isn't even listed by name."

"No," she said.

"And he isn't going to change the will for you?"

"The Disty won't do business with clones."

"I didn't know you had business with the Disty," I said.

She shrugged. "The Disty, the Emin, the Revs. You name them, we have business with them. And we have to be careful of some customs."

"Won't the stockholders be suspicious when you don't inherit?"

Her mouth formed a thin line. "That's why I'm hiring you," she said. "You need to find my sister."

I nodded. Then, for the first time in the meeting, I sat down. The chair was softer than I had expected it would be. I put my feet on the nearest chair. She glanced at them as if they were a lower life-form.

"In order to search for people," I said, "I need to know who they're running from. If they're running from the Disty, for example, I'll avoid the Martian colonies, because they're overrun with Disty. No one would hide there.

It would be impossible. If they were running from the Revs, I would start looking at plastic surgeons and doctors who specialize in genetic alteration because anyone who looks significantly different from the person the Revs have targeted is considered, by the Revs, to be a different being entirely."

She started to say something, but I held up my hand to silence her.

"Human spouses abuse each other," I said. "It seems to be part of the human experience. These days, the abused spouse moves out, and sometimes leaves the city, and sometimes leaves the plant, but more often than not stays in the same area. It's unusual to run, to go through a complete identity change, and to start a new life, especially in your parents' income bracket. So tell me, why did your mother really leave?"

Nothing changed in Anetka's expression. It remained so immobile that I knew she was struggling for control. The hardness that had been so prevalent the day before was gone, banished, it seemed, so that I wouldn't see anything amiss.

"My father has a lot of money," she said.

"So do other people. Their spouses don't disappear."

"He also controls a powerful megacorp with fingers all over the developing worlds. He has access to more information than anyone. He vowed to never let my mother out of his sight. My father believed that marriage vows were sacred, and no matter how much the parties wanted out, they were obligated by their promises to each other and to God to remain." Anetka's tone was flat too. "If she had just moved out, he would have forced her to move back in. If she had moved to the Moon, he would have come after her. If she had moved to some of the planets in the next solar system, he would have come for her. So she had no choice."

"According to your father."

"According to anyone who knew her." Anetka's voice was soft. "You saw the vids."

I nodded.

"That was mild, I guess, for what he did to her."

I leaned back in the chair, lifting the front two legs off the ground. "So how come he didn't treat his other women that way?"

Something passed through her eyes so quickly that I wasn't able to see what the expression was. Suspicion? Fear? I couldn't tell.

"My father never allowed himself to get close to anyone else."

"Not even his Broadway actress?"

She frowned, then said, "Oh, Linda? No. Not even her. They were using each other to throw off the media. She had a more significant relationship with one of the major critics, and she didn't want that to get out."

"What about you?" I asked that last softly. "If he hurt your mother, why didn't he hurt you?"

She put her other hand on the chair as if she were steadying herself. "Who says he didn't?"

And in that flatness of tone, I heard all the complaints I'd ever heard from clones. She had legal protection, of course. She was fully human. But she didn't have familial protection. She wasn't part of any real group. She didn't have defenders, except those she hired herself.

But I didn't believe it, not entirely. She was still lying to me. She was still keeping me slightly off balance. Something was missing, but I couldn't find it. I'd done all the digging I could reasonably do. I had no direction to go except after the missing wife—if I chose to continue working on this case. This was the last point at which I could comfortably extricate myself from the entire mess.

"You're not telling me everything," I said.

Again, the movement with the eyes. So subtle. So quick. I wondered if she had learned to cover up her emotions from her father.

"My father won't harm her," she said. "If you want, I'll even sign a waiver guaranteeing that."

It seemed the perfect solution to a superficial problem. I had a hunch there were other problems lurking below.

"I'll have one sent to you," I said.

"Are you still taking the case?"

"Are you still lying to me?"

She paused, the dress billowing around her in the static-charged air. "I need you to find my sister," she said.

And that much, we both knew to be true.

VI

My work is nine-tenths research and one-tenth excitement. Most of the research comes in the beginning, and it's dry to most people, although I still find the research fascinating. It's also idiosyncratic and part of the secret behind my reputation. I usually don't describe how I do the research—and I never explain it to clients. I usually summarize it, like this:

It took me four months to do the preliminary research on Sylvy Sobol. I started from the premise that she was pregnant with a single girl child. A pregnant woman did one of three things: she carried the baby to term, she miscarried, or she aborted. After dealing with hospital records for what seemed like weeks, I determined that she carried the baby to term. Or at least, she hadn't gotten rid of it before she disappeared.

A pregnant woman had fewer relocation options than a non-pregnant one. She couldn't travel as far or on as many forms of transport because it might harm the fetus. Several planets, hospitable to humans after they'd acclimatized, were not places someone in the middle of pregnancy was allowed to go. The pregnancy actually made my job easier, and I was glad for it.

Whoever had hidden her was good, but no disappearance service was perfect. They all had cracks in their systems, some revealing themselves in certain types of disappearance, others in all cases past a certain layer of complexity. I knew those flaws as well as I knew the scars and blemishes on my own hands. And I exploited them with ease.

At the end of four months, I had five leads on the former Mrs. Sobol. At the end of five months, I had eliminated two of those leads. At the end of six months, I had a pretty good idea which of the remaining three leads was the woman I was looking for.

I got in my ship, and headed for Mars.

VII

In the hundred years since the Disty first entered this solar system, they have taken over Mars. The human-run mineral operations and the ship bases are still there, but the colonies are all Disty-run, and some are Disty-built.

The Emmeline has clearance on most planets where humans make their homes. Mars is no different. I docked at the Dunes, above the Artic Circle, and wished I were going elsewhere. It was the Martian winter, and here, in the largest field of sand dunes in the solar system, that meant several months of unrelenting dark.

I had never understood how the locals put up with this. But I hadn't understood a lot of things. The domes here, mostly of human construction, had an artificial lighting system built in, but the Disty hated the approximation of a twenty-four-hour day. Since the Disty had taken over the northernmost colonies, darkness outside and artificial lights inside were the hallmarks of winter.

The Disty made other alterations as well. The Disty were small creatures with large heads, large eyes, and narrow bodies. They hated the feeling of wide open spaces, and so in many parts of the Sahara Dome, as Terrans called this place, false ceilings had been built in, and corridors had been compressed. Buildings were added into the wider spaces, getting rid of many passageways and making the entire place seem like a rat's warren. Most adult humans had to crouch to walk comfortably through the city streets and some, in disgust, had bought small carts so that they could ride. The result was a congestion that I found claustrophobic at the best of times. I hated crouching when I walked, and I hated the stink of so many beings in such a confined space.

Many Terran buildings rose higher than the ceiling level of the street, but to discourage that wide-open-spaces feel, the Disty built more structures, many of them so close together that there was barely enough room for a human to stick his arm between them. Doors lined the crowded streets, and the only identifying marks on most places were carved into the frame along the door's side. The carvings were difficult to see in the weird lighting, even if there weren't the usual crowds struggling to get through the streets to God knew where.

My candidate lived in a building owned by the Disty. It took me two passes to find the building's number, and another to realize that I had found the right place. A small sign, in English, advertised accommodations fit for humans, and my back and I hoped that the sign was right.

It was. The entire building had been designed with humans in mind. The Disty had proven themselves to be able interstellar traders, and quite willing to adapt to local customs when it suited them. It showed in the interior design of this place. Once I stepped through the door, I was able to stand upright, although the top of my head did brush the ceiling. To my left, a sign pointed toward the main office, another pointed to some cramped stairs, and a third pointed to the recreation area.

I glanced at the main office before I explored any farther. The office was up front, and had the same human-sized ceilings. In order to cope, the Disty running the place sat on its desk, its long feet pressed together in concentration. I passed it, and went to the recreation area. I would look for the woman here before I went door to door upstairs.

The recreation area was about half the size of an human-made room for the same purpose. Still, the Disty managed to cram a lot of stuff in here, and the closeness of everything—while comfortable for the Disty—made it uncomfortable for any human. All five humans in the room were huddled near the bar on the far end. It was the only place with a walking path large enough to allow a full-grown man through.

To get here, I had to go past the Ping-Pong table, and a small section set aside for Go players. Several Disty were playing Go—they felt it was the best thing they had discovered on the planet Earth, with Ping-Pong a close second—sitting on the tables so that their heads were as near the ceiling as they could get. Two more Disty were standing on the table, playing Ping-Pong. None of them paid me any attention at all.

I wound my way through the tight space between the Go players and the Ping-Pong table, ducking once to avoid being whapped in the head with an out-of-control Ping-Pong ball. I noted three other Disty watching the games with rapt interest. The humans, on the other hand, had their backs to the rest of the room. They were sitting on the tilting bar stools, drinking, and not looking too happy about anything.

A woman who could have been anywhere from thirty to seventy-five sat at one end of the bar. Her black hair fell to the middle of her back, and she wore makeup, an affectation that the Disty seemed to like. She was slender—anyone who wanted to live comfortably here had to be—and she wore a silver beaded dress that accented that slimness. Her legs were smooth, and did not bear any marks from mining or other harsh work.

"Susan Wilcox?" I asked as I put my hand on her shoulder and showed her my license.

I felt the tension run through her body, followed by several shivers, but her face gave no sign that anything was wrong.

"Want to go talk?"

She smiled at me, a smooth professional smile that made me feel a little more comfortable. "Sure."

She stood, took my hand as if we'd been friends a long time, and led me onto a little patio someone had cobbled together in a tiny space behind the recreation area. I didn't see the point of the thing until I looked up. This was one of the few places in Sahara where the dome was visible, and through its clear surface, you could see the sky. She pulled over a chair, and I grabbed one as well.

"How did you find me?" she asked.

"I'm not sure I did." I held out my hand. In it was one of my palmtops. "I want to do a DNA check."

She raised her chin slightly. "That's not legal."

"I could get a court order."

She looked at me. A court order would ruin any protection she had, no matter who—or what—she was running from.

"I'm not going to see who you are. I want to see if you're who I'm looking for. I have comparison DNA."

"You're lying," she said softly.

"Maybe," I said. "If I am, you're in trouble either way."

She knew I was right. She could either take her chances with me, or face the court order where she had no chance at all.

She extended her hand. I ran the edge of the computer along her palm, removing skin cells. The comparison program ran, and as I turned the palmtop face up, I saw that there was no match. The only thing this woman shared in common with the former Mrs. Sobol was that they were both females of a similar age, and that they had both disappeared twenty-nine years ago while pregnant. Almost everything else was different.

I used my wrist-top for a double-check, and then I

sighed. She was watching me closely, her dark eyes reflecting the light from inside.

I smiled at her. "You're in the clear," I said. "But if it was this easy for me to find you, chances are that it'll be as easy for someone else. You might want to move on."

She shook her head once, as if the very idea were repugnant.

"Your child might appreciate it," I said.

She looked at me as if I had struck her. "She's not who—"

"No," I said. "She's safe. From me, at least. And maybe from whoever's after you. But you've survived out here nearly thirty years. You know the value of caution."

She swallowed, hard. "You know a lot about me."

"Not really." I stood. "I only know what you have in common with the woman I'm looking for." I slipped the palmtop into my pocket and bowed slightly. "I appreciate your time."

Then I went back inside, slipped through the recreation area, walked past two more Disty in the foyer, and headed into the narrow passageway they called a street. There I shuddered. I hated the Disty. I'd worked so many cases in which people ran to avoid being caught by the Disty that I'd become averse to them myself.

At least, that was my explanation for my shudder. But I knew that it wasn't a real explanation. I had put a woman's life in jeopardy, and we both knew it. I hoped no one had been paying attention. But I was probably wrong. The only solace I had was that since she was hiding amongst the Disty, she probably wasn't being sought by one of them. If she had been pursued by a Disty, my actions probably would have signed her death warrant.

I spent a night in a cramped hotel room since the Disty didn't allow takeoffs within thirty-six hours of landing. And then I got the hell away from Sahara Dome—and Mars.

VIII

My second possible was in New Orleans, which made my task a lot easier. I had former clients there who felt they owed me, some of whom were in related businesses. I had one of those clients break into the Disappeared's apartment, remove a strand of hair, and give it to another former client. A third brought me the strand in my room in the International Space Station. Because the strand proved not to be a match, and because I was so certain it would be, I repeated the procedure once more, this time getting another old friend to remove another hair strand from the suspect's person. Apparently, he passed her in a public place, and plucked. The strand matched the first one, but didn't belong to Sylvy Sobol.

I didn't warn this woman at all because I didn't feel as if I had put her in danger. If she were suspicious about the hair pulling incident, I felt it was her responsibility to leave town on her own.

The third candidate was on the Moon, in Hadley. I had no trouble finding her, which seemed odd, but she didn't check out either. I returned to Armstrong, both stumped and annoyed.

The logical conclusion was that my DNA sample was false—that it wasn't the sample for Sylvy Sobol. I had taken the sample from the Interstellar DNA database, and there was the possibility that the sample had been changed or tainted. I had heard of such a thing being done, but had always dismissed it as impossible. Those samples were the most heavily guarded in the universe. Even if someone managed to get into the system, they would encounter back-ups upon back-ups, and more encryption than I wanted to think about.

So I contacted Anetka and asked her to send me a DNA sample of her mother. She did, and I ran it against the sample I had. Mine had been accurate. The women I had seen were not Sylvy Sobol.

I had never, in my entire career, made an error of this magnitude. One of those women should have been the former Mrs. Sobol. Unless my information was wrong. Unless I was operating from incorrect assumptions. Still, the assumptions shouldn't have mattered in this search. A pregnant woman wasn't that difficult to hide, not when she was taking transport elsewhere. I'd even found the one who'd remained on Earth.

No. The incorrect assumption had to come after the pregnancy ended. The children. Transport registries always keep track of the sex of the fetus, partly as a response to a series of lawsuits where no one could prove that the woman who claimed she'd lost a fetus on board a transport had actually been pregnant. The transports do not do a DNA check—such things are considered violations of privacy in all but criminal matters—but they do require pregnant women to submit a doctor's report on the health of the mother and the fetus before the woman is allowed to board.

I'd searched out pregnant women, but only those carrying a single daughter. Not twins or multiples. And no males.

Anetka had mentioned failed clones. Clones failed for a variety of reasons, but they only failed in large numbers when someone was using a defective gene or was trying to make a significant change on the genetic level. If the changes didn't work at the genetic level, surgery was performed later to achieve the same result and the DNA remained the same.

I had Anetka's DNA. I'd taken it that first day without her knowing it. I ran client DNA only when I felt I had no other choice; sometimes to check identity, sometimes to check for past crimes. I hadn't run Anetka's—photographic, vid, and those enhancements made it obvious that she was who she said she was. I knew she wasn't concealing her identity, and there was no way she was fronting for a Disty or any other race. She had told me she was a clone.

So I felt a DNA check was not only redundant, it was also unnecessary because it didn't give me the kind of information I was searching for.

But now things were different. I needed to check it to see if she was a repaired child, if there had been some flaw in the fetus that couldn't have been altered in the womb. I hadn't looked for repaired children when I'd done the hospital records scans. I hadn't looked for anything that complicated at all.

So I ran the DNA scan. It only took a second, and the results were not what I expected.

Anetka Sobol wasn't a repaired child, at least not in the sense that I had been looking for. Anetka Sobol was an altered child.

According to her DNA, Anetka Sobol had once been male.

IX

If the trail hadn't been so easy to follow once I realized I was looking for a woman pregnant with a boy, I wouldn't have traced it. I would have gone immediately to Anetka and called her on it. But the trail was easy to follow, and any one of my competitors would have done so—perhaps earlier because they had different methods than I did. I knew at least three of them that ran DNA scans on clients as a matter of course.

If Anetka went to any of them after I refused to complete the work, they would find her mother. It would take them three days. It took me less, but that was because I was better.

X

Sylvy Sobol ran a small private university in the Gagarin Dome on the Moon. She went by the name Celia Walker, and she had transferred from a school out past the Disty homeworld where she had spent the first ten years of her exile. She had run the university for fifteen years.

Gagarin had been established fifty years after Armstrong, and was run by a governing board, the only colony that had such a government. The board placed covenants on any person who owned or rented property within the interior of the dome. The covenants covered everything from the important, such as oxygen regulators, to the unimportant, such as a maintenance schedule for each building, whether the place needed work or not. Gagarin did not tolerate any rules violations. If someone committed three such violations—whether they be failing to follow the maintenance schedule or murder—that person was banned from the dome for life.

The end result was that residents of Gagarin were quiet, law-abiding, and suspicious. They watched me as if I were a particularly distasteful bug when I got off the high speed train from Armstrong. I learned later that I didn't meet the dome's strict dress code.

I had changed into something more appropriate after I got my hotel room, and then went to campus. The university was a technical school for undergraduates, most of them local, but a few came in from other parts of the Moon. The administrative offices were in a low building with fake adobe facades. The classrooms were in some of Gagarin's only high rises, and were off limits to visitors.

I didn't care about that. I went straight to the Chancellor's office and buzzed myself in, even though I didn't have an appointment. Apparently, the open campus policy that the on-line brochures proudly proclaimed extended to the administrative offices as well.

Sylvy Sobol sat behind a desk made of Moon clay. Ancient Southwestern tapestries covered the walls, and matching rugs covered the floor. The permaplastic here had been covered with more fake adobe, and the net effect was to make this seem like the American Southwest hundreds of years before.

She looked no different than the age-enhancement programs on my computer led me to believe she'd look. Her dark hair was laced with silver, her eyes had laugh lines in the corners, and she was as slender as she had been when she disappeared. She wore a blouse made of the same weave as the tapestries, and a pair of tan cargo pants. Beneath the right sleeve of her blouse a stylist wrist-top glistened. When she saw me, she smiled. "May I help you?"

I closed the door, walked to her desk, and showed her my license. Her eyes widened ever so slightly, and then she covered the look.

"I came to warn you," I said.

"Warn me?" She straightened almost imperceptibly, but managed to look perplexed. Behind the tightness of her lips, I sensed fear.

"You and your son need to use a new service, and disappear again. It's not safe for you any more."

"I'm sorry, Mr.—Flint?—but I'm not following you."

"I can repeat what I said, or we can go somewhere where you'd feel more comfortable talking."

She shook her head once, then stood. "I'm not sure I know what we'd be talking about."

I reached out my hand. I had my palm scanner in it. Anyone who'd traveled a lot, anyone who had been on the run, would recognize it. "We can do this the old-fashioned way, Mrs. Sobol, or you can listen to me."

She sat down slowly. Her lower lip trembled. She didn't object to my use of her real name. "If you're what your identification says you are, you don't warn people. You take them in."

I let my hand drop. "I was hired by Anetka Sobol," I said. "She wanted me to find you. She claimed that she wanted to share her inheritance with her Original. She's a clone. The record supports this claim."

"So, you want to take us back." Her voice was calm, but her eyes weren't. I watched her hands. They remained on the desktop, flat, and she was without enhancement. So far, she hadn't signaled anyone for help.

"Normally, I would have taken you back. But when I discovered that Anetka's Original was male, I got confused."

Sylvy licked her lower lip, just like her cloned daughter did. An hereditary nervous trait.

I rested one leg on the corner of the desk. "Why would a man change the sex of a clone when the sex didn't matter? Especially if all he wanted was the child. A man with no violent tendencies, who stood accused of attacking his wife so savagely all she could do was leave him, all she could do was disappear. Why would he do that?"

She hadn't moved. She was watching me closely. Beads of perspiration had formed on her upper lip.

"So I went back through the records and found two curious things. You disappeared just after his business on Korsve failed. And once you moved to Gagarin, you and your son were often in other domed Moon colonies at the same time as your husband. Not a good way to hide from someone, now is it, Mrs. Sobol?"

She didn't respond.

I picked up a clay pot. It was small and very, very old. It was clearly an original, not a Moon-made copy. "And then there's the fact that your husband never bothered to change his will to favor the child he had raised. It wouldn't have mattered to most parents that the child was a clone, especially when the Original was long gone. He could have arranged a dispensation, and then made certain that the business remained in family hands." I set the pot down. "But he had already done that, hadn't he? He hoped that the Wygnin would forget."

She made a soft sound in the back of her throat, and backed away from me, clutching at her wrist. I reached across the desk and grabbed her left arm, keeping her hand away from her wrist-top. I wasn't ready for her to order someone to come in here. I still needed to talk to her alone.

"I'm not going to turn you in to the Wygnin," I said. "I'm not going to let anyone know where you are. But if you don't listen to me, someone else will find you, and soon."

She stared at me, the color high in her cheeks. Her arm was rigid beneath my hand.

"The will was your husband's only mistake," I said. "The Wygnin never forget. They targeted your firstborn, didn't they? The plants on Korsve didn't open and close without a fuss. Something else happened. The Wygnin only target firstborns for a crime that can't be undone."

She shook her arm free of me. She rubbed the spot where my hand had touched her flesh, then she sighed. She seemed to know I wouldn't go away. When she spoke, her voice was soft. "No Wygnin were on the site planning committee. We bought the land, and built the plants according to our customs. At that point, the Wygnin didn't understand the concept of land purchase."

I noted the use of the word "we." She had been involved with the Third Dynasty, more involved than the records said.

"We built a haven for nestlings. You understand nestlings?"

"I thought they were a food source."

She shook her head. "They're more than that. They're part of Wygnin society in a way we didn't understand. They become food only after they die. It's the shells that are eaten, not the nestlings themselves. The nestlings themselves are considered sentient."

I felt myself grow cold. "How many were killed?"

She shrugged. "The entire patch. No one knows for sure. We were told, when the Wygnin came to us, that they were letting us off easily by taking our firstborn—Carson's and mine. They could easily take all the children of anyone who was connected with the project, but they didn't."

They could have, too. It was the Third Dynasty that acted without regard to local custom, which made it liable to local laws. Over the years, no interstellar court had overturned a ruling in instances like that.

"Carson agreed to it," she said. "He agreed so no one else would suffer. Then we got me out."

"And no one came looking for you until I did."

"That's right," she said.

"I don't think Anetka's going to stop," I said. "I suspect she wants her father to change the will—"

"What?" Sylvy clenched her collar with her right hand, revealing the wrist-top. It was one of the most sophisticated I'd seen.

"Anetka wants control of the Third Dynasty, and I was wondering why her father hadn't done a will favoring her. Now I know. She was probably hoping I couldn't find you so that her father would change the will in her favor."

"He can't," Sylvy said.

"I'm sure he might consider it, if your son's life is at stake," I said. "The Wygnin treat their captives like family—indeed, make them into family, but the techniques they use on adults of other species are—"

"No," she said. "It's too late for Carson to change his will."

She was frowning at me as if I didn't understand anything. And it took me a moment to realize how I'd been used.

Anetka Sobol had tricked me in more ways than I cared to think about. I wasn't half as good as I thought I was. I felt the beginnings of an anger I didn't need. I suppressed it. "He's dead, isn't he?"

Sylvy nodded. "He died three years ago. He installed a personal alarm that notified me the moment his heart stopped. My son has been voting his shares through a proxy program my husband set up during one of his trips here."

I glanced at the wrist-top. No wonder it was so sophisticated. Too sophisticated for a simple administrator. Carson Sobol had given it to her, and through it, had notified her of his death. Had it broken her heart? I couldn't tell, not from three years' distance.

She caught me staring at it, and brought her arm down. I turned away, taking a deep breath as the reality of my situation hit me. Anetka Sobol had outmaneuvered me. She had put me in precisely the kind of case I never wanted.

I was working for the Tracker. I was leading a Disappeared to her death and probably the death of her son. "I don't get it," I said, "if something happens to your son, Anetka still won't inherit."

Sylvy's smile was small. "She inherits by default. My son will disappear, and stop voting the proxy program. She'll set up a new proxy program and continue to vote the shares. I'm sure the Board thinks she's the person behind the votes anyway. No one knows about our son."

"Except for you, and me, and the Wygnin." I closed my eyes. "Anetka had no idea you'd had a son."

"No one did," Sylvy said. "Until now."

I rubbed my nose with my thumb and forefinger. Anetka was good. She had discovered that I was the best and the quickest Retrieval Artist in the business. She had studied me and had known how to reach me. She had also known how to play at being an innocent, how to use my past history to her advantage. She hired me to find her Original, and once I did, she planned to get rid of him. It would have been easy for her too; no hitman, no attempt at killing. She wouldn't have had to do anything except somehow—surreptitiously—let the Wygnin know how to find the Original. They would have taken him in payment for the Third Dynasty's crimes, he would have stopped voting his shares, and she would have controlled the corporation.

Stopping Anetka wasn't going to be easy. Even if I refused to report, even if Sylvy and her son returned to hiding, Anetka would continue looking for them.

I had doomed them. If I left this case now, I ensured that one of my colleagues would take it. They would find Sylvy and her son. They would find Sylvy and her son. My colleagues weren't as good as I was, but they were good. And they were smart enough to follow the bits of my trail that I couldn't erase.

The only solution was to get rid of Anetka. I couldn't kill her. But I could think of one other way to stop her.

I opened my eyes. "If I could get Anetka out of the business, and allow you and your son to return home, would you do so?"

Sylvy shook her head. "This is my home," she said. She glanced at the fake adobe walls, the southwestern decor. Her fingers touched a blanket hanging on the wall behind her. "But I can't answer for my son."

"If he doesn't do anything, he'll be running for the rest of his life?"

She nodded. "I still can't answer for him. He's an adult now. He makes his own choices."

As we all did.

"Think about it," I said, handing her a card with my chip on it. "I'll be here for two days."

XI

They hired me, of course. What thinking person wouldn't? I had to guarantee that I wouldn't kill Anetka when I got her out of the business—and I did that, by assuring Sylvy that I wasn't now nor would I ever been an assassin—and I had to guarantee that I would get the Wygnin off her son's trail.

I agreed to both conditions, and for the first time in years, I did something other than tracking a Disappeared.

Through channels, I let it drop that I was searching for the real heir to Carson Sobol's considerable fortune. Then I showed some of my actual research—into the daughter's history, the falsified birth date, the inaccurate records. I managed to dump information about Anetka's cloning and her sex change, and I tampered with the records to show that her clone mark had been faked just as her sex had. Alterations, done at birth, made her look like a clone when she really wasn't.

I made sure that my own work on-line looked like sloppy detecting, but I hid the changes I made in other files. I did all of this quickly and thoroughly, and by the time I was done, it appeared as though Carson Sobol had hidden his own heir—originally a son—by making him into a daughter and passing him off as a clone.

At that point, I could have sat back and let events move forward by themselves. But I didn't. This had become personal.

I had to see Anetka one last time.

I set an appointment to hand-deliver my final bill.

XII

This time she was wearing emeralds, an entire sheath covered with them. I had heard that there would be a gala event honoring one of the galaxy's leaders, but I had forgotten that the event would be held in Armstrong, at one of the poshest restaurants on the Moon.

She was sweeping up her long hair, letting it fall just below the mark on the back of her head, when I entered. As she turned, she stabbed an emerald haircomb into the bun at the base of her neck.

"I don't have much time," she said.

"I know," I closed the door. "I wanted to give you my final bill."

"You found my sister?" There was a barely concealed excitement in her voice.

"No." The room smelled of an illegal perfume, I was surprised no one had confiscated it when she got off the shuttle and then I realized she probably hadn't taken a shuttle. Even the personal items bag she wore that first day had been part of her act. "I'm resigning."

She shook her head slightly. "I might have known you would. You have enough money now, so you're going to quit."

"I have enough information now to know you're not the kind of person I relish working for."

She raised her eyebrows. The movement dislodged the tiny emerald attached to her left cheek. She caught it just before it fell to the floor. "I thought you were done investigating me."

"Your father's dead," I said. "He has been for three years, although the Third Dynasty has managed to keep the information secret, knowing the effect his death would have had on galactic confidence in the business."

She stared at me for a moment, clearly surprised. "Only five of us knew that."

"Six," I said.

"You found my mother." She stuck the emerald in its spot.

"You found the alarm. You knew she'd been notified of your father's death."

The emerald wasn't staying on her cheek. Anetka let out a puff of air, then set the entire kit down. "I really didn't appreciate the proxy program," she said. "It notified me of my insignificance an hour after my father breathed his last. It told me to go about my life with my own fortune and abandon my place in the Third Dynasty to my Original."

"Which you didn't do."

"Why should I? I knew more about the business than she ever would."

"Including the Wygnin."

She leaned against the dressing table. "You're much better than I thought."

"And you're a lot more devious than I gave you credit for."

She smiled and tapped her left cheek. "It's the face. Youth still fools."

Perhaps it did. I usually didn't fall for it, though. I couldn't believe I had this time. I had simply thought I was being as cautious as usual. What Anetka Sobol had taught me was that being as cautious as usual wasn't cautious enough.

"Pay me, and I'll get out of here," I said.

"You've found my mother. You may as well tell me where she is."

"So you can turn your Original over to the Wygnin?"

That flat look came back into her eyes. "I wouldn't do that."

"How would you prevent it? The Wygnin have a valid debt."

"It's twenty-seven years old."

"The Wygnin hold onto markers for generations." I paused, then added, "As you well know."

"You can't prove what I do and do not know."

I nodded. "True enough. Information is always tricky. It's so easy to tamper with."

Her eyes narrowed. She was smart, probably one of the smartest people I'd ever come up against. She knew I was referring to something besides our discussion.

"So I'm getting out," I handed her a paper copy of the bill—rare, unnecessary, and expensive. She knew that as well as I did. Then, as soon as she took the paper from my hand, I pressed my wrist-top to send the electronic version. "You owe me money. I expect payment within the hour."

She crumpled the bill. "You'll get it."

"Good." I pulled open the door.

"You know," she said, just loud enough for me to hear, "if you can find my mother, anyone can."

"I've already thought of that," I said, and left.

XIII

The Wygnin came for her later that night, toward the end of the gala. Security tried to stop them until they showed a valid warrant for the heir of Carson Sobol. The entire transaction caused an interstellar incident, and the vidnets were filled with it for days. The Third Dynasty used its attorneys to try to prove that Anetka was the eighth clone, just as everyone thought she was, but the Wygnin didn't believe it.

The beautiful thing about a clone is that it is a human being. It's simply one whose heritage matches another person's exactly, and whose facts of birth are odder than most. These are facts, yes, but they are facts that can be explained in other ways. The Wygnin simply chose to believe my explanations, not Anetka's. It was the sex change that did it. The Wygnin believed that anyone who would change a child's sex to protect it would also brand it with a clone mark, even if the mark wasn't accurate.

Over time, the lawyers lost all of their appeals, and Anetka disappeared into the Wygnin culture, never to be heard from again.

Oh, of course, the Third Dynasty still believes it's being run by Anetka Sobol voting her shares, as she always has, through a proxy program. Her Original apparently decided not to return to claim his prize. He acts as he always planned to, secretly. Only Sylvy Sobol, her son, and I know the person voting those shares isn't Anetka.

After Anetka's future was sealed, I stopped paying attention to the business of the Third Dynasty. I still don't look. I don't want to know if I have traded one monster for another. Some cold-heartedness is trained—and I can make myself think that Carson Sobol never once treated young Anetka with love, affection, or anything bordering on civility—but I am smart enough to know that most cold-heartedness is bred into the genes. Just because

Anetka is gone, doesn't mean the Original won't act the same way in similar circumstances.

And what is my excuse for my coldheartedness? I'd like to say I've never done anything like this before, but I have—always in the name of my client, or a Disappeared. This time, though, this time, I did it for me.

Anetka Sobol had out-thought me, had compromised me, and had made me do the kind of work I'd vowed I'd never do. I let a front use me to open a door that would allow other Trackers to find a Disappeared.

People disappear because they want to. They disappear to escape a bad life, or a mistake they've made, or they disappear to save themselves from a horrible death. A person who has disappeared never wants to be found.

I always ignored that simple fact, thinking I knew better. But one man is never a good judge of another, even if he thinks he is.

I tell myself Anetka Sobol would have destroyed her Original if she had had the chance. I tell myself Anetka Sobol was greedy and self-centered. I tell myself Anetka Sobol deserved her fate.

But I can't ignore the fact that when I learned that Anetka Sobol had used me, this case became personal, in a way I would never have expected. Maybe, just maybe, I might have found a different solution, if she hadn't angered me so.

And now she haunts me in the middle of the night. She wakes me out of many a sound sleep. She keeps me restless and questioning. Because I didn't go after her for who she was or what she was planning. I had worked with people far worse than she was. I had met others who had done horrible things, things that made me wonder if they were even human. Anetka Sobol wasn't in their league.

No. I had gone after her for what she had done to me. For what she had made me see about myself. And because I hadn't liked my reflection in the mirror she held up, I destroyed her.

I can't get her back. No one comes back intact from the Wygnin. She will spend the rest of her days there. And I will spend the rest of mine thinking about her.

Some would say that is justice. But I have come to realize, in a universe as complex as this one, justice no longer exists.

"REPENT, HARLEQUIN!"
SAID THE
TICKTOCKMAN

Harlan Ellison

One of the most acclaimed and controversial figures in modern letters, Harlan Ellison has produced over fifty books and over a thousand stores, articles, essays, and film and television scripts and is considered by many to be one of the fathers of modern urban horror. He is the editor of Dangerous Visions (*perhaps the most famous single anthology in the history of the genre*); Again, Dangerous Visions; Medea: Harlan's World; *and the forthcoming* The Last Dangerous Visions. *His short story collections include* Partners in Wonder, Alone Against Tomorrow, The Beast That Shouted Love at the Heart of the World, Approaching Oblivion, Deathbird Stories, Strange Wine, Shatterday, *and* Angry Candy. *He has won multiple Nebula and Hugo Awards, the Edgar Award, and several Writer's Guild of America Awards for Most Outstanding Television Script. His most recent books are the collections* Troublemakers *and* The Essential Ellison: A 50-Year Retrospective.

The famous story that follows, about an intensely regimented society where it's a crime even to be late, won both the Nebula and the Hugo Awards when it was first published. And in a day when people seem willing to trade freedom for security, to tolerate any degree of governmental control and scrutiny if it keeps them safe, it's more germane than it ever was.

There are always those who ask, what is it all about? For those who need to ask, for those who need points sharply made, who need to know "where it's at," this:

> *The mass of men serve the state thus, not as men mainly, but as machines, with their bodies. They are the standing army, and the militia, jailors, constables, posse comitatus, etc. In most cases there is no free exercise whatever of the judgment or of the moral sense; but they put themselves on a level with wood and earth and stones; and wooden men can perhaps be manufactured that will serve the purpose as well. Such command no more respect than men of straw or a lump of dirt. They have the same sort of worth only as horses and dogs. Yet such as these even are commonly esteemed good citizens. Others—as most legislators, politicians, lawyers, ministers, and officeholders—serve the state chiefly with their heads; and, as they rarely make any moral distinctions, they are as likely to serve the Devil, without intending it, as God. A very few, as heroes, patriots, martyrs, reformers in the great sense, and men, serve the state with their consciences also, and so necessarily resist it for the most part; and they are commonly treated as enemies by it.*

> Henry David Thoreau
> CIVIL DISOBEDIENCE

That is the heart of it. Now begin in the middle, and later learn the beginning; the end will take care of itself.

• • •

But because it was the very world it was, the very world
they had allowed it to become, for months his activities did
not come to the alarmed attention of The Ones Who Kept
The Machine Functioning Smoothly, the ones who poured
the very best butter over the cams and mainsprings of the
culture. Not until it had become obvious that somehow,
someway, he had become a notoriety, a celebrity, perhaps
even a hero for (what Officialdom inescapably tagged) "an
emotionally disturbed segment of the populace," did they
turn it over to the Ticktockman and his legal machinery.
But by then, because it was the very world it was, and they
had no way to predict he would happen—possibly a strain
of disease long-defunct, now, suddenly, reborn in a system
where immunity had been forgotten, had lapsed—he had
been allowed to become too real. Now he had form and
substance.

He had become a *personality,* something they had filtered out of the system many decades before. But there it
was, and there *he* was, a very definitely imposing personality. In certain circles—middle-class circles—it was thought
disgusting. Vulgar ostentation. Anarchistic. Shameful. In
others, there was only sniggering: those strata where
thought is subjugated to form and ritual, niceties, propri-
eties. But down below, ah, down below, where the people
always needed their saints and sinners, their bread and cir-
cuses, their heroes and villains, he was considered a Boli-
var; a Napoleon; a Robin Hood; a Dick Bong (Ace of
Aces); a Jesus; a Jomo Kenyatta.

And at the top—where, like socially-attuned Shipwreck
Kellys, every tremor and vibration threatening to dislodge
the wealthy, powerful and titled from their flagpoles—he
was considered a menace; a heretic; a rebel; a disgrace; a
peril. He was known down the line, to the very heart-meat
core, but the important reactions were high above and far
below. At the very top, at the very bottom.

So his file was turned over, along with his time-card
and his cardioplate, to the office of the Ticktockman.

The Ticktockman: very much over six feet tall, often silent, a soft purring man when things went timewise. The Ticktockman.

Even in the cubicles of the hierarchy, where fear was generated, seldom suffered, he was called the Ticktockman. But no one called him that to his mask.

You don't call a man a hated name, not when that man, behind his mask, is capable of revoking the minutes, the hours, the days and nights, the years of your life. He was called the Master Timekeeper to his mask. It was safer that way.

"This is *what* he is," said the Ticktockman with genuine softness, "but not *who* he is. This time-card I'm holding in my left hand has a name on it, but it is the name of *what* he is, not *who* he is. The cardioplate here in my right hand is also named, but not *whom* named, merely *what* named. Before I can exercise proper revocation, I have to know *who* this *what* is."

To his staff, all the ferrets, all the loggers, all the finks, all the commex, even the mineez, he said, "Who is this Harlequin?"

He was not purring smoothly. Timewise, it was jangle.

However, it *was* the longest speech they had ever heard him utter at one time, the staff, the ferrets, the loggers, the finks, the commex, but not the mineez, who usually weren't around to know, in any case. But even they scurried to find out.

Who is the Harlequin?

High above the third level of the city, he crouched on the humming aluminum-frame platform of the air-boat (foof! air-boat, indeed! swizzleskid is what it was, with a tow-rack jerry-rigged) and he stared down at the neat Mondrian arrangement of the buildings.

Somewhere nearby, he could hear the metronomic left-right-left of the 2:47 PM shift, entering the Timkin roller-bearing plant in their sneakers. A minute later, precisely, he heard the softer right-left-right of the 5:00 AM formation, going home.

An elfin grin spread across his tanned features, and his dimples appeared for a moment. Then, scratching at his thatch of auburn hair, he shrugged within his motley, as though girding himself for what came next, and threw the joystick forward, and bent into the wind as the air-boat dropped. He skimmed over a slidewalk, purposely dropping a few feet to crease the tassles of the ladies of fashion, and—inserting thumbs in large ears—he stuck out his tongue, rolled his eyes and went wugga-wugga-wugga. It was a minor diversion. One pedestrian skittered and tumbled, sending parcels everywhichway, another wet herself, a third keeled slantwise and the walk was stopped automatically by the servitors till she could be resuscitated. It was a minor diversion.

Then he swirled away on a vagrant breeze, and was gone. Hi-ho. As he rounded the cornice of the Time-Motion Study Building, he saw the shift, just boarding the slidewalk. With practiced motion and an absolute conservation of movement, they sidestepped up onto the slow-strip and (in a chorus line reminiscent of a Busby Berkeley film of the antedivulian 1930s) advanced across the strips ostrich-walking till they were lined up on the expresstrip.

Once more, in anticipation, the elfin grin spread, and there was a tooth missing back there on the left side. He dipped, skimmed, and swooped over them; and then, scrunching about on the air-boat, he released the holding pins that fastened shut the ends of the home-made pouring troughs that kept his cargo from dumping prematurely. And as he pulled the trough-pins, the air-boat slid over the factory workers and one hundred and fifty thousand dollars' worth of jelly beans cascaded down on the expresstrip.

Jelly beans! Millions and billions of purples and yellows and greens and licorice and grape and raspberry and mint and round and smooth and crunchy outside and soft-mealy inside and sugary and bouncing jouncing tumbling clittering clattering skittering fell on the heads and shoulders and hardhats and carapaces of the Timkin workers, tinkling on the slidewalk and bouncing away and rolling about underfoot and filling the sky on their way down with all the colors of joy and childhood and holidays, coming down in a steady rain, a solid wash, a torrent of color and sweetness out of the sky from above, and entering a universe of sanity and metronomic order with quite-mad cuckoo newness. Jelly beans!

The shift workers howled and laughed and were pelted, and broke ranks, and the jelly beans managed to work their way into the mechanism of the slidewalks after which there was a hideous scraping as the sound of a million fingernails rasped down a quarter of a million blackboards, followed by a coughing and a sputtering, and then the slidewalks all stopped and everyone was dumped thisawayandthataway in a jackstraw tumble, still laughing and popping little jelly bean eggs of childish color into their mouths. It was a holiday, and a jollity, an absolute insanity, a giggle. But . . .

The shift was delayed seven minutes.

They did not get home for seven minutes.

The master schedule was thrown off by seven minutes.

Quotas were delayed by inoperative slidewalks for seven minutes.

He had tapped the first domino in the line, and one after another, like *chik chik chik*, the others had fallen.

The System had been seven minutes' worth of disrupted. It was a tiny matter, one hardly worthy of note, but in a society where the single driving force was order and unity and equality and promptness and clocklike precision and attention to the clock, reverence of the gods of the passage of time, it was a disaster of major importance.

So he was ordered to appear before the Ticktockman. It was broadcast across every channel of the communications web. He was ordered to be *there* at 7:00 dammit on time.

And they waited, and they waited, but he didn't show up till almost ten-thirty, at which time he merely sang a little song about moonlight in a place no one had ever heard of, called Vermont, and vanished again. But they had all been waiting since seven, and it wrecked *hell* with their schedules. So the question remained: Who is the Harlequin?

But the *unasked* question (more important of the two) was: how did we get *into* this position, where a laughing, irresponsible japer of jabberwocky and jive could disrupt our entire economic and cultural life with a hundred and fifty thousand dollars' worth of jelly beans . . .

Jelly for God's sake *beans!* This is madness! Where did he get the money to buy a hundred and fifty thousand dollars' worth of jelly beans? (They knew it would have cost that much, because they had a team of Situation Analysts pulled off another assignment, and rushed to the slidewalk scene to sweep up and count the candies, and produce findings, which disrupted *their* schedules and threw their entire branch at least a day behind.) Jelly beans! Jelly . . . *beans?* Now wait a second—a second accounted for—no one has manufactured jelly beans for over a hundred years. Where did he get jelly beans?

That's another good question. More than likely it will never be answered to your complete satisfaction. But then, how many questions ever are?

The middle you know. Here is the beginning. How it starts:

A desk pad. Day for day, and turn each day. 9:00— open the mail. 9:45—appointment with planning commission board. 10:30—discuss installation progress charts with J.L. 11:45—pray for rain. 12:00—lunch. *And so it goes.*

"I'm sorry, Miss Grant, but the time for interviews was set at 2:30, and it's almost five now. I'm sorry you're late, but those are the rules. You'll have to wait till next year to submit application for this college again." *And so it goes.*

The 10:10 local stops at Cresthaven, Gatesville, Tonawanda Junction, Selby and Farnhurst, but not at Indiana City, Lucasville and Colton, except on Sunday. The 10:35 express stops at Gatesville, Selby and Indiana City, except on Sundays & Holidays, at which time it stops at . . . *and so it goes.*

"I couldn't wait, Fred. I had to be at Pierre Cartain's by 3:00, and you said you'd meet me under the clock in the terminal at 2:45, and you weren't there, so I had to go on. You're always late, Fred. If you'd been there, we could have sewed it up together, but as it was, well, I took the order alone . . . And so it goes.

Dear Mr. and Mrs. Atterley: In reference to your son Gerold's constant tardiness. I am afraid we will have to suspend him from school unless some more reliable method can be instituted guaranteeing he will arrive at his classes on time. Granted he is an exemplary student, and his marks are high, his constant flouting of the schedules of this school makes it impractical to maintain him in a system where the other children seem capable of getting where they are supposed to be on time *and so it goes.*

YOU CANNOT VOTE UNLESS YOU APPEAR AT 8:45 AM.

"I DON'T CARE IF THE SCRIPT IS <u>GOOD</u>, I NEED IT THURSDAY!"

"CHECK-OUT TIME IS 2:00 PM.

"You got here late. The job's taken. Sorry."

YOUR SALARY HAS BEEN DOCKED FOR TWENTY MINUTES TIME LOST.

"God, what time is it, I've gotta run!"

And so it goes. And so it goes. And so it goes goes goes goes goes tick tock tick tock tick tock and one day we no longer let time serve us, we serve time and we are slaves of the schedule, worshippers of the sun's passing, bound into a life predicated on restrictions because the system will not function if we don't keep the schedule tight.

Until it becomes more than a minor inconvenience to be late. It becomes a sin. Then a crime. Then a crime punishable by this:

> **EFFECTIVE 15 JULY 2389 12:00:00 midnight, the office of the Master Timekeeper will require all citizens to submit their time-cards and cardioplates for processing. In accordance with Statute 555-7-SGH-999 governing the revocation of time per capita, all cardioplates will be keyed to the individual holder and—**

What they had done was devise a method of curtailing the amount of life a person could have. If he was ten minutes late, he lost ten minutes of his life. An hour was proportionately worth more revocation. If someone was consistently tardy, he might find himself, on a Sunday night, receiving a communiqué from the Master Timekeeper that his time had run out, and he would be "turned off" at high noon on Monday, please straighten your affairs, sir, madame or bisex.

And so, by this simple scientific expedient (utilizing a scientific process held dearly secret by the Ticktockman's office) the System was maintained. It was the only expedient thing to do. It was, after all, patriotic. The schedules had to be met. After all, there *was* a war on!

But, wasn't there always?

• • •

"Now that is really disgusting," the Harlequin said, when Pretty Alice showed him the wanted poster. "Disgusting and highly improbable. After all, this isn't the Day of the Desperado. A wanted poster!"

"You know," Pretty Alice noted, "you speak with a great deal of inflection."

"I'm sorry," said the Harlequin, humbly.

"No need to be sorry. You're always saying 'I'm sorry.' You have such massive guilt, Everett, it's really very sad."

"I'm sorry," he said again, then pursed his lips so the dimples appeared momentarily. He hadn't wanted to say that at all. "I have to go out again. I have to *do* something."

Pretty Alice slammed her coffee-bulb down on the counter. "Oh for God's *sake,* Everett, can't you stay home just *one* night! Must you always be out in that ghastly clown suit, running around an*noy*ing people?"

"I'm—" He stopped, and clapped the jester's hat onto his auburn thatch with a tiny tinkling of bells. He rose, rinsed out his coffee-bulb at the spray, and put it into the dryer for a moment. "I have to go."

She didn't answer. The faxbox was purring, and she pulled a sheet out, read it, threw it toward him on the counter. "It's about you. Of course. You're ridiculous."

He read it quickly. It said the Ticktockman was trying to locate him. He didn't care, he was going out to be late again. At the door, dredging for an exit line, he hurled back petulantly, "Well, *you* speak with inflection, *too!*"

Pretty Alice rolled her pretty eyes heavenward. "You're ridiculous."

The Harlequin stalked out, slamming the door, which sighed shut softly, and locked itself.

There was a gentle knock, and Pretty Alice got up with an exhalation of exasperated breath, and opened the door. He stood there. "I'll be back about ten-thirty, okay?"

She pulled a rueful face. "Why do you tell me that? Why? You *know* you'll be late! You *know* it! You're *always*

late, so why do you tell me these dumb things?" She closed
the door.

On the other side, the Harlequin nodded to himself:
*She's right. She's always right. I'll be late. I'm always late.
Why do I tell her these dumb things?*

He shrugged again, and went off to be late once more.

He had fired off the firecracker rockets that said: I will attend the 115th annual International Medical Association
Invocation at 8:00 pm precisely. I do hope you will all be
able to join me.

The words had burned in the sky, and of course the authorities were there, lying in wait for him. They assumed,
naturally, that he would be late. He arrived twenty minutes
early, while they were setting up the spiderwebs to trap and
hold him. Blowing a large bullhorn, he frightened and un-
nerved them so, their own moisturized encirclement webs
sucked closed, and they were hauled up, kicking and
shrieking, high above the amphitheater's floor. The Harlequin laughed and laughed, and apologized profusely. The
physicians, gathered in solemn conclave, roared with
laughter, and accepted the Harlequin's apologies with exaggerated bowing and posturing, and a merry time was had
by all, who thought the Harlequin was a regular foofaraw
in fancy pants; all, that is, but the authorities, who had
been sent out by the office of the Ticktockman; they hung
there like so much dockside cargo, hauled up above the
floor of the amphitheater in a most unseemly fashion.

(In another part of the same city where the Harlequin
carried on his "activities," totally unrelated in every way to
what concerns us here, save that it illustrates the Ticktockman's power and import, a man named Marshall Delahanty received his turn-off notice from the Ticktockman's
office. His wife received the notification from the gray-
suited minee who delivered it, with the traditional "look of
sorrow" plastered hideously across his face. She knew

what it was, even without unsealing it. It was a billet-doux
of immediate recognition to everyone these days. She
gasped, and held it as though it were a glass slide tinged
with botulism, and prayed it was not for her. Let it be
for Marsh, she thought, brutally, realistically, or one of
the kids, but not for me, please dear God, not for me. And
then she opened it, and it *was* for Marsh, and she was at
one and the same time horrified and relieved. The next
trooper in the line had caught the bullet. "Marshall," she
screamed, "Marshall! Termination, Marshall! OhmiGod,
Marshall, whatttl we do, whattl we do, Marshall omigod-
marshall . . ." and in their home that night was the sound of
tearing paper and fear, and the stink of madness went up
the flue and there was nothing, absolutely nothing they
could do about it.

(But Marshall Delahanty tried to run. And early the next
day, when turn-off time came, he was deep in the Canadian
forest two hundred miles away, and the office of the Ticktockman blanked his cardioplate, and Marshall Delahanty
keeled over, running, and his heart stopped, and the blood
dried up on its way to his brain, and he was dead that's all.
One light went out on the sector map in the office of the
Master Timekeeper, while notification was entered for fax
reproduction, and Georgette Delahanty's name was entered on the dole roles till she could remarry. Which is the
end of the footnote, and all the point that need be made, except don't laugh, because that is what would happen to the
Harlequin if ever the Ticktockman found out his real name.
It isn't funny.)

The shopping level of the city was thronged with the
Thursday-colors of the buyers. Women in canary yellow
chitons and men in pseudo-Tyrolean outfits that were jade
and leather and fit very tightly, save for the balloon pants.

When the Harlequin appeared on the still-being-
constructed shell of the new Efficiency Shopping Center,

his bullhorn to his elfishly-laughing lips, everyone pointed
and stared, and he berated them:

"Why let them order you about? Why let them tell you
to hurry and scurry like ants or maggots? Take your time!
Saunter a while! Enjoy the sunshine, enjoy the breeze, let
life carry you at your own pace! Don't be slaves of time,
it's a helluva way to die, slowly, by degrees . . . down with
the Ticktockman!"

Who's the nut? most of the shoppers wanted to know.
Who's the nut oh wow I'm gonna be late I gotta run . . .

And the construction gang on the Shopping Center received an urgent order from the office of the Master Timekeeper that the dangerous criminal known as the Harlequin
was atop their spire, and their aid was urgently needed in
apprehending him. The work crew said no, they would lose
time on their construction schedule, but the Ticktockman
managed to pull the proper threads of governmental web-
bing, and they were told to cease work and catch that
nitwit up there on the spire; up there with the bullhorn. So
a dozen and more burly workers began climbing into their
construction platforms, releasing the a-grav plates, and rising toward the Harlequin.

After the debacle (in which, through the Harlequin's attention to personal safety, no one was seriously injured), the
workers tried to reassemble, and assault him again, but it
was too late. He had vanished. It had attracted quite a
crowd, however, and the shopping cycle was thrown off by
hours, simply hours. The purchasing needs of the system
were therefore falling behind, and so measures were taken
to accelerate the cycle for the rest of the day, but it got
bogged down and speeded up and they sold too many
float-valves and not nearly enough wegglers, which meant
that the popli ratio was off, which made it necessary to
rush cases and cases of spoiling Smash-O to stores that
usually needed a case only every three or four hours. The

shipments were bollixed, the transshipments were mis-routed, and in the end, even the swizzleskid industries felt it.

"Don't come back till you have him!" the Ticktockman said, very quietly, very sincerely, extremely dangerously.

They used dogs. They used probes. They used cardio-plate crossoffs. They used teepers. They used bribery. They used stiktytes. They used intimidation. They used torment. They used torture. They used finks. They used cops. They used search&seizure. They used fallaron. They used betterment incentive. They used fingerprints. They used the Bertillon system. They used cunning. They used guile. They used treachery. They used Raoul Mitgong, but he didn't help much. They used applied physics. They used techniques of criminology.

And what the hell: they caught him.

After all, his name was Everett C. Marm, and he wasn't much to begin with, except a man who had no sense of time.

"Repent, Harlequin!" said the Ticktockman.

"Get stuffed!" the Harlequin replied, sneering.

"You've been late a total of sixty-three years, five months, three weeks, two days, twelve hours, forty-one minutes, fifty-nine seconds, point oh three six one one one microseconds. You've used up everything you can, and more. I'm going to turn you off."

"Scare someone else. I'd rather be dead than live in a dumb world with a bogeyman like you."

"It's my job."

"You're full of it. You're a tyrant. You have no right to order people around and kill them if they show up late."

"You can't adjust. You can't fit in."

"Unstrap me, and I'll fit my fist into your mouth."

"You're a nonconformist."

"That didn't used to be a felony."

"It is now. Live in the world around you."

"I hate it. It's a terrible world."

"Not everyone thinks so. Most people enjoy order."

"I don't, and most of the people I know don't."

"That's not true. How do you think we caught you?"

"I'm not interested."

"A girl named Pretty Alice told us who you were."

"That's a lie."

"It's true. You unnerve her. She wants to belong; she wants to conform; I'm going to turn you off."

"Then do it already, and stop arguing with me."

"I'm not going to turn you off."

"You're an idiot!"

"Repent, Harlequin!" said the Ticktockman.

"Get stuffed."

So they sent him to Coventry. And in Coventry they worked him over. It was just like what they did to Winston Smith in Nineteen Eighty-Four, which was a book none of them knew about, but the techniques are really quite ancient, and so they did it to Everett C. Marm; and one day, quite a long time later, the Harlequin appeared on the communications web, appearing elfin and dimpled and bright-eyed, and not at all brainwashed, and he said he had been wrong, that it was a good, a very good thing indeed, to belong, to be right on time hip-ho and away we go, and everyone stared up at him on the public screens that covered an entire city block, and they said to themselves, well, you see, he was just a nut after all, and if that's the way the system is run, then let's do it that way, because it doesn't pay to fight city hall, or in this case, the Ticktockman. So Everett C. Marm was destroyed, which was a loss, because of what Thoreau said earlier, but you can't make an omelet without breaking a few eggs, and in every revolution a few die who shouldn't, but they have to, because that's the way it happens, and if you make only a little change, then it seems to be worthwhile. Or, to make the point lucidly:

"Uh, excuse me, sir, I, uh, don't know how to uh, to uh, tell you this, but you were three minutes late. The schedule is a little, uh, bit off."

He grinned sheepishly.

"That's ridiculous!" murmured the Ticktockman behind his mask. "Check your watch." And then he went into his office, going *mrmee, mrmee, mrmee, mrmee.*

TIME BUM

C. M. Kornbluth

*Some of the details in this story, first published all the way
back in 1953, may be a bit dated today, but the idea behind
it is as fresh as it ever was. In fact, it's likely that this con
would work better today than it would have in 1953, here
in an age when dismayingly large portions of the population believe in angels, astrology, and alien abductions, and
it wouldn't be surprising if somebody was running it on the
internet even as you read these words—so keep a wary eye
on your spam!*

*The late C. M. Kornbluth first started selling stories as
a teenage prodigy in 1940, making his first sale to* Super
Science Stories, *and wrote vast amounts of pulp fiction
under many different pseudonyms in the years before
World War II, most of it unknown today. Only after the war,
in the booming SF scene of the early '50s, did Kornbluth
begin to attract some serious attention. As a writer, C. M.
Kornbluth first came to widespread prominence with a series of novels written in collaboration with Frederik Pohl,
including the* Space Merchants *(one of the most famous SF
novels of the '50s),* Gladiator-at-Law, Search the Sky, *and*
Wolfbane; *he also produced two fairly routine novels in
collaboration with Judith Merill as "Cyril Judd,"* Outpost
Mars *and* Gunner Cade, *that were moderately well received at the time but largely forgotten today, as well as
several long-forgotten mainstream novels in collaboration
with Pohl. As a solo writer—in addition to several mainstream novels under different pseudonyms—he produced
three interesting but largely unsuccessful novels (*Not This
August, The Syndic, *and* Takeoff*) that had little impact on
the SF world of the day.*

What did *have a powerful impact on the SF world,*

though, was Kornbluth's short fiction. Kornbluth was a master of the short story, working with a sophistication, maturity, elegance, and grace rarely seen in the genre, then or now, one of those key authors—one also thinks of Damon Knight, Theodore Sturgeon, Alfred Bester, Algis Budrys, and a few others—who were busy in the '50s redefining what you could do with the instrument known as the science fiction short story, and greatly expanding its range. In the years before his tragically early death in 1958 Kornbluth created some of the best short work of the '50s, including the classic "The Little Black Bag," "The Marching Morons," "Shark Ship," "Two Dooms," "Gomez," "The Last Man Left in the Bar," "The Advent of Channel Twelve," "MS. Found in a Chinese Fortune Cookie," "With These Hands," and dozens of others.

Kornbluth won no major awards during his lifetime, but one story of his, "The Meeting," completed from a partial draft by Pohl years after Kornbluth's death, won a Hugo Award in 1972. Kornbluth's solo short work was collected in The Explorers, A Mile Beyond the Moon, The Marching Morons, Thirteen O'Clock and Other Zero Hours, *and* The Best of C. M. Kornbluth. *Pohl and Kornbluth's collaborative short work has been collected in* The Wonder Effect, Critical Mass, Before the Universe, *and* Our Best. *Until recently, I would have said that everything by Kornbluth was long out of print, but, fortunately, in 1996 NESFA Press published a massive retrospective Kornbluth collection,* His Share of the Glory: The Complete Short Fiction of C. M. Kornbluth *(NESFA Press, P.O. Box 809, Framingham, MA 07101-0203, $27.00 plus postage). True to its title, this collection assembles almost everything Kornbluth ever wrote under his own name, and it belongs in every serious SF reader's library.*

Harry Twenty-Third Street suddenly burst into laughter. His friend and sometimes roper Farmer Brown looked inquisitive.

"I just thought of a new con," Harry Twenty-Third Street said, still chuckling.

Farmer Brown shook his head positively. "There's no such thing, my man," he said. "There are only new switches on old cons. What have you got—a store con? Shall you be needing a roper?" He tried not to look eager as a matter of principle, but everybody knew the Farmer needed a connection badly. His girl had two-timed him on a badger game, running off with the chump and marrying him after an expensive, month-long buildup.

Harry said, "Sorry, old boy. No details. It's too good to split up. I shall rip and tear the suckers with this con for many a year, I trust, before the details become available to the trade. Nobody, but nobody, is going to call copper after I take him. It's beautiful and it's mine. I will see you around, my friend."

Harry got up from the booth and left, nodding cheerfully to a safeblower here, a fixer there, on his way to the locked door of the hangout. Naturally he didn't nod to such small fry as pickpockets and dope peddlers. Harry had his pride.

The puzzled Farmer sipped his lemon squash and concluded that Harry had been kidding him. He noticed that Harry had left behind him in the booth a copy of a magazine with a space ship and a pretty girl in green bra and pants on the cover.

"A furnished . . . bungalow?" the man said hesitantly, as though he knew what he wanted but wasn't quite sure of the word.

"Certainly, Mr. Clurg," Walter Lachlan said. "I'm sure we can suit you. Wife and family?"

"No," said Clurg. "They are . . . far away." He seemed to get some secret amusement from the thought. And then, to Walter's horror, he sat down calmly in empty air beside the desk and, of course, crashed to the floor looking ludicrous and astonished.

Walter gaped and helped him up, sputtering apologies and wondering privately what was wrong with the man. There wasn't a chair there. There was a chair on the other side of the desk and a chair against the wall. But there just wasn't a chair where Clurg had sat down.

Clurg apparently was unhurt; he protested against Walter's apologies, saying: "I should have known, Master Lachlan. It's quite all right; it was all my fault. What about the bang—the bungalow?"

Business sense triumphed over Walter's bewilderment. He pulled out his listings and they conferred on the merits of several furnished bungalows. When Walter mentioned that the Curran place was especially nice, in an especially nice neighborhood—he lived up the street himself—Clurg was impressed. "I'll take that one," he said. "What is the . . . feoff?"

Walter had learned a certain amount of law for his real-estate license examination; he recognized the word. "The *rent* is seventy-five dollars," he said. "You speak English very well, Mr. Clurg." He hadn't been certain that the man was a foreigner until the dictionary word came out. "You have hardly any accent."

"Thank you," Clurg said, pleased. "I worked hard at it. Let me see—seventy-five is six twelves and three." He opened one of his shiny-new leather suitcases and calmly laid six heavy little paper rolls on Walter's desk. He broke open a seventh and laid down three mint-new silver dollars. "There I am," he said. "I mean, there you are."

Walter didn't know what to say. It had never happened before. People paid by check or in bills. They just didn't pay in silver dollars. But it was money—why shouldn't Mr. Clurg pay in silver dollars if he wanted to? He shook himself, scooped the rolls into his top desk drawer and said: "I'll drive you out there if you like. It's nearly quitting time anyway."

Walter told his wife Betty over the dinner table: "We ought to have him in some evening. I can't imagine where on Earth he comes from. I had to show him how to turn on the kitchen range. When it went on he said, 'Oh, yes—electricity!' and laughed his head off. And he kept ducking the question when I tried to ask him in a nice way. Maybe he's some kind of a political refugee."

"Maybe . . ." Betty began dreamily, and then shut her mouth. She didn't want Walter laughing at her again. As it was, he made her buy her science-fiction magazines downtown instead of at neighborhood newsstands. He thought it wasn't becoming for his wife to read them. He's so eager for success, she thought sentimentally.

That night, while Walter watched a television variety show, she read a story in one of her magazines. (Its cover, depicting a space ship and a girl in green bra and shorts, had been prudently torn off and thrown away.) It was about a man from the future who had gone back in time, bringing with him all sorts of marvelous inventions. In the end the Time Police punished him for unauthorized time traveling. They had come back and got him, brought him back to his own time. She smiled. It *would* be nice if Mr. Clurg, instead of being a slightly eccentric foreigner, were a man from the future with all sorts of interesting stories to tell and a satchelful of gadgets that could be sold for millions and millions of dollars.

After a week they did have Clurg over for dinner. It started badly. Once more he managed to sit down in empty air and crash to the floor. While they were brushing him off he said fretfully: "I can't get used to not—" and then said no more.

He was a picky eater. Betty had done one of her mother's specialties, veal cutlet with tomato sauce, topped by a poached egg. He ate the egg and sauce, made a clumsy attempt to cut up the meat, and abandoned it. She served a plate of cheese, half a dozen kinds, for dessert, and Clurg tasted them uncertainly, breaking off a crumb from each, while Betty wondered where that constituted good manners. His face lit up when he tried a ripe cheddar. He popped the whole wedge into his mouth and said to Betty: "I will have that, please."

"Seconds?" asked Walter. "Sure. Don't bother, Betty. I'll get it." He brought back a quarter-pound wedge of the cheddar.

Walter and Betty watched silently as Clurg calmly ate every crumb of it. He sighed. "Very good. Quite like—" The word, Walter and Bettery later agreed, was *see-mon-joe*. They were able to agree quite early in the evening, because Clurg got up after eating the cheese, said warmly, "Thank you so much!" and walked out of the house.

Betty said, *"What—on—Earth!"*

Walter said uneasily, "I'm sorry, doll. I didn't think he'd be quite that peculiar—"

"—But after *all!*"

"—Of course he's a foreigner. What was that word?"

He jotted it down.

While they were doing the dishes Betty said, "I think he was drunk. Falling-down drunk."

"No," Walter said. "It's exactly the same thing he did in my office. As though he expected a chair to come to him instead of him going to a chair." He laughed and said uncertainly, "Or maybe he's royalty. I read once about Queen Victoria never looking around before she sat down, she was so sure there'd be a chair there."

"Well, there isn't any more royalty, not to speak of," she

said angrily, hanging up the dish towel. "What's on TV tonight?"

"Uncle Miltie. But . . . uh . . . I think I'll read. Uh . . . where do you keep those magazines of yours, doll? Believe I'll give them a try."

She gave him a look that he wouldn't meet, and she went to get him some of her magazines. She also got a slim green book which she hadn't looked at for years. While Walter flipped uneasily through the magazines she studied the book.

After about ten minutes she said: "Walter. *Seemonjoe.* I think I know what language it is."

He was instantly alert. "Yeah? What?"

"It should be spelled c-i-m-a-n-g-o, with little jiggers over the C and G. It means 'universal food' in Esperanto."

"Where's Esperanto?" he demanded.

"Esperanto isn't anywhere. It's an artificial language. I played around with it a little once. It was supposed to end war and all sorts of things. Some people called it 'the language of the future.'" Her voice was tremulous.

Walter said, "I'm going to get to the bottom of this."

He saw Clurg go into the neighborhood movie for the matinee. That gave him about three hours.

Walter hurried to the Curran bungalow, remembered to slow down and tried hard to look casual as he unlocked the door and went in. There wouldn't be any trouble—he was a good citizen, known and respected—he could let himself into a tenant's house and wait for him to talk about business if he wanted to.

He tried not to think of what people would think if he should be caught rifling Clurg's luggage, as he intended to do. He had brought along an assortment of luggage keys. Surprised by his own ingenuity, he had got them at a locksmith's by saying his own key was lost and he didn't want to haul a heavy packed bag downtown.

But he didn't need the keys. In the bedroom closet the two suitcases stood, unlocked.

There was nothing in the first except uniformly new clothes, bought locally at good shops. The second was full of the same. Going through a rather extreme sports jacket, Walter found a wad of paper in the breast pocket. It was a newspaper page. A number had been penciled on a margin; apparently the sheet had been torn out and stuck into the pocket and forgotten. The dateline on the paper was July 18th, 2403.

Walter had some trouble reading the stories at first, but found it was easy enough if he read them aloud and listened to his voice.

One said:

TAIM KOP NABD:
PROSKYOOTR ASKS DETH

Patrolm'n Oskr Garth 'v thi Taim Polis w'z arest'd toodei at hiz hom, 4365 9863th Strit, and bookd at 9768th Prisint on tchardg'z 'v Polis-Ekspozh'r. Thi aledjd Ekspozh'r okur'd hwaile Garth w'z on dooti in thi Twenti-Furst Sentch'ri. It konsist'd 'v hiz admish'n too a sit'zen 'v thi Twenti-Furst Sentch'ri that thi Taim Polis ekzisted and woz op'rated fr'm thi Twenti-Fifth Sentch'ri. Thi Proskyoot'rz Ofis sed thi deth pen'lti will be askt in vyoo 'v thi heinus neitch'r 'v thi ofens, hwitch thret'nz thi hwol fabrik 'v Twenti-Fifth-Sentch'ri eksiztens.

There was an advertisement on the other side:

BOIZ 'ND YUNG MEN!
SERV EUR SENTCH'RI!
ENLIST IN THI TAIM POLIS RISURV NOW!
            RIMEMB'R—

ONLI IN THI TAIM POLIS KAN EU SI THI PA-
JENT 'V THI AJEZ! ONLY IN THI TAIM POLIS
KAN EU PROTEKT EUR SIVILIZASH'N FR'M
VARI'NS! THEIR IZ NO HAIER SERVIS TOO AR
KULTCH'R! THEIR IZ NO K'REER SO FAS'-
NATING AZ A K'REER IN THI TAIM POLIS!

Underneath it another ad asked:

HWAI BI ASHEIM'D 'V EUR TCHAIRZ? GET
ROLFASTS!
   No uth'r tcheir haz thi immidjit respons 'v a Rol-
fast. Sit enihweir—eor Rolfast iz their!

Eur Rolfast met'l partz ar solid gold to avoid tairsum
polishing. Eur Rolfast beirings are thi fain'st six-
intch dupliks di'mondz for long wair.

Walter's heart pounded. Gold—to avoid tiresome polishing! Six-inch diamonds—for long wear!
   And Clurg must be a time policeman. "Only in the time
police can you see the pageant of the ages!" What did a
time policeman do? He wasn't quite clear about that. But
what they *didn't* do was let anybody else—anybody earlier—know that the Time Police existed. He, Walter Lachlan of the twentieth century, held in the palm of his hand
Time Policeman Clurg of the twenty-fifth century—the
twenty-fifth century where gold and diamonds were common as steel and glass in this!

He was there when Clurg came back from the matinee.
   Mutely, Walter extended the page of newsprint. Clurg
snatched it incredulously, stared at it and crumpled it in his
fist. He collapsed on the floor with a groan. "I'm done
for!" Walter heard him say.

"Listen, Clurg," Walter said. "Nobody ever needs to know about this—*nobody*."

Clurg looked up with sudden hope in his eyes. "You will keep silent?" he asked wildly. "It is my life!"

"What's it worth to you?" Walter demanded with brutal directness. "I can use some of those diamonds and some of that gold. Can you get it into this century?"

"It would be missed. It would be over my mass-balance," Clurg said. "But I have a Duplix. I can copy diamonds and gold for you; that was how I made my feoff money."

He snatched an instrument from his pocket—a fountain pen, Walter thought. "It is low in charge. It would Duplix about five kilograms in one operation—"

"You mean," Walter demanded, "that if I brought you five kilograms of diamonds and gold you could duplicate it? And the originals wouldn't be harmed? Let me see that thing. Can I work it?"

Clurg passed over the "fountain pen." Walter saw that within the case was a tangle of wires, tiny tubes, lenses—he passed it back hastily. Clurg said, "That is correct. You could buy or borrow jewelry and I could Duplix it. Then you could return the originals and retain the copies. You swear by your contemporary God that you would say nothing?"

Walter was thinking. He could scrape together a good thirty thousand dollars by pledging the house, the business, his own real estate, the bank account, the life insurance, the securities. Put it all into diamonds, of course, and then—*doubled! Overnight!*

"I'll say nothing," he told Clurg. "If you come through." He took the sheet from the twenty-fifth-century newspaper from Clurg's hands and put it securely in his own pocket. "When I get those diamonds duplicated," he said, "I'll burn this and forget the rest. Until then, I want you to stay close to home. I'll come around in a day or so with the stuff for you to duplicate."

Clurg nervously promised.

• • •

The secrecy, of course, didn't include Betty. He told her when he got home and she let out a yell of delight. She demanded the newspaper, read it avidly, and then demanded to see Clurg.

"I don't think he'll talk," Walter said doubtfully. "But if you really want to . . ."

She did, and they walked to the Curran bungalow. Clurg was gone, lock, stock and barrel, leaving not a trace behind. They waited for hours, nervously.

At last Betty said, "He's gone back."

Walter nodded. "He wouldn't keep his bargain, but by God I'm going to keep mine. Come along. We're going to the *Enterprise*."

"Walter," she said. "You wouldn't—would you?"

He went alone, after a bitter quarrel.

At the *Enterprise* office he was wearily listened to by a reporter, who wearily looked over the twenty-fifth-century newspaper. "I don't know what you're peddling, Mr. Lachlan," he said, "but we like people to buy their ads in the *Enterprise*. This is a pretty bare-faced publicity grab."

"But—" Walter sputtered.

"Sam, would you please ask Mr. Morris to come up here if he can?" the reporter was saying into the phone. To Walter he explained, "Mr. Morris is our press-room foreman."

The foreman was a huge, white-haired old fellow, partly deaf. The reporter showed him the newspaper from the twenty-fifth century and said, "How about this?"

Mr. Morris looked at it and smelled it and said, showing no interest in the reading matter: "American Type Foundry Futura number nine, discontinued about ten years ago. It's been hand-set. The ink—hard to say. Expensive stuff, not a news ink. A book ink, a job-printing ink. The paper, now, I know. A nice linen rag that Benziger jobs in Philadelphia."

"You see, Mr. Lachlan? It's a fake." The reporter shrugged.

Walter walked slowly from the city room. The press-room foreman *knew*. It was a fake. And Clurg was a faker.

Suddenly Walter's heels touched the ground after twenty-four hours and stayed there. Good God, the diamonds! Clurg was a conman! He would have worked a package switch! He would have had thirty thousand dollars' worth of diamonds for less than a month's work!

He told Betty about it when he got home and she laughed unmercifully. "Time Policeman" was to become a family joke between the Lachlans.

Harry Twenty-Third Street stood, blinking, in a very peculiar place. Peculiarly, his feet were firmly encased, up to the ankles, in a block of clear plastic.

There were odd-looking people and a big voice was saying: "May it please the court. The People of the Twenty-Fifth Century versus Harold Parish, alias Harry Twenty-Third Street, alias Clurg, of the Twentieth Century. The charge is impersonating an officer of the Time Police. The Prosecutor's Office will ask the death penalty in view of the heinous nature of the offense, which threatens the whole fabric—"

MERCURIAL

Kim Stanley Robinson

Kim Stanley Robinson sold his first story in 1976 and quickly established himself as one of the most respected and critically acclaimed writers of his generation. His story "Black Air" won the World Fantasy Award in 1984, and his novella "The Blind Geometer" won the Nebula Award in 1987. His novel The Wild Shore *was published in 1984 and was quickly followed up by other novels such as* Icehenge; The Memory of Whiteness; A Short, Sharp Shock; The Gold Coast; The Pacific Shore; *and* Antarctica; *and by collections such as* The Planet on the Table, Escape from Kathmandu, *and* Remaking History.

Robinson's already distinguished literary reputation would take a quantum jump in the decade of the '90s, though, with the publication of his acclaimed Mars trilogy, Red Mars, Green Mars, *and* Blue Mars; Red Mars *would win a Nebula Award, both* Green Mars *and* Blue Mars *would win Hugo Awards, and the trilogy would be widely recognized as the genre's most accomplished, detailed, sustained, and substantial look at the colonization and terraforming of another world, rivaled only by Arthur C. Clarke's* The Sands of Mars. *Robinson's latest books are a collection of stories and poems set on his fictional Mars,* The Martians, *and a major new Alternate History novel,* The Days of Rice and Salt. *He lives with his family in Davis, California.*

The Mars trilogy will probably associate Robinson's name forever with the Red Planet, but in the story that follows he takes us instead to an equally vivid and brilliantly realized future Mercury, where a strange and very intriguing game is afoot. . . .

"She rules all of Oz," said Dorothy, "and so she rules your city and you, because you are in the Winkie Country, which is part of the Land of Oz."

"It may be," returned the High Coco-Lorum, "for we do not study geography and have never inquired whether we live in the Land of Oz or not. And any Ruler who rules us from a distance, and unknown to us, is welcome to the job."

—L. Frank Baum, *The Lost Princess of Oz*

I *am not*, despite the appearances, fond of crime detection. In the past, it is true, I occasionally accompanied my friend Freya Grindavik as she solved her cases, and admittedly this watsoning gave me some good material for the little tales I have written for the not-very-discriminating markets on Mars and Titan. But after the Case of the Golden Sphere or the Lion of Mercury, in which I ended up hanged by the feet from the clear dome of Terminator, two hundred meters above the rooftops of the city, my native lack of enthusiasm rose to the fore. And following the unfortunate Adventure of the Vulcan Accelerator, when Freya's arch-foe Jan Johannsen tied us to a pile of hay under a large magnifying glass in a survival tent, there to await Mercury's fierce dawn, I put my face down: no more detecting. That, so to speak, was the last straw.

So when I agreed to accompany Freya to the Solday party of Heidi van Seegeren, it was against my better judgment. But Freya assured me there would be no business involved; and despite the obvious excesses, I enjoy a Solday party as much as the next esthete. So when she came by my villa, I was ready.

"Make haste," she said. "We're late, and I must be before Heidi's Monet when the Great Gates are opened. I adore that painting."

"Your infatuation is no secret," I said, panting as I trailed her through the crowded streets of the city. Freya, as those of you who have read my earlier tales know, is two and a half meters tall, and broad-shouldered; she barged through the shoals of Solday celebrants rather like a whale, and I, pilot fish-like, dodged in her wake. She led me through a group of Grays, who with carpetbeaters were busy pounding rugs saturated with yellow dust. As I coughed and brushed off my fine burgundy suit, I said, "My feeling is that you have taken me to view that antique canvas once or twice too often."

She looked at me sternly. "As you will see, on Solday it transcends even its usual beauty. You look like a bee drowning in pollen, Nathaniel."

"Whose fault is that?" I demanded, brushing my suit fastidiously.

We came to the gate in the wall surrounding Van Seegeren's town villa, and Freya banged on it loudly. The gate was opened by a scowling man. He was nearly a meter shorter than Freya, and had a balding head that bulged rather like the dome of the city. In a mincing voice he said, "Invitations?"

"What's this?" said Freya. "We have permanent invitations from Heidi."

"I'm sorry," the man said coolly. "Ms. Van Seegeren has decided her Solday parties have gotten overcrowded, and this time she sent out invitations, and instructed me to let in only those who have them."

"Then there has been a mistake," Freya declared. "Get Heidi on the intercom, and she will instruct you to let me in. I am Freya Grindavik, and this is Nathaniel Sebastian."

"I'm sorry," the man said, quite unapologetically. "Every person turned away says the same thing, and Ms. Van Seegeren prefers not to be disturbed so frequently."

"She'll be more disturbed to hear we've been held up," Freya shifted toward the man. "And who might you be?"

"I am Sander Musgrave, Ms. Van Seegeren's private secretary."

"How come I've never met you?"

"Ms. Van Seegeren hired me two months ago," Musgrave said, and stepped back so he could look Freya in the eye without straining his neck. "That is immaterial, however—"

"I've been Heidi's friend for over forty years," Freya said slowly, once again shifting forward to lean over the man. "And I would wager she values her friends more than her secretaries."

Musgrave stepped back indignantly. "I'm sorry!" he snapped. "I have my orders! Good day!"

But alas for him, Freya was now standing well in the gateway, and she seemed uninclined to move; she merely cocked her head at him. Musgrave comprehended his problem, and his mouth twitched uncertainly.

The impasse was broken when Van Seegeren's maid Lucinda arrived from the street. "Oh, hello, Freya, Nathaniel. What are you doing out here?"

"This new Malvolio of yours is barring our entrance," Freya said.

"Oh, Musgrave," said Lucinda. "Let these two in, or the boss will be mad."

Musgrave retreated with a deep scowl. "I've studied the ancients, Ms. Grindavik," he said sullenly. "You need not insult me."

"Malvolio was a tragic character," Freya assured him. "Read Charles Lamb's essay concerning the matter."

"I certainly will," Musgrave said stiffly, and hurried to the villa, giving us a last poisonous look.

"Of course, Lamb's father," Freya said absently, staring after the man, "was a house servant. Lucinda, who is that?"

Lucinda rolled her eyes. "The boss hired him to restore some of her paintings, and get the records in order. I wish she hadn't."

The bell in the gate sounded. "I've got it, Musgrave," Lucinda shouted at the villa. She opened the gate, revealing the artist Harvey Washburn.

"So you do," said Harvey, blinking. He was high again; a bottle of the White Brother hung from his hand. "Freya! Nathaniel! Happy Solday to you—have a drink?"

We refused the offer, and then followed Harvey around the side of the villa, exchanging a glance. I felt sorry for Harvey. Most of Mercury's great collectors came to Harvey's showings, but they dissected his every brushstroke for influences, and told him what he *should* be painting, and then among themselves they called his work amateurish and unoriginal, and never bought a single canvas. I was never surprised to see him drinking.

We rounded the side of the big villa and stepped onto the white stone patio, which was made of a giant slab of England's Dover cliffs, cut out and transported to Mercury entire. Malvolio Musgrave had spoken the truth about Heidi reducing the size of her Solday party: where often the patio had been jammed, there were now fewer than a dozen people. I spotted George Butler, Heidi's friend and rival art collector, and Arnold Ohman, the art dealer who had obtained for many of Mercury's collectors their ancient masterpieces from Earth. As I greeted them Freya led us all across the patio to the back wall of the villa, which was also fronted with white slabs of the Dover cliffs. There, all alone, hung Claude Monet's *Rouen Cathedral—Sun Effect*. "Look at it, Nathaniel!" Freya commanded me. "Isn't it beautiful?"

I looked at it. Now you must understand that, as owner of the Gallery Orientale, and by deepest personal esthetic conviction, I am a connoisseur of Chinese art, a style in which a dozen artfully spontaneous brushstrokes can serve to delineate a mountain or two, several trees, a small village and its inhabitants, and perhaps some birds. Given my predilection, you will not be surprised to learn that to look at the antique rectangle of color that Freya so admired was to risk damaging my eyes. Thick scumbled layers of grainy paint scarcely revealed the cathedral of the title, which wavered under a blast of light so intense that I doubted Mercury's midday could compete with it. Small blobs of every color served to represent both the indistinct stone and a pebbly sky, both were composed of combinations principally of white, yellow, and purple, though as I say every other color made an appearance.

"Stunning," I said, with a severe squint. "Are you sure this Monet wasn't a bit nearsighted?"

Freya glared at me, ignoring Butler's chuckles. "I suppose your comment might have been funny the first time you made it. To children, anyway."

"But I heard it was actually *true*," I said, shielding my eyes with one hand. "Monet *was* nearsighted, and so, like Goya, his vision affected his painting—"

"I should hope so," Harvey said solemnly.

"—so all he could see were those blobs of color; isn't that sad?"

Freya shook her head. "You won't get a rise out of me today, Nathaniel. You'll have to think up your dinner conversation by yourself."

Momentarily stopped by this riposte, I retired with Arnold Ohman to Heidi's patio bar. After dialing drinks from the bartender we sat on the blocks of Dover cliffs that made up the patio's outer wall. We toasted Solday, and contemplated the clouds of yellow talc that swirled over the orange tile rooftops below us. For those of you who have never visited it, Terminator is an oval city. The forward half of the city is flat, and projects out under the clear dome. The rear half of the oval is terraced, and rises to the tall Dawn Wall which supports the upper rim of the dome, and shields the city from the perpetually rising sun. The Great Gates of Terminator are near the top of the Dawn Wall, and when they are opened shafts of Sol's overwhelming light spear through the city's air, illuminating everything in a yellow brilliance. Heidi van

Seegeren's villa was about halfway up the terraced slope; we looked upon gray stone walls, orange tile roofs, and the dusty vines and lemon trees of the terrace gardens that dotted the city. Outside the dome the twelve big tracks of the city extended off to the horizon, circling the planet like a slender silver wedding band. It was a fine view, and I lifted my glass remembering that Claude Monet wasn't there to paint it. For sometimes, if you ask me, reality is enough.

Ohman downed his drink in one swallow. Rumor had it that he was borrowing heavily to finance one of his big Terran purchases; it was whispered he was planning to buy the closed portion of the Louvre—or the Renaissance room of the Vatican museum—or Amsterdam's Van Gogh collection. But rumors like that circulated around Arnold continuously. He was that kind of dealer. It was unlikely any of them were true; still, his silence seemed to reveal a certain tension.

"Look at the way Freya is soaking in that painting you got for Heidi," I said, to lift his spirits. Freya's face was within centimeters of the canvas, where she could examine it blob by blob; the people behind her could see nothing but her white-blond hair. Ohman smiled at the sight. He had brought the Monet back from his most recent Terran expedition, and apparently it had been a great struggle to obtain it. Both the English family that owned it and the British government had had to be paid enormous sums to secure its release, and only the fact that Mercury was universally considered humanity's greatest art museum had cleared the matter with the courts. It had been one of Arnold's finest hours.

Now he said, "Maybe we should pull her away a bit, so that others can see."

"If both of us tug on her it may work," I said. We stood and went to her side. Harvey Washburn, looking flushed and frazzled, joined us, and we convinced Freya to share the glory. Ohman and Butler conferred over something, and entered the villa through the big French doors that led into the concert room. Inside, Heidi's orchestra rolled up and down the scales of Moussorgsky's *Hut of Baba Yaga*. That meant it was close to the time when the Great Gates would open (Heidi always gets inside information about this).

Sure enough, as Moussorgsky's composition burst from *The Hut of Baba Yaga* into *The Great Gates of Kiev*, two splinters of white light split the air under the dome. Shouts and fanfares rose everywhere, nearly drowning the amplified sound of our orchestra. Slowly the Great Gates opened, and as they did the shafts of light grew to thick buttery gold bars of air. By their rich, nearly blinding glare, Heidi van Seegeren made her first entrance from her villa, timing her steps to the exaggerated Maazel *ritard* that her conductor Hiu employed every Solday when *Pictures at an Exhibition* was performed. This *ritard* shifted the music from the merely grandiose to the utterly bombastical, and it took Heidi over a minute to cross her own narrow patio; but I suppose it was not entirely silly, given the ritual nature of the moment, and the flood of light that was making the air appear a thick, quite tangible gel. What with the light, and the uproar created by the keening Grays and the many orchestras in the neighborhood, each playing their own overture or fanfare (the *Coriolan* came from one side of us, the *1812* from the other), it was a complex and I might even say *noisy* esthetic moment, and the last thing I needed was to take another look at the Monet monstrosity, but Freya would not have it otherwise.

"You've never seen it when the Great Gates are opened," she said. "That was the whole point in bringing you here today."

"I see." Actually I barely saw anything; as Freya had guided me by the arm to the painting I had accidentally looked directly at the incandescent yellow bars of sunlight and brilliant blue afterimages bounced in my sight. I heard rather than saw Harvey Washburn join us. Many blinks later I was able to join the others in devoting my attention to the big canvas.

Well. The Monet positively *glowed* in the dense, lambent air; it gave off light like a lamp, vibrating with a palpable energy of its own. At the sight of it even I was impressed.

"Yes," I admitted to Freya and Harvey, "I can see how precisely he placed all those little chunks of color, and I can see how sharp and solid the cathedral is under all that goo, but it's like Solday, you know, it's a heightened effect. The result is garish, really; it's too much."

"But this is a painting of midday," Harvey said. "And as you can see, midday can get pretty garish."

"But this is Terminator! The Grays have put a lot of talc in the air to make it look this way!"

"So what?" Freya demanded impatiently. "Stop thinking so much, Nathaniel. Just *look* at it. *See* it. Isn't it beautiful? Haven't you felt things look that way sometimes, seeing stone in sunlight?"

"Well . . ." And, since I am a strictly honest person, if I had said anything at all I would have had to admit that it did have a power about it. It drew the eye; it poured light onto us as surely as the beams of sunlight extending from the gates in the Dawn Wall to the curved side of the clear dome.

"Well?" Freya demanded.

"Well yes," I said. "Yes I see that cathedral front—I feel it. But there must have been quite a heat wave in old Rouen. It's as if Monet had seen Terminator on Solday, the painting fits so well with this light."

"No," Freya said, but her left eye was squinted, a sign she was thinking.

Harvey said, "We make the conditions of light in Terminator, and so it is an act of the imagination, like this painting. You shouldn't be surprised if there are similari-

ties. We value this light because the old masters created it
on their canvases."

I shook my head, and indicated the brassy bedlam
around us. "No. I believe we made this one up ourselves."

Freya and Harvey laughed, with the giddiness that Solday inspires.

Suddenly a loud screech came from inside the villa.
Freya hurried across the patio into the music room, and I
followed her. Both of us, however, had forgotten the
arrangements that Heidi made on Soldays to cast the brilliant light throughout her home, and as we ran past the si-
lenced orchestra into a hallway we were blasted by light
from a big mirror carefully placed in the villa's central
atrium. Screams still echoed from somewhere inside, but
we could only stumble blindly through bright pulsing afterimages, retinal Monets if you will, while unidentified
persons bowled into us, and mirrors crashed to the floor.
And the atrium was raised, so that occasional steps up in
the hallway tripped us.

"Murder!" someone cried. "Murder! There he goes!"
And with that a whole group of us were off down the halls
like hounds—blind hounds—baying after unknown prey.
A figure leaped from behind a mirror glaring white, and
Freya and I tackled it just inside the atrium.

When my vision swam back I saw it was George Butler. "What's going on?" he asked, very politely for a man
who had just been jumped on by Freya Grindavik.

"Don't ask us," Freya said irritably.

"Murder!" shrieked Lucinda, from the hallway that led
from the atrium directly back to the patio. We jumped up
and crowded into the hallway. Just beyond a mirror shattered into many pieces lay a man's body; apparently he
had been crawling toward the patio when he collapsed,
and one arm and finger extended ahead of him, still pointing to the patio. Freya approached, gingerly turned the
body's head. "It's that Musgrave fellow," she said, blink-

ing to clear her sight. "He's dead, all right. Struck on the head with the mirror there, no doubt."

Heidi van Seegeren joined us. "What's going on?"

"That was my question," George Butler said.

Freya explained the situation to her.

"Call the police," Heidi said to Lucinda. "And I suppose no one should leave."

I sighed.

And so crime detection ensnared me once again. I helped Freya by circulating on the patio, calming the shocked and nervous guests. "Um, excuse me, very sorry to inform you, yes, sorry—hard to believe, yes—somebody had it in for the secretary Musgrave, it appears"—all the while watching to see if anyone would jump, or turn pale, or start to run when I told them. Then, of course, I had to lead gently to the idea that everyone had gone from guest to suspect, soon to be questioned by Freya and the police. "No, no, of course you're not suspected of anything, farthest thing from our minds, it's just that Freya wants to know if there's anything you saw that would help," and so on. Then I had to do the difficult scheduling of Freya's interviews, at the same time I was supposed to keep an eye out for anything suspicious.

Oh, the watson does the dirty work, all right. No wonder we always look dense when the detective unveils the solutions; we never have the time even get the facts straight, much less meditate on their meaning. All I got that day were fragments: Lucinda whispered to me that Musgrave had worked for George Butler before Heidi hired him. Harvey Washburn told me that Musgrave had once been an artist, and that he had only recently moved to Mercury from Earth; this was his first Solday. That didn't give him much time to be hired by Butler, fired, and then hired by Van Seegeren. But was that of significance?

Late in the day I spoke with one of the police officers

handling the case. She was relieved to have the help of
Freya Grindavik. Terminator's police force is small, and
often relies on the help of the city's famous detective for
the more difficult cases. The officer gave me a general outline of what they had learned: Lucinda had heard a shout
for help, had stepped into the atrium and seen a bloodied
figure crawling down the hallway toward the patio. She
had screamed and run for help, but only in the hallway was
clear vision possible, and she had quickly gotten lost. After
that, chaos; everyone at the party had a different tale of
confusion.

Following that conversation I had nothing more to do,
so I got all the sequestered guests coffee, and helped pick
up some of the broken hall mirrors, and passed some time
prowling Heidi's villa, getting down on my hands and
knees with the police robots to inspect a stain or two.

When Freya was finished with her interrogations, she
promised Heidi and the police that she would see the case
to its end—at least provisionally: "I only do this for entertainment," she told them irritably. "I'll stay with it as long
as it entertains me. And I shall entertain myself with it."

"That's all right," said the police, who had heard this
before. "Just so long as you'll take the case." Freya nodded, and we left.

The Solday celebration was long since over; the Great
Gates were closed, and once again through the dome shone
the black sky. I said to Freya, "Did you hear about Musgrave working for Butler? And how he came from Earth
just recently?" For you see, once on the scent I am committed to seeing a case solved.

"Please, Nathaniel," Freya said. "I heard all of that and
more. Musgrave stole the concept of Harvey Washburn's
first series of paintings, he blackmailed both Butler and
our host Heidi to obtain his jobs from them—or so I de-
duce, from their protestations, and from certain facts concerning their recent questionable merger that I am privy to.
And he tried to assault Lucinda, who is engaged to the

cook Delaurence—" She let out a long sigh. "Motives are everywhere."

Bemused, I said, "It seems this Musgrave was a thoroughly despicable sort."

"Yes. An habitual blackmailer."

"Nothing *suggests* itself to you?"

"No. Not only that, but it seems almost every person at the party had a good alibi for the moment of the murder! Oh, I don't know why I agree to solve these things. Here I am committed to this head-bashing, and my best clue is something that *you* suggested."

"I wasn't aware that I had suggested anything!"

"There is a fresh perspective to ignorance that can be very helpful."

"So it *is* important that Musgrave just arrived from Earth?"

She laughed. "Let's stop in the Plaza Dubrovnik and get something to eat. I'm starving."

Almost three weeks passed without a word from Freya, and I began to suspect that she was ignoring the case. Freya has no real sense of right and wrong, you see; she regards her cases as games, to be tossed aside if they prove too taxing. More than once she has cheerfully admitted defeat, and blithely forgotten any promises she may have made. She is not a moral person.

So I dropped by her home near Plaza Dubrovnik one evening, to rouse her from her irresponsible indifference. When she answered the door there were paint smudges on her face and hands.

"Freya," I scolded her. "How could you take up an entirely new hobby when there is a *case* to be solved?"

"Generously I allow you entrance after such a false accusation," she said. "But you will have to eat your words."

She led me downstairs to her basement laboratory, which extended the entire length and breadth of her villa.

There on a big white-topped table lay Heidi van Seegeren's Monet, looking like the three-dimensional geologic map of some minerally blessed country.

"What's this?" I exclaimed. "Why is this here?"

"I believe it is a fake," she said shortly, returning to a computer console.

"Wait a moment!" I cried. On the table around the painting were rolls of recording chart paper, lab notebooks, and what looked like black-and-white photos of the painting. "What do you mean?"

After tapping at the console she turned to me. "I mean I believe it's a fake!"

"But I thought art forgery was extinct. It is too easy to discover a fake."

"Ha!" She waved a finger at me angrily. "You pick a bad time to say so. It is a common opinion, of course, but not necessarily true."

I regarded the canvas more closely. "What makes you think this a fake? I thought it was judged a masterpiece of its period."

"Something you said first caused me to question it," she said. "You mentioned that the painting seemed to have been created by an artist familiar with the light of Terminator. This seemed true to me, and it caused me to reflect that one of the classic signs of a fake was anachronistic sensibility—that is to say, the forger injects into his vision of the past some element of his time that is so much a part of his sensibility that he cannot perceive it. Thus the Victorians faked Renaissance faces with a sentimentality that only they could not immediately see."

"I see." I nodded sagely. "It did seem that cathedral had been struck with Solday light, didn't it?"

"Yes. The trouble is, I have been able to find no sign of forgery in the physical properties of the painting." She shook her head. "And after three weeks of uninterrupted chemical analysis, that is beginning to worry me."

"But Freya," I said, as something occurred to me. "Does all this have a bearing on the Musgrave murder?"

"I think so," she replied. "And if not, it is certainly more interesting. But I believe it does."

I nodded. "So what, exactly, have you found?"

She smiled ironically. "You truly want to know? Well. The best test for anachronisms is the polonium 210, radium 226 equilibrium—"

"Please, Freya. No jargon."

"Jargon!" She raised an eyebrow to scorn me. "There is no such thing. Intelligence is like mold in a petri dish—as it eats ever deeper into the agar of reality, language has to expand with it to describe what has been digested. Each specialty provides the new vocabulary for its area of feeding, and gets accused of fabricating jargon by those who know no better. I'm surprised to hear such nonsense from you. Or perhaps not."

"Very well," I said, hands up. "Still, you must communicate your meaning to me."

"I shall. First I analyzed the canvas. The material and its weave match the characteristics of the canvas made by the factory outside Paris that provided Monet throughout the painting of the Rouen cathedral series. Both the fabric and the glue appear very old, though there is no precise dating technique for them. And there was no trace of solvents that might have been used to strip paint off a genuine canvas of the period.

"I then turned to the paint. Follow so far?" she asked sharply. "Paint?"

"You may proceed without further sarcasm, unless unable to control yourself."

"The palette of an artist as famous as Monet has been studied in detail, so that we know he preferred cadmium yellow to chromium yellow or Naples yellow, that he tended to use Prussian blue rather than cobalt blue, and so on." She tapped the flecks of blue at the base of the cathedral. "Prussian blue."

"You've taken paint off the canvas?"

"How else test it? But I took very small samples, I assure you. Whatever the truth concerning the work, it remains a masterpiece, and I would not mar it. Besides, most of my tests were on the white paint, of which there is a great quantity, as you can see."

I leaned over to stare more closely at the canvas. "Why the white paint?"

"Because lead white is one of the best dating tools we have. The manufacturing methods used to make it changed frequently around Monet's time, and each change in method altered the chemical composition of the paint. After 1870, for instance, the cheaper zinc white was used to adulterate lead white, so there should be over one percent zinc in Monet's lead white."

"And is that what you found?"

"Yes. The atomic absorption spectrum showed—" She dug around in the pile of chart paper on the table. "Well, take my word for it—"

"I will."

"Nearly twelve percent. And the silver content for late-nineteenth-century lead white should be around four parts per million, the copper content about sixty parts per million. So it is with this paint. There is no insoluble antimony component, as there would be if the paint had been manufactured after 1940. The X-ray diffraction pattern"—she unrolled a length of chart paper and showed me where three sharp peaks in a row had been penned by the machine—"is exactly right, and there is the proper balance of polonium 210 and radium 226. That's very important, by the way, because when lead white is manufactured the radioactive balance of some of its elements is upset, and it takes a good three hundred years for them to decay back to equilibrium. And this paint is indeed back to that equilibrium."

"So the paints are Monet's," I concluded. "Doesn't that prove the work authentic?"

"Perhaps," Freya admitted. "But as I was doing all this analysis, it occurred to me that a modern forger has just as much information concerning Monet's palette as I do. With a modern laboratory it would be possible to *use such information as a recipe,* so to speak, and then to synthesize paints that would match the recipe exactly. Even the radioactively decayed lead white could be arranged, by avoiding the procedures that disrupt the radioactive balance in the first place!"

"Wouldn't that be terrifically complicated?"

Freya stared at me. "*Obviously,* Nathaniel, we are dealing with a very, very meticulous faker here. But how else could it be done, in this day and age? Why else do it at all? The complete faker must take care to anticipate every test available, and then in a modern laboratory create the appropriate results for every one of them. It's admirable!"

"Assuming there ever was such a forger," I said dubiously. "It seems to me that what you have actually done here is prove the painting genuine."

"I don't think so."

"But even with these paints made by recipe, as you call them, the faker would still have to paint the painting!"

"Exactly. Conceive the painting, and execute it. It becomes very impressive, I confess." She walked around the table to look at the work from the correct angle. "I do believe this is one of the *best* of the Rouen cathedral series—astonishing, that a forger would be capable of it."

"That brings up another matter," I said. "Doesn't this work have a five-hundred-year-old pedigree? How could a whole history have been provided for it?"

"Good question. But I believe I have discovered the way. Let's go upstairs—you interrupted my preparations for lunch, and I'm hungry."

I followed her to her extensive kitchen, and sat in the window nook that overlooked the tile rooftops of the lower city while she finished chopping up the vegetables for a large salad.

"Do you know the painting's history?" Freya asked, looking up from a dissected head of lettuce.

I shook my head. "Up until now the thing has not been of overwhelming interest to me."

"A confession of faulty esthetics. The work was photographed at the original exhibit in 1895, Durand-Ruel photo 5828 L8451. All of the information appended to the photo fits our painting—same name, size, signature location. Then for a century it disappeared. Odd. But it turned out to have been in the estate of an Evans family, in Aylesbury, England. When the family had some conservation work done on one corner it returned to public knowledge, and was photographed for a dozen books of the twenty-first and twenty-second centuries. After that it slipped back into obscurity, but it is as well documented as any of the series belonging to private estates."

"Exactly my point," I said. "How could such a history be forged?"

As Freya mixed the salad she smiled. "I sat and thought about that for quite some time myself. But consider it freshly, Nathaniel. How do we know what we know of the past?"

"Well," I said, somewhat at a loss. "From data banks, I suppose. And books—documents—historians—"

"From historians!" She laughed. She provided us both with bowls, and sat across from me. As I filled mine she said, "So we want to know something of the past. We go to our library and sit at its terminal. We call up general reference works, or a bibliographical index, and we choose, if we want, books that we would like to have in our hands. We type in the appropriate code, our printer prints up the appropriate book, and the volume slides out of the computer into our waiting grasp." She paused to fork down several mouthfuls of salad. "So we learn about the past using computer programs. And a clever programmer, you see, can change a program. It would be possible to *insert*

extra pages into these old books on Monet, and thus add
the forged painting to the record of the past."

I paused, a cherry tomato hovering before my mouth.
"But—"

"I searched for an original of *any* of these books containing photos of our painting," Freya said. "I called all
over Mercury, and to several incunabulists in libraries on
Earth—you wouldn't believe the phone bill I've run up.
But the original printings of these art volumes were very
small, and although first editions probably remain *somewhere,* they are not to be found. Certainly there are no first
editions of these books on Mercury, and none immediately
locatable on Earth. It began to seem a very unlikely coincidence, as if these volumes contained pictures of our
painting precisely because they existed only in the data
banks, and thus could be altered without discovery."

She attended to her salad, and we finished eating in silence. All the while my mind was spinning furiously, and
when we were done I said, "What about the original exhibit photo?"

She nodded, pleased with me. "That, apparently, is genuine. But the Durand-Ruel photos include four or five of
paintings that have never been seen since. In that sense the
Rouen cathedral series is a good one for a faker; from the
first it has never been clear how many cathedrals Monet
painted. The usual number given is thirty-two, but there
are more in the Durand-Ruel list, and a faker could examine the list and use one of the lost items as a prescription
for his fake. Providing a later history with the aid of these
obscure art books would result in a fairly complete pedigree."

"But could such an addition to the data banks be
made?"

"It would be easiest done on Earth," Freya said. "But
there is no close security guarding the banks containing
old art books. No one expects them to be tampered with."

"It's astonishing," I said with a wave of my fork, "it is baroque, it is *byzantine* in its ingenuity!"

"Yes," she said. "Beautiful, in a way."

"However," I pointed out to her, "you have no proof—only this perhaps overly complex theory. You have found no first edition of a book to confirm that the computer-generated volumes add Heidi's painting, and you have found no physical anachronism in the painting itself."

Gloomily she clicked her fork against her empty salad bowl, then rose to refill it. "It is a problem," she admitted. "Also, I have been working on the assumption that Sandor Musgrave discovered evidence of the forgery. But *I* can't find it."

Never let it be said that Nathaniel Sebastian has not performed a vital role in Freya Grindavik's great feats of detection. I was the first to notice the anachronism if sensibility in Heidi's painting; and now I had a truly inspired idea. "He was pointing to the patio!" I exclaimed. "Musgrave, in his last moment, struggled to point to the patio!"

"I had observed that," Freya said, unimpressed.

"But Heidi's patio—you know—it is formed out of blocks of the Dover cliffs! And thus Musgrave indicated *England!* Is it not possible? The Monet was owned by Englishmen until Heidi purchased it—perhaps Musgrave meant to convey that the original owners were the forgers!"

Freya's mouth hung open in surprise, and her left eye was squinted shut. I leaped from the window nook in triumph. "I've solved it! I've solved a mystery at last."

Freya looked up at me and laughed.

"Come now, Freya, you must admit I have given you the vital clue."

She stood up, suddenly all business. "Yes, yes, indeed you have. Now out with you, Nathaniel; I have work to do."

"So I did give you the vital clue?" I asked. "Musgrave was indicating the English owners?"

As she ushered me to her door Freya laughed. "As a detective your intuition is matched only by your confidence. Now leave me to work, and I will be in contact with you soon, I assure you." And with that she urged me into the street, and I was left to consider the case alone.

Freya was true to her word, and only two days after our crucial luncheon she knocked on the door of my town villa. "Come along," she said. "I've asked Arnold Ohman for an appointment; I want to ask him some questions about the Evans family. The city is passing the Monet museum, however, and he asked us to meet him out there."

I readied myself quickly, and we proceeded to North Station. We arrived just in time to step across the gap between the two platforms, and then we were on the motionless deck of one of the outlying stations that Terminator is always passing. There we rented a car and sped west, paralleling the dozen massive cylindrical rails over which the city slides. Soon we had left Terminator behind, and when we were seventy or eighty kilometers onto the nightside of Mercury we turned to the north, to Monet Crater.

Terminator's tracks lie very close to the thirtieth degree of latitude, in the northern hemisphere, and Monet Crater is not far from them. We crossed Endeavor Rupes rapidly, and passed between craters named after the great artists, writers, and composers of Earth's glorious past: traversing a low pass between Holbein and Gluck, looking down at Melville and the double crater of Rodin. "I think I understand why a modern artist on Mercury might turn to forgery," Freya said. "We are dwarfed by the past as we are by this landscape."

"But it is still a crime," I insisted. "If it were done often, we would not be able to distinguish the authentic from the fake."

Freya did not reply.

I drove our car up a short rise, and we entered the sub-

mercurial garage of the Monet museum, which is set deep
in the southern rim of the immense crater named after the
artist. One long wall of the museum is a window facing out
over the crater floor, so that the central knot of peaks is visible, and the curving inner wall of the crater defines the
horizon in the murky distance. Shutters slid down to protect these windows from the heat of Mercury's long day,
but now they were open and the black wasteland of the
planet formed a strange backdrop to the colorful paintings
that filled the long rooms of the museum.

There were many Monet originals there, but the canvases of the Rouen cathedral series were almost all reproductions, set in one long gallery. As Freya and I searched
for Arnold we also viewed them.

"You see, they're not just various moments of a single
day," Freya said.

"Not unless it was a very strange day for weather." The
three reproductions before us all depicted foggy days: two
bluish and underwater-looking, the third a bright burning-
off of yellow noontime fog. Obviously these were from a
different day than the ones across the room, where a cool
clear morning gave way to a midday that looked as if the sun
were just a few feet above the cathedral. The museum had
classified the series in color groups: "Blue Group," "White
Group," "Yellow Group," and so on. To my mind that system was stupid—it told you nothing you couldn't immediately see. I myself classified them according to weather.
There was a clear day that got very hot; a clear winter day,
the air chill and pure; a foggy day; and a day when a rain-
storm had grown and then broken.

When I told Freya of my system she applauded it. "So
Heidi's painting goes from the king of the White Group to
the hottest moment of the hot day."

"Exactly. It's the most extreme in terms of sunlight
blasting the stone into motes of color."

"And thus the forger extends Monet's own thinking,

you see," she said, a bit absently. "But I *don't* see Arnold, and I think we have visited every room."

"Could he be late?"

"We are already quite late ourselves. I wonder if he has gone back."

"It seems unlikely," I said.

Purposefully we toured the museum one more time, and I ignored the color-splashed canvases standing before the dark crater, to search closely in all the various turns of the galleries. No Arnold.

"Come along," Freya said. "I suspect he stayed in Terminator, and now I want to speak with him more than ever."

So we returned to the garage, got back in our car, and drove out onto Mercury's bare, baked surface once again. Half an hour later we had Terminator's tracks in sight. They stretched before us from horizon to horizon, twelve fat silvery cylinders set five meters above the ground on narrow pylons. To the east, rolling over the flank of Valàzquez Crater so slowly that we could not perceive its movement without close attention, came the city itself, a giant clear half-egg filled with the colors of rooftops, gardens, and the gray stone of the building crowding the terraced Dawn Wall.

"We'll have to go west to the next station," I said. Then I saw something, up on the city track nearest us: spread-eagled over the top of the big cylinder was a human form in a light green daysuit. I stopped the car. "Look!"

Freya peered out her window. "We'd better go investigate."

We struggled quickly into the car's emergency daysuits, clamped on the helmets, and slipped through the car's lock onto the ground. A ladder led us up the nearest cylinder pylon and through a tunnel in the cylinder itself. Once on top we could stand safely on the broad hump of the rail.

The figure we had seen was only thirty meters away from us, and we hurried to it.

It was Arnold, spread in cruciform fashion over the cylinder's top, secured in place by three large suction plates that had been cuffed to his wrists and ankles, and then stuck to the cylinder. Arnold turned from his contemplation of the slowly approaching city, and looked at us wide-eyed through his faceplate. Freya reached down and turned on his helmet intercom.

"—am I glad to see you!" Arnold cried, voice harsh. "These plates won't move!"

"Tied to the tracks, eh?" Freya said.

"Yes!"

"Who put you here?"

"I don't know! I went out to meet you at the Monet museum, and the last thing I remember I was in the garage there. When I came to, I was here."

"Does your head hurt?" I inquired.

"Yes. Like I was gassed, though, not hit. But—the city—it just came over the horizon a short time ago. Perhaps we could dispense with discussion until I am freed?"

"Relax," Freya said, nudging one of the plates with her boot. "Are you sure you don't know who did this, Arnold?"

"Of course! That's what I just said! Please, Freya, can't we talk after I get loose?"

"In a hurry, Arnold?" Freya asked.

"Of course."

"No need to be too worried," I assured him. "If we can't free you the cowcatchers will be out to pry you loose." I tried lifting a plate, but could not move it. "Surely they will find a way—it's their job, after all."

"True," Arnold said.

"Usually true," said Freya. "Arnold is probably not aware that the cowcatchers have become rather unreliable recently. Some weeks ago a murderer tied his victim to a track just as you have been, Arnold, and then somehow disengaged the cowcatchers' sensors. The unfortunate victim was shaved into molecules by one of the sleeves of the city. It was kept quiet to avoid any attempted repetitions, but since then the cowcatchers' sensors have continued to function erratically, and two or three suicides have been entirely too successful."

"Perhaps this isn't the best moment to tell us about this," I suggested to Freya.

Arnold choked over what I took to be his agreement.

"Well," Freya said, "I thought I should make the situation clear. Now listen, Arnold. We need to talk."

"Please," Arnold said. "Free me first, *then* talk."

"No, no—"

"But Terminator is only a kilometer away!"

"Your perspective from that angle is deceptive," Freya told him. "The city is at least three kilometers away."

"More like two," I said, as I could now make out individual rooftops under the Dawn Wall. In fact the city glowed like a big glass lamp, and illuminated the entire landscape with a faint green radiance.

"And at three point four kilometers an hour," Freya said, "that gives us almost an hour, doesn't it. So listen to me, Arnold. The Monet cathedral that you sold to Heidi is a fake."

"What?" Arnold cried. "It certainly is not! And I insist this isn't the time—"

"It is a fake. Now I want you to tell me the truth, or I will leave you here to test the cowcatchers." She leaned over to stare down at Arnold face to face. "I know who painted the fake, as well."

Helplessly Arnold stared up at her.

"He put you on the track here, didn't he."

Arnold squeezed his eyes shut, nodded slowly. "I think so."

"So if you want to be let up, you must swear to me that you will abide by my plan for dealing with this forger. You *will* follow my instructions, understand?"

"I understand."

"Do you agree?"

"I agree," Arnold said, forcing the words out. "Now let me up!"

"All right," Freya straightened.

"How are we going to do it?" I asked.

Freya shrugged. "I don't know."

At this Arnold howled, he shouted recriminations, he began to wax hysterical—

"Shut up!" Freya exclaimed. "You're beginning to sound like a man who has made too many brightside crossings. These suction plates are little different from children's darts." She leaned down, grasped a plate, pulled up with all of her considerable strength. No movement. "Hmm," she said thoughtfully.

"Freya," Arnold said.

"One moment," she replied, and walked back down the hump of the cylinder to the ladder tunnel, there to disappear down it.

"She's left me," Arnold groaned. "Left me to be crushed."

"I don't think so," I said. "No doubt she has gone to the car to retrieve some useful implement." I kicked heartily at the plate holding Arnold's feet to the cylinder, and even managed to slide it a few centimeters down the curve, which had the effect of making Arnold suddenly taller. But other than that I made no progress.

When Freya returned she carried a bar bent at one end. "Crowbar," she explained to us.

"But where did you get it?"

"From the car's tool chest, naturally. Here." She stepped over Arnold. "If we just insinuate this end of it under your cuffs, I believe we'll have enough leverage to do the trick. The cylinder being curved, the plates' grasp should be weakened . . . about here." She jammed the short end of the bar under the edge of the footplates' cuff, and pulled on the upper end of it. Over the intercom, breathless silence; her fair cheeks reddened; then suddenly Arnold's legs flew up and over his head, leaving his arms twisted and his neck at an awkward angle. At the same time Freya staggered off the cylinder, performed a neat somersault and landed on her feet, on the ground below us. While she made her way back up to us I tried to ease the weight on Arnold's neck, but by his squeaks of distress I judged he was still uncomfortable. Freya rejoined us, and quickly wedged her crowbar under Arnold's right wrist cuff, and freed it. That left Arnold hanging down the side of the cylinder by his left wrist; but with one hard crank Freya popped that plate free as well, and Arnold disappeared. By leaning over we could just see him, collapsed in a heap on the ground. "Are you all right?" Freya asked. He groaned for an answer.

I looked up and saw that Terminator was nearly upon us. Almost involuntarily I proceeded to the ladder tunnel; Freya followed me, and we descended to the ground. "Disturbing not to be able to trust the cowcatchers," I remarked as my heartbeat slowed.

"Nathaniel," Freya said, looking exasperated. "I made all that up, you know that."

"Ah. Yes, of course."

As we rejoined Arnold he was just struggling to a seated position. "My ankle," he said. Then the green wash of light from Terminator disappeared, as did the night sky; the city slid over us, and we were encased in a gloom interrupted by an occasional running light. All twelve of the city's big tracks had disappeared, swallowed by the sleeves in the city's broad metallic foundation. Only the open slots that allowed passage over the pylons showed where the sleeves were; for a moment in the darkness it seemed we stood between two worlds held apart by a field of pylons.

Meanwhile the city slid over us soundlessly, propelled by the expansion of the tracks themselves. You see, the alloy composing the tracks is capable of withstanding the 425 degree Centigrade heat of the Mercurial day, but the cylinders do expand just a bit in this heat. Here in the Terminator is the forward edge of the cylinders' expansion, and the smooth-sided sleeves above us at that moment fit so snugly over the cylinders that as the cylinders expand, the city is pushed forward toward the cooler, thinner railing to the west; and so the city is propelled by the sun, while never being fully exposed to it. The motive force is so strong, in fact, that resistance to it arranged in the sleeves generates the enormous reserves of energy that Terminator has sold so successfully to the rest of civilization.

Though I had understood this mechanism for decades, I had never before observed it from this angle, and despite the fact that I was somewhat uneasy to be standing under our fair city, I was also fascinated to see its broad, knobby silver underside gliding majestically westward. For a long time I did nothing but stare at it.

"We'd better get to the car," Freya said. "The sun will be up very soon after the city passes, and then we'll be in trouble."

Since Arnold was still cuffed to the plates, and had at least a sprained ankle, walking with him slung between us was a slow process. While we were at it the Dawn Wall passed over us, and suddenly the twelve tracks and the stars between them were visible again. "Now we'd better hurry," said Freya. Above us the very top of the Dawn Wall flared a brilliant white; sunlight was striking that surface, only two hundred meters above us. Dawn was not far away. In the glare of reflected light we could see the heavily tireprinted ground under the cylinders perfectly, and for a while our eyes were nearly overwhelmed. "Look!" Freya cried, shielding her eyes with one hand and pointing up at the sun-washed slope of the city wall with the other. "It's the inspiration of our Monet, don't you think?"

Despite our haste, the great Rouen cathedral of Mercury pulled away from us. "This won't do," Freya said. "Only a bit more to the car, but we have to hurry. Here, Arnold, let me carry you—" and she ran, carrying Arnold piggyback, the rest of the way to the car. As we maneuvered him

through the lock, a tongue of the sun's corona licked
briefly over the horizon, blinding us. I felt scorched; my
throat was dry. We were now at the dawn edge of the Terminator zone, and east-facing slopes burned white while
west-facing slopes were still a perfect black, creating a
chaotic patchwork that was utterly disorienting. We rolled
into the car after Arnold, and quickly drove west, passing
the city, returning to the night zone, and arriving at a station where we could make the transfer into the city again.
Freya laughed at my expression as we crossed the gap.
"Well, Nathaniel," she said, "home again."

The very next day Freya arranged for those concerned with
the case to assemble on Heidi's patio again. Four police officials were there, and one took notes. The painting of the
cathedral of Rouen was back in its place on the villa wall;
George Butler and Harvey Washburn stood before it, while
Arnold Ohman and Heidi paced by the patio's edge. Lucinda and Delaurence, the cook, watched from behind the
patio bar.

Freya called us to order. She was wearing a severe blue
dress, and her white-blond hair was drawn into a tight
braid that fell down her back. Sternly she said, "I will suggest to you an explanation for the death of Sandor Musgrave. All of you except for the police and Mr. Sebastian
were to one extent or another suspected of killing him, so
I know this will be of great interest to you."

Naturally there was an uneasy stir among those listening.

"Several of you had reason to hate Musgrave, or to fear
him. The man was a blackmailer by profession, and on
Earth he had obtained evidence of illegalities in the merger
Heidi and George made five years ago, that gave him
leverage over both of you. This and motives for the rest of
you were well established during the initial investigation,
and we need not recapitulate the details.

"It is also true, however, that subsequent investigations have confirmed that all of you had alibis for the moment when Musgrave was struck down. Lucinda and Delaurence were together in the kitchen until Lucinda left to investigate the shout she heard; this was confirmed by caterers hired for the Solday party. Heidi left the patio shortly before Musgrave was found, but she was consulting with Hiu and the orchestra during the time in question. George Butler went into the house with Arnold Ohman, but they were together for most of the time they were inside. Eventually George left to go to the bathroom, but luckily for him the orchestra's first clarinetist was there to confirm his presence. And fortunately for Mr. Ohman, I myself could see him from the patio, standing in the hallway until the very moment when Lucinda screamed.

"So you see—" Freya paused, eyed us one by one, ran a finger along the frame of the big painting. "The problem took on a new aspect. It became clear that, while many had a motive to kill Musgrave, no one had the opportunity. This caused me to reconsider. How, exactly, had Musgrave been killed? He was struck on the head by the frame of one of Heidi's hall mirrors. Though several mirrors were broken in the melee following Lucinda's screams, we know the one that struck Musgrave; it was at the bend in the hallway leading from the atrium to the patio. And it was only a couple of meters away from a step down in the hallway."

Freya took a large house plan from a table and set it before the policeman. "Sandor Musgrave, you will recall, was new to Mercury. He had never seen a Solday celebration. When the Great Gates opened and the reflected light filled this villa, my suggestion is that he was overwhelmed by fright. Lucinda heard him cry for help—perhaps he thought the house was burning down. He panicked, rushed out of the study, and blindly began to run for the patio. Unable to see the step down or the mirror, he must have pitched forward, and his left temple struck the frame with a fatal blow. He crawled a few steps farther, then collapsed and died."

Heidi stepped forward. "So Musgrave died by accident?"

"This is my theory. And it explains how it was that no one had the opportunity to kill him. In fact, no one did kill him." She turned to the police. "I trust you will follow up on this suggestion?"

"Yes," said the one taking notes. "Death declared accidental by consulting investigator. Proceed from there." He exchanged glances with his colleagues. "We are satisfied this explains the facts of the case."

Heidi surveyed the silent group. "To tell you the truth, I am very relieved." She turned to Delaurence. "Let's open the bar. It would be morbid to celebrate an accidental death, but here we can say we are celebrating the absence of a murder."

The others gave a small cheer of relief, and we surrounded the bartender.

A few days later Freya asked me to accompany her to North Station. "I need your assistance."

"Very well," I said. "Are you leaving Terminator?"

"Seeing someone off."

When we entered the station's big waiting room, she inspected the crowd, then cried, "Arnold!" and crossed the room to him. Arnold saw her and grimaced. "Oh, Arnold," she said, and leaned over to kiss him on each cheek. "I'm very proud of you."

Arnold shook his head, and greeted me mournfully. "You're a hard woman, Freya," he told her. "Stop behaving so cheerfully; you make me sick. You know perfectly well this is exile of the worst sort."

"But Arnold," Freya said, "Mercury is not the whole of civilization. In fact it could be considered culturally dead, an immense museum to the past that has no real life at all."

"Which is why you choose to live here, I'm sure," he said bitterly.

"Well of course it does have some pleasures. But the really vital centers of any civilization are on the frontier, Arnold, and that's where you're going."

Arnold looked completely disgusted.

"But Arnold," I said. "Where are you going?"

"Pluto," he said curtly.

"*Pluto?*" I exclaimed. "But whatever for? What will you do there?"

He shrugged. "Dig ditches, I suppose."

Freya laughed. "You certainly will not." She addressed me. "Arnold has decided, very boldly I might add, to abandon his safe career as a dealer here on Mercury, to become a real artist on the frontier."

"But *why?*"

Freya wagged a finger at Arnold. "You must write us often."

Arnold made a strangled growl. "Damn you, Freya. I refuse. I refuse to go."

"You don't have that option," Freya said. "Remember the chalk, Arnold. The chalk was your signature."

Arnold hung his head, defeated. The city interfaced with the spaceport station. "It isn't fair," Arnold said. "What am I going to do out on those barbaric outworlds?"

"You're going to live," Freya said sternly. "You're going to live and you're going to paint. No more hiding. Understand?"

I, at any rate, was beginning to.

"You should be thanking me profusely," Freya went on, "but I'll concede you're upset and wait for gratitude by mail." She put a hand on Arnold's shoulder, and pushed him affectionately toward the crossing line. "Remember to write."

"But," Arnold said, a panicked expression on his face. "But—"

"Enough!" Freya said. "Be gone! Or else."

Arnold sagged, and stepped across the divide between the stations. Soon the city left the spaceport station behind.

"Well," Freya said. "That's done."

I stared at her. "You just helped a murderer to escape!"

She lifted an eyebrow. "Exile is a very severe punishment; in fact in my cultural tradition it was the usual punishment for murder committed in anger or self-defense."

I waved a hand dismissively. "This isn't the Iceland of Eric the Red. And it wasn't self-defense—Sandor Musgrave was outright murdered."

"Well," she said. "*I* never liked him."

I told you before; she has no sense of right and wrong. It is a serious defect in a detective. I could only wave my arms in incoherent outrage; and my protests have never carried much weight with Freya, who claims not even to believe them.

We left the station. "What's that you were saying to Arnold about chalk?" I said, curiosity getting the better of me.

"That's the clue you provided, Nathaniel—somewhat transformed. As you reminded me, Musgrave was pointing at the patio, and Heidi's patio is made of a block of the Dover cliffs. Dover cliffs, as you know, are composed of *chalk.* So I returned to the painting, and cut through the back to retrieve samples of the chalk used in the underdrawing, which had been revealed to me by infrared photography." She turned a corner and led me uptown. "Chalk, you see, has its own history of change. In Monet's time chalk was made from natural sources, not from synthetics. Sure enough, the chalk I took from the canvas was a natural chalk. But natural chalk, being composed of marine ooze, is littered with the fossil remains of unicellular algae called coccoliths. These coccoliths are different depending upon the source of the chalk. Monet used Rouen chalk, appropriately enough, which was filled with the coccoliths *Maslovella barnesae* and *Cricolithus pemmatoidens.* The coccoliths in our painting, however, are *Neococcolithes dubius*. Very dubious indeed—for this is a North American chalk, first mined in Utah in 1924."

"So Monet couldn't have used this chalk! And there you had your proof that the painting is a fake."

"Exactly."

I said doubtfully. "It seems a subtle clue for the dying Musgrave to conceive of."

"Perhaps," Freya said cheerfully. "Perhaps he was only pointing in the direction of the patio by the accident of his final movements. But it was sufficient that the coincidence gave me the idea. The solution of a crime often depends upon imaginary clues."

"But how did you know Arnold was the forger?" I asked. "And why, after taking the trouble to concoct all those paints, did he use the wrong chalk?"

"The two matters are related. It could be that Arnold only knew he needed a natural chalk, and used the first convenient supply without knowing there are differences between them. In that case it was a mistake—his only mistake. But it seems unlike Arnold to me, and I think rather that it was the forger's signature. In effect, the forger said, if you take a slide of the chalk trapped underneath the paint, and magnify it five thousand times with an electron microscope, you will find me. This chalk never used by Monet is my sign. —For on some level every forger hopes to be discovered, if only in the distant future—to receive credit for the work.

"So I knew we had a forger on Mercury, and I was already suspicious of Arnold, since he was the dealer who brought the painting to Mercury, and since he was the only guest at Heidi's party with the opportunity to kill Musgrave; he was missing during the crucial moments—"

"You *are* a liar!"

"And it seems Arnold was getting desperate; I searched among his recent bills, and found one for three suction plates. So when we found him on the track I was quite sure."

"He stuck himself to the track?"

"Yes. The one on his right wrist was electronically controlled, so after setting the other two he tripped the third between his teeth. He hoped that we would discover him there after missing him at the museum, and think that there was someone else who wished him harm. And if not, the cowcatchers would pull him free. It was a silly plan, but he was desperate after I set up that appointment with him. When I confronted him with all this, after we rescued him from the tracks, he broke down and confessed. Sandor Musgrave had discovered that the Monet was a fake while blackmailing the Evans family in England, and after forcing Heidi to give him a job, he worked on the painting in secret until he found proof. Then he blackmailed Arnold into bankruptcy, and when on Solday he pressed Arnold for more money, Arnold lost his composure and took advantage of the confusion caused by the opening of the Great Gates to smack Musgrave on the head with one of Heidi's mirrors."

I wagged a finger under her nose. "And you set him free. You've gone too far this time, Freya Grindavik."

She shook her head. "If you consider Arnold's case a bit longer, you might change your mind. Arnold Ohman has been the most important art dealer on Mercury for over sixty years. He sold the Vermeer collection to George Butler, and the Goyas to Terminator West Gallery, and the Pissarros to the museum in Homer Crater, and those Chinese landscapes you love so much to the city park, and the Kandinskys to the Lion of the Grays. Most of the finest paintings on Mercury were brought here by Arnold Ohman."

"So?"

"So how many of those, do you think, were painted by Arnold himself?"

I stopped dead in the street, stunned at the very idea. "But—but that only makes it worse! Inestimably worse! It means there are fakes all over the planet!"

"Probably so. And no one wants to hear that. But it also means Arnold Ohman is a very great artist. And in our age that is no easy feat. Can you imagine the withering reception his painting would have received if he had done original work? He would have ended up like Harvey Washburn and all the rest of them who wander around the galleries like dogs. The great art of the past crashes down on our artists like meteors, so that their minds resemble the blasted landscape we roll over. Now Arnold has escaped that fate, and his work is universally admired, even loved. That Monet, for instance—it isn't just that it passes for one of the cathedral series; it could be argued that it is the *best* of them. Now is this a level of greatness that Arnold could have achieved—would have been *allowed* to achieve—if he had done original work on this museum planet? Impossible. He was forced to forge old masters to be able to fully express his genius."

"All this is no excuse for forgery or murder."

But Freya wasn't listening. "Now that I've exiled him, he may go on forging old paintings, but he may begin painting something new. That possibility surely justified ameliorating his punishment for killing such a parasite as Musgrave. And there is Mercury's reputation as art museum of the system to consider. . . ."

I refused to honor her opinions with a reply, and looking around, I saw that during our conversation she had led me far up the terraces. "Where are we going?"

"To Heidi's," she said. And she had the grace to look a little shamefaced—for a moment, anyway. "I need your help moving something."

"Oh, no."

"Well," Freya explained, "when I told Heidi some of the facts of the case, she insisted on giving me a token of her gratitude, and she overrode all my refusals, so . . . I was forced to accept." She rang the wall bell.

"You're joking," I said.

"Not at all. Actually, I think Heidi preferred not to own

a painting she knew to be a fake, you see. So I did her a favor by taking it off her hands."

When Delaurence let us in, we found he had almost finished securing *Rouen Cathedral—Sun Effect* in a big plastic box. "We'll finish this," Freya told him.

While we completed the boxing I told Freya what I thought of her conduct. "You've taken liberties with the *law*—you lied right and left—"

"Well boxed," she said. "Let's go before Heidi changes her mind."

"And I suppose you're proud of yourself."

"Of course. A lot of lab work went into this."

We maneuvered the big box through the gate and into the street, and carried it upright between us, like a short flat coffin. We reached Freya's villa, and immediately she set to work unboxing the painting. When she had freed it she set it on top of a couch, resting against the wall.

Shaking with righteous indignation, I cried, "That *thing* isn't a product of the past! It isn't *authentic*. It is only a *fake*. Claude Monet *didn't paint it*."

Freya looked at me with a mild frown, as if confronting a slightly dense and very stubborn child. "So what?"

After I had lectured her on her immorality a good deal more, and heard all of her patient agreement, I ran out of steam. "Well," I muttered, "you may have destroyed all my faith in you, and damaged Mercury's art heritage forever, but at least I'll get a good story out of it." This was some small comfort. "I believe I'll call it The Case of the Thirty-third Cathedral of Rouen."

"What's this?" she exclaimed. "No, of course not!" And then she insisted that I keep everything she had told me that day a secret.

I couldn't believe it. Bitterly I said, "You're like those forgers. You want *somebody* to witness your cleverness, and I'm the one who is stuck with it."

She immediately agreed, but went on to list all the reasons no one else could ever learn of the affair—how so many people would be hurt—including her, I added acerbically—how so many valuable collections would be ruined, how her plan to transform Arnold into a respectable honest Plutonian artist would collapse, and so on and so forth, for nearly an hour. Finally I gave up and conceded to her wishes, so that the upshot of it was, I promised not to write down a single word concerning this particular adventure of ours, and I promised furthermore to say nothing of the entire affair, and to keep it a complete secret, forever and ever.

But I don't suppose it will do any harm to tell you.

TAKING THE PISS

Brian Stableford

Critically acclaimed British "hard science" writer Brian Stableford is the author of more than thirty books, including Cradle of the Sun, The Blind Worm, Days of Glory, In the Kingdom of the Beasts, Day of Wrath, The Halcyon Drift, The Paradox of the Sets, The Realms of Tatarus, Serpent's Blood, The Empire of Fear, The Angel of Pain, The Carnival of Destruction, Year Zero, *and* The Eleventh Hour. *His most recent novels are part of his ongoing future history sequence, dealing with the effect of genetic engineering on the human race:* Inherit the Earth, Architects of Emortality, The Fountains of Youth, The Cassandra Complex, Dark Ararat, *and, most recently,* The Omega Expedition. *His short fiction has been collected in* Sexual Chemistry: Sardonic Tales of the Genetic Revolution. *His nonfiction books include* The Sociology of Science Fiction *and, with David Langford,* The Third Millennium: A History of the World A.D. 2000–3000. *His acclaimed novella "Les Fleurs du Mal" was a finalist for the Hugo Award in 1994. A biologist and sociologist by training, Stableford lives in Reading, England.*

In the wry and ingenious story that follows, one that introduces an entirely new *sort of crime, he shows us how sometimes a Man's Got to Do What a Man's Got to Do— even in a high-tech future where some surprisingly basic things are Against the Law. . . .*

Modern town centers are supposed to be very safe places. There are CC-TV cameras everywhere, in the street as well as in the shops, all of them feeding video tapes that can be requisitioned by the police as soon as a crime is reported. Unfortunately, the promise of safety draws people to the High Street like a magnet, in such numbers that mere population density becomes a cloak sheltering all manner of clandestine skullduggery. Which was how I came to be kidnapped in broad daylight, at two o'clock on a Saturday afternoon, as I came out of Sainsbury's clutching two bags of assorted foodstuffs.

If I'd had any warning, I might have been able to figure out how to handle the situation, but who could possibly expect a dumpy and lumpy peroxide blonde with a Primark raincoat draped over her right arm to snuggle up to a well-built lad beside the trolley-rack and stick an automatic pistol under his ribs? It's not the kind of situation you rehearse in idle moments, even if you have been warned that you might be a target for industrial espionage.

"Make for the parking lot, Darren," she whispered. "Nice and easy." The woman looked almost as old and homely as my mum, but the gun barrel digging into my solar plexus seemed to me to be more a wicked-stepmother kind of thing.

"You have *got* to be joking," I said, more stupidly than courageously.

"On the contrary," she retorted. "If I weren't extremely serious, I wouldn't be taking the risk."

I started walking toward the parking lot, nice and easy. It was partly the shock. I couldn't quite get my head together, and when your thinking engine stalls, you tend to follow ready-made scripts. I'd never been kidnapped before, but I'd seen lots of movies and my legs knew exactly how scenes of that sort were supposed to go. On top of that, it was exciting. People talk about going numb with shock, as if that were the usual effect, but I didn't. Once my thinking engine had restarted after the momentary stall, it told me that this was the most exciting thing that had ever happened to me. In my twenty years of life I'd never been able to think of myself as the kind of person who might get kidnapped, and actually *being* kidnapped had to be perceived as a compliment. It was like a promotion: I felt that I'd leapt a good few thousand places in the pecking order of human society.

Parking lots are lousy with CC-TV cameras, so I wasn't particularly astonished when a white Transit slid past the EXIT barrier as we approached and slowed almost to a halt as we neared it. The side door opened as it eased past us, and the blonde reached out with her free hand to force my head down before using the concealed gun to shove me forward. Two hands reached out from the dark interior to haul me into the back of the van, without the least care for elegance or comfort. The woman slammed the door behind me. I presume she walked on, a picture of innocence, as if she hadn't a care in the world.

By the time I'd sorted myself out and got myself into a sitting position on the hardboard-covered floor, I'd taken due note of the fact that the hands belonged to a stout man wearing a Honey Monster party-mask. His ears stuck out from the sides, though, and the way they'd been flattened suggested to me that the guy had probably gone more than a few rounds in a boxing ring, maybe one of the unlicensed kind where the fighters don't wear gloves. I'm no weed, but I figured that he probably didn't need a gun to keep me in line.

I was tempted to tell him that he must have got the wrong Darren, but I knew I wouldn't like hearing the obvious reply.

"You could have tried bribery," I said, instead. "Kidnapping's not nice."

"I don't *do* nice," the masked pugilist informed me. "But don't wet yourself yet—there'll be time for that later."

The back of the driver's head was stubbornly uninformative, and from where I was sitting, I couldn't see his face in the mirror. So far as I could tell, though, his was also the head of a man who didn't do nice. The van was

And now, to add injury to insult, I was being kidnapped.

Somehow, the man with the magic syringe had failed to include that in his list of don'ts. If he *had* included the possibility in his presentation he'd probably have fed me a line of bullshit about trying to keep track of the turns the van made, and listening out for any tell-tale sounds, like trains going over bridges and street-markets and church clocks, but I didn't bother with any of that. As far as I was concerned, if the kidnappers wanted to steal a bucketful of my piss they were more than welcome, and if GSKC plc didn't like it, they ought to have been more careful with that fucking dustbuster.

Mercifully, the man who didn't do nice didn't start to fiddle with my apparatus while we were still in the van. I couldn't have stood that. It was bad enough having to walk around all day with a tube and a glorified hot-water bottle attached to my inside leg and a double-duty condom hermetically sealed to my prick, and I'd had my fill of embarrassment the day before, when I'd handed over my first set of sample bottles to GSKC's collection service. Having some pervert do a removal job in the back of a white van would definitely have added yet more insult to the injury that had already been added to the first insult.

I tried to lie back against the side-panel of the van and think of England, but it wasn't the kind of situation that was conducive to a shrewd analysis of our chances in the upcoming World Cup. I concentrated on telling myself that once the kidnappers had gotten what they wanted, they'd have no further use for me and they'd turn me loose again. I even started rehearsing the statement I'd have to give to the police. No, officer, I wouldn't recognize the woman again, officer—all fat middle-aged peroxide blondes look alike to me. No, I didn't get the index number of the van and I didn't see any distinguishing marks inside or out.

The need to piss got steadily worse, but I wanted to hold on, for propriety's sake. It didn't occur to me that if I went there and then they *might* just take the bottle and let me go, without even bothering to take me all the way to their destination, but that wasn't what the plug-ugly had implied when he'd advised me to hang on.

I wondered what he'd done with the shopping bags. I had to hope that they'd let me have them all back when the deal was done—but even if they did, Mum wouldn't be pleased if anything was broken, or even slightly bruised. As if in answer to my unspoken question, I heard my captor say: "Naughty, naughty. You're not supposed to be drinking alcohol." He'd obviously found Mum's bottle of Hungarian pinot noir.

I heard the sound of a cork being withdrawn.

Somehow, the idea of a kidnapper carrying a corkscrew was deeply unreassuring. I couldn't believe that he'd been carrying it on the off-chance that I had a bottle of wine in my shopping bag when his ugly girlfriend had intercepted me.

If it hadn't been for the duct tape, I'd have told the presumably unmasked Honey Monster that the pinot noir wasn't for me, and that Mum would have his guts for garters if she ever found out who'd deprived her of her Sunday treat, but as things were, I had no alternative but to let the ex-pugilist believe that I was the kind of person who didn't take obligatory employment contracts too seriously.

Maybe, I thought, that was the kind of person I really should have been, given that piss-artists are right at the bottom of the totem-pole in the bioreactor hierarchy. I'd always thought that was completely unfair. I suppose one can understand the social status that attaches to pretty girls with loaded tits, but why blood donors should be reckoned a cut above the rest of us is beyond me. Where's the virtue in being vampires' prey?

"This stuff is *disgusting*," the man who didn't do nice informed me, effortlessly living up to his self-confessed reputation. "It's been dosed with washing soda to neutralize excess acid, then sugared to cover up the residual soapiness. There's no excuse, you know, with Calais just the other side of the tunnel and a resident smuggler on every housing estate from Dover to Coventry. It's not as if we're living in fucking Northumberland."

He was displaying his age and his origins as well as his ignorance. I might have failed geography GCSE, but even I knew that there was no such county as Northumberland any more, and hadn't been in my lifetime. Years of exile had weakened his accent, but I guessed that he had probably been born somewhere not a million miles from Carlisle. Anyway, Mum liked her wine sweet as well as fruity. She wouldn't have thanked me for a classy claret.

The van rolled to a final halt then, and I heard the driver get out. It must have been the driver who opened the side door, although it was the wine connoisseur who seized me by the scruff of the neck and thrust me out into the open again. Wherever we were, there couldn't have been many CC-TV cameras around. I couldn't tell whose hand it was that grabbed my arm and steered me along a pavement and down a flight of steps, then along a corridor, and up a second staircase, through God only knows how many doorways. In the end, though, I felt the pile of a decent carpet under my running shoes before I was thrust into a perfectly serviceable armchair.

The strip of tape that had sealed my mouth was removed with an abruptness that left me wishing I'd shaved a little more carefully that morning, but the strips sealing my eyes and securing my wrists were left untouched.

"Sorry about the precautions, Darren," said a male voice I hadn't heard before, "but it's for your own good. You really don't want to know too much about us." I guessed that this man too was from up north, though not nearly so far north as the one who didn't do nice. Derby maybe, or Nottingham: what real northerners would call the Midlands.

"I can go any time you want me to," I told him, meaning *go* rather than literally go. "Just take the bottle and

drop me off—anywhere you want, although somewhere
near home would be nice."

"It's not that simple," said the Midlander. "We'll need a
more generous sample than you can provide just like that."

"Oh shit," I murmured. It's amazing how half a dozen
marathon water-drinking sessions can put you right off the
idea of thirst. "How long are you going to keep me here?"

"A few hours. You'll be home in time for dinner. We'll
put the pizzas and the other perishables in the fridge for
you. Sorry about the wine—but you really aren't supposed
to be drinking."

"It's for my Mum," I told him, exasperatedly. "You'd
better be telling the truth. Mum'll report me missing if I
don't turn up by six—that's when the supermarket shuts."

"No problem, Darren," the voice said, softly. "We'll
need to do a few little tests—but we won't hurt you. I
promise."

There was something in that seemingly insincere promise that immediately made me think of dustbusters and
catheters. "Aw, come *on*," I said, finally giving way to
pent-up terror. "I'm nothing special. Just one more con-
script in Wilie's barmy army, doing my bit for king and
country. I don't know what I'm pissing, apart from the fact
that it's pink, but I'm absolutely bloody certain that it can't
be worth much, or the boys at GSKC plc wouldn't be letting me roam the streets and do Mum's shopping in Sainsbury's."

"You might be right," was the amiable reply. "But it
might just be GSKC that have miscalculated. Our employers' hackers think so, at any rate—and when the hackers
say *frog,* we all jump. Way of the world, old son. You'll
just have to be patient for a few hours. You can manage
that, can't you? I can put the radio on for you, if you like,
or a CD. How about a little bit of Vivaldi? Wagner might
be a little too stimulating."

I knew that he was mocking me, but it didn't seem to
matter.

"Vivaldi will be fine," I said, with as much dignity as I could muster. "A pot of coffee would be nice, if I've got to do a lot of drinking. Cream, no sugar. A few bourbon biscuits wouldn't come amiss."

"It's not the Ritz, Darren," he told me—and I could tell from the direction of his voice that he'd got up and was moving toward the door—"but I guess we can stretch to tea if you'd rather have that than water. Lots and lots of lovely tea."

Personally, I'd always thought that tea was for chimpanzees, but I was right off water, especially the kind that came from the tap. Tea was probably the best offer I was going to get.

"Tea's okay," I assured him, trying to put a brave face on things.

"But there's one more thing we need to take care of first," he said, in a way that told me loud and clear that I wasn't going to like it one little bit.

"What?" I said, although I'd already guessed.

When I'd handed in the first batch of samples, GSKC's delivery-boy had been careful not to make any comments, but I hadn't been able to stop myself imagining what he must be thinking. If you're a sperm-donor, so rumor has it, they just give you a Dutch magazine and a plastic cup and leave you to it, but it's not as easy as that when your eyes and hands are taped up. I told them that I wouldn't try anything, but they weren't taking any chances.

"Think of it as phone sex," the Vivaldi fan said, as he left me in the capable hands of his female accomplice—but I'd never gone in for phone sex and even in phone sex you get to use your own hand. It didn't help matters that I had to assume that she was the same woman who'd stuck a gun in my ribs: fat, fifty-five, and fake blonde.

After that, drinking tea by the quart so that I could piss like a champion didn't seem as much like torture as it

might have. The long wait thereafter was positively relax-
ing, and not because of bloody Vivaldi tinkling away in the
background.

I was really looking forward to another ride in the back
of the van, even though my arms were aching like crazy,
when I heard the mobile phone playing the old *Lone
Ranger* theme-tune. It was the Midland accent that exclaimed: "What? You have *got* to be joking." I knew something must have gone wrong, and I spent a couple of
minutes wallowing in terror while my captor listened to
the rest of the bad news.

Mercifully, it turned out that he wasn't being instructed
to bump me off.

"I'm sorry, Darren," the Midlander informed me—and
he really did sound regretful—"but there's been a bit of a
hitch. We may need to hang on to you a little longer."

"What kind of hitch?" I wanted to know.

"You were right and we were wrong, Darren. We should
have tried bribery. We were trying to save on expenses. Is
it too late to start over, do you think?"

It was an interesting idea. I knew I ought to tell him to
go fuck himself, if only for appearances' sake, but I hadn't
quite got over the complimentary implications of being a
kidnap victim. This new departure seemed like another
promotion, a chance to skip another few thousand rungs of
the status ladder.

"How big a bribe did you have in mind?" I said, trying
with all my might to sound like a man who was accus-
tomed to being on the ball. "I mean, given the inconvenience, not to mention the insult . . . and this is a
multimillion-euro business, after all."

"Don't push it, Darren," he said. "We all have to make
a profit on the deal, and we know exactly what GSKC
were paying you. It wasn't enough, even before . . . but we
have our choices to make too. We *could* put you up for
auction. That's what the Honey Monster wants to do—but

I'm not like him. I *can* do nice, if it seems worthwhile. How would you like to work for us?"

"As a piss-artist?" I said, wearily.

"As a spy. You were right, you see, when you said that if you were making anything valuable GSKC wouldn't have turned you loose on to the streets—but our employers' hackers were right when they said that GSKC might have made a mistake. If it weren't for their cumbersome bureaucratic procedures, GSKC's troubleshooters would have got to you before we did, but we're leaner and quicker. The thing is, they don't know yet that you've been snatched. Maybe we can fix things so that they never have to find out. They'll take you into residential care anyway, so you can forget your mum's Sunday roast, but you still have a choice: you can work for them, under the contract, you've already signed—which included a sheaf of self-serving contingency clauses that you probably didn't bother to read—or you can work for them *and us,* for three times the money. We pay in cash, so the Inland Revenue won't be taking a bite out of our contribution."

Three times the pittance that GSKC were paying me didn't sound like a fortune to me, but these things are relative.

"I want to know what's going on," I said, trying hard to be sensible. "Why are my bodily fluids suddenly worth so much more than they were before the delivery van picked up that first crateload?"

"I'm not sure you'd understand. GSKC are supposed to be operating under the principle of informed consent, so they were obliged by law to tell you exactly what they were proposing to do to you, but my guess is that they didn't make much effort to make it comprehensible, and that you just nodded your head when they asked you if you understood. Am I right?"

I hesitated, but there was no point in denying it. "I'm not stupid," I told him. "Maybe I did only get three GCSEs, with not an ology among them, but that's because

I didn't like school, okay? Maybe I have been unemployed long enough to fall into the national service trap, but that's because I won't take the kind of shit you have to take with the kind of jobs people think you're fit for if you only have three GCSEs. I'm not some sort of idiot you can peddle any kind of bullshit to."

"Okay, Darren—I believe you. So how much *do* you know about the kind of manufacturing process you're involved in?"

"They shot some kind of virus into me to modify the cells of my bladder wall," I said. "The idea was to make them secrete something into the stored urine. The pink stuff is just a marker—what they really want is some kind of protein to which the dye's attached. They said they weren't obliged to tell me exactly what it was, but they told me it wouldn't do me any harm. They weren't wrong about that, were they?"

"Not as far as we can tell," was the far-from-reassuring answer. "How much background did you manage to take in?"

"Not a lot," I admitted.

"Then we'd better start from scratch. It really would be a good idea if you listened this time, and tried really hard to understand. You need to know, for your own sake, why you're a more valuable commodity than they expected you to be."

I tried. It wasn't easy, but with my eyes still taped up, I had no alternative but to concentrate on what I was hearing, and I knew I'd have to make good on my boast that I wasn't stupid.

Apparently, the first animals genetically modified to excrete useful pharmaceuticals along with their liquid wastes had been mice. The gimmick had promised advantages that sheep and cows modified to secrete amplified milk didn't have. All the individuals in a population produce urine all the time, and urine is much simpler, chemically speaking, than milk. Extraction and purification of the target proteins was a doddle—but it had never become economically viable because mice were simply too small. Cows and sheep weren't as useful as urine-producers as they were milk-producers, for reasons far too technical for me to grasp—it had something to do with the particular digestion processes of specialist herbivores—and interest had soon switched to somatically modified human bioreactors. Or, to put it another way, to the ever-growing ranks of the unemployed. It was one of the few kinds of modern manufacturing that robots couldn't do better.

The pioneering mice had mostly had their genes tweaked while they were still eggs in a flat dish, but you can't do that to the unemployed, so biotech companies like GSKC could only do "somatic engineering": which means that they used viruses to cause temporary local transformations in specialized tissues. In effect, what they had done was give me a supposedly harmless bladder infection. It was supposed to be an "invisible" infection—which meant that my immune system wouldn't fight it off, although I could be cured by GSKC's own anti-bug devices as and when required. In the meantime, the cells in the bladder would pump the target protein into the stored urine, ready for export.

Once I'd grasped the explanation that the Vivaldi fan was so eager to put across, I thought I could see a thousand ways it might go horribly wrong, but he assured me that the procedure was much safer than it seemed. In nine hundred and fifty cases out of a thousand, he told me, it all went like clockwork, and in forty-nine of the remaining fifty the whole thing was a straightforward bust.

Fortunately or unfortunately, *I* was the thousandth. What I was producing wasn't the expected product, and the difference was "interesting."

"How interesting?" I wanted to know. "Cure-for-cancer interesting? Elixir-of-life interesting?"

"Biotech isn't the miracle-working business it's sometimes cracked up to be," the Midland accent assured me. "Interesting, in this context, means *we need more time to figure out what the hell is going on.* Where we are now, as you've probably guessed, is just a collection point. We can do simple analytical tests on the kitchen table, but we don't have a secret research lab in the basement. We could probably sell you on with the samples we've collected, but that would move our employers into much more dangerous and complicated territory, crimewise, and they're very image-conscious. It would be a lot easier for them, as well as more profitable for everyone concerned, if we were to handle you. That's why you and I need to renegotiate our relationship."

"Okay," I said, way too quickly. "You convinced me. What's your offer, and what do you want me to do?"

"We want you to take a couple of tiny tape recorders with you when GSKC take you back in. And we want you to take the principle of informed consent a *lot* more seriously. Demand to see the documentation—they're legally obliged to show it to you. They'll probably be quite prepared to believe that you can't read the stuff without moving your lips, so don't be afraid of spelling out the complicated words loudly to make an impression on the tape. We can't use transmitters because they'll almost certainly have detectors in place, but the simple methods are always the best. We'll make arrangements to have the first recorder picked up tomorrow—hide it behind the bedhead, if you can. Left hand side—*your* left, that is. Can you remember all that?"

"I'm not stupid," I reminded him. How could I be? I'd just become a secret agent: an industrial mole.

"If we take the tape off your eyes and wrists, Darren," my oh-so-friendly captor pointed out, "we'll be taking a big risk—but you'll have to take your share of that risk. Once you're in a position to put us in deep trouble, we'll have to take precautions to make sure you don't."

Or to put it another way, I thought, *once I've seen your faces, the only way you can stop me describing them is to shoot me. Once I'm in the gang, resigning could seriously damage my health.* It might be easier, I realized, to call their bluff about selling me on as I was—but my arms were aching horribly, and there was a possibility that GSKC might not be the highest bidder.

"I'm in," I assured him. "Just get this fucking tape off, will you."

"We know where you and your mum live, Darren," the Vivaldi fan reminded me. "We even know where your gran lives."

I couldn't quite imagine them sending a hitman all the way up to Whitby with instructions to break into an old people's home and shoot a ninety-two-year-old who usually didn't know what day it was, but I could see the point he was trying to make.

"It's okay," I assured. "I'm on your side. One hundred percent committed. I always wanted a more interesting job. Who wouldn't, when the alternative's having the piss taken out of you relentlessly, literally as well as metaphorically?"

I knew he'd be impressed by the fact that I knew what "metaphorically" meant.

"Okay, Darren," he said, after a few more seconds' hesitation. "I'll trust you. You're in."

The first surprise was that the female kidnapper not only had real blonde hair under the peroxide wig, but wasn't really fat or fifty-five. I could almost have wished I'd known that earlier, although it wasn't a train of thought I wanted to follow.

After that revelation, it wasn't quite as surprising to find out that the man who supposedly didn't do nice had also been heavily padded and that his cauliflower ears were as fake as his Honey Monster grin. He really did look fifty-ish, but he seemed more bookish than brutal.

The team leader turned out to look more like a twenty-five-year-old nerd than a gangster. I wouldn't have cared to estimate how many GCSEs the three of them had between them.

The gun, on the other hand, was real.

Once they'd made up their minds, they moved swiftly to get me home before anyone knew I'd gone. The only one who told me his name was the Vivaldi fan, and I was far from convinced that "Matthew Jardine" wasn't a pseudonym, but it seemed like a friendly gesture anyway.

Jardine lectured me all the way home, but I tried to take in as much of it as I could. I had no option but to be the gang clown, but I knew that I had to make an effort to keep up if I were going to build a proper career as a guinea-pig-cum-industrial-spy. He dropped me on the edge of the estate. Because it's a designated high crime/zero tolerance area, we have almost as many hidden CC-TV cameras around as the average parking lot, even though the kids have mastered six different techniques for locating and disabling them.

The repacked shopping bags didn't look too bad, but I had to hope that Mum wouldn't make too much fuss about the missing wine or the frozen peas and fish fingers being slightly defrosted. I needn't have worried; she was much too annoyed about the phone ringing off the hook. She hadn't answered it, of course—she always used the answerphone to screen her calls—but she was paranoid about the tape running out. GSKC had left seven messages in less than four hours.

I called back immediately, as requested.

"Mr. Hepplewhite," the doctor said, letting his relief show in his voice. "At last. Thanks for getting back to us."

I had my story ready. "That's okay, mate," I said. "I'm sorry I was out, but I was watching the match on the big screen down at the Hare and Hounds. Not a drop of alcohol passed my lips, though—it was bitter lemons all the way, especially when the opposition got that penalty."

"That's all right, Mr. Hepplewhite," he assured me. "It's just that something's come up as a result of the samples you delivered yesterday. It's nothing to worry about, but we'd like you to come in as soon as possible. In fact, we'd like to send a taxi to pick you up now, if it's not inconvenient."

"Well," I said, acting away like a trooper, "I don't know about that. I had plans for later—and Mum was just about to put a ham and mushroom pizza in the oven."

"We'll pay you overtime, of course, as per your contract. We'll even send out for a pizza." He carefully refrained from mentioning that they wouldn't be letting me out again, and I carefully refrained from letting on that I already knew.

"Okay," I said. "If it's that important."

I took Mum into the bathroom to brief her and turned the taps on, just in case. You can't be too careful when you live in a high crime/zero tolerance area.

The taxi was round inside ten minutes, but it didn't take me to the general hospital where I'd signed on. It dropped me at a clinic way out in the country, halfway to Newbury. As soon as I saw the place, I knew how far I'd come up in the world. It was a private clinic—the sort that you have to pay through the nose to get into if you don't have an organization like GSKC to pay your way. It was the sort of place where someone like me would normally expect to be hanging around in reception for at least half an hour, but I got the VIP treatment instead. Two doctors—one male, one female—pounced on me as soon as I was through the door and led me away.

The room they led me to wasn't quite as palatial as I'd hoped, but the bed seemed comfortable enough, and it did have a wooden bedhead rather than a tubular steel frame.

The TV was a twenty-six-inch widescreen. There was a highly visible CC-TV camera in the corner, with its red light on, but I guessed that it probably wasn't the only one.

The male doctor asked me to undress, and an orderly took away my clothes as soon as I had, but by that time I'd already managed to secrete one of Jardine's bugs behind the bedhead and another in the jacket of the green pajamas they provided.

When the female doctor offered me a cup of tea, having condescended to tell me that her name was Dr. Finch, she tried hard to make it sound as if she were merely being polite, but I'd seen enough movies to know what a hidden agenda was.

"I'd rather have coffee," I said. "Cream, no sugar. A few bourbon biscuits would be nice, while I'm waiting for my pizza."

I got tea, and lots of it. Mercifully, they didn't want any other samples just then.

Dr. Finch really was plump and fiftyish, but she was far from blonde. I waited patiently while they did their stuff, munching on the ham and mushroom pizza they'd ordered in for me—which, to be fair, was a little bit better than the one I'd bought in Sainsbury's—but I was ready for them by the time they braced themselves to tell me that they were enforcing the clause in my contract that allowed them to admit me for twenty-four-hour observation whether I liked it or not.

"I suppose it's okey," I said, by way of brightening their day before I began biting back, "but I need to understand what you're doing. You have to tell me why, don't you? I believe you mentioned the principle of informed consent. It's the law."

"You didn't seem very interested last time," the male doctor said, suspiciously. His name was Hartman. I'd never seen him before but I didn't bother to ask him how he knew.

"I've been thinking about it a lot," I told him. "I've

even done some reading. Something's gone wrong, hasn't it? Your virus has turned rogue. I'm infectious, aren't I? You've gone and given me some kind of horrible disease." It was all claptrap, but they didn't know that I knew that. They had to set my mind at rest.

"No, no, no, it's nothing like that," Dr. Hartman hastened to assure me. "It's just that we're not getting the protein we expected. We think we may know why, but we need to be sure. If there are any awkward side-effects, of course, we can kill the virus off just like *that*. We need to monitor the situation, at least until we've confirmed our hypothesis as to why the translocated gene isn't behaving the way we expected it to."

"Well," I said, temptingly, "I guess that would probably be all right . . . but you have to tell me exactly what's going on. It's my body, when all's said and done, and I have to look after it. Do you think I might be able to patent my bladder?"

He looked at me suspiciously again, but all he saw was a twenty-year-old benefit scrounger with three GCSEs, and not an ology among them.

"Okay," he said, finally. "I'll explain what we're doing. How much do you know about the Human Genetic Diversity Project?"

"What I've read in the papers," I told him. "Second phase of the Genome Project. Greatest scientific achievement ever, blueprint of the soul, key to individuality, etcetera, etcetera. Individually tailored cures for everyone, just as soon as the wrinkles have all been ironed out. I take it that I've just been officially declared a wrinkle."

"What the first phase of the HGP gave us," Dr. Hartman said, putting on his best let's-blind-the-bugger-with-bullshit voice, "was a record of the genes distributed on each of the twenty-four kinds of human chromosomes. There are twenty-three pairs, you see, but the sex chromosomes aren't alike. We've managed to identify about fifty thousand exons—they're sequences that can be turned into proteins, or bits of proteins—but not nearly as many as we'd expected. Before we'd completed the first draft, way back in 2000, we figured that there might be anything up to a hundred and fifty thousand, but we were wrong-footed." He paused.

"The reason for that, we now know, is that we'd drastically underestimated the number of *versatile exons*—expressed sequences that contribute to whole sets of proteins. Twentieth-century thinking was a bit crude, you see: we thought of genes as separate entities, definite lengths of DNA laid out on the chromosomes like strings of beads, separated by junk. The reality turned out to be a lot messier. All genes have introns as well as exons, which cut them up into anything up to a dozen different bits, and some genes are so widely scattered that they have other genes inside their introns. Some so-called *collaborative genes* producing proteins of the same family share exons with one another, and we're even beginning to find cases where genes on different chromosomes collaborate.

"The HGDP is gradually compiling a catalogue of all the different forms of the individual exons that are present in the human population. A directory of mutations, if you like. Before we knew how many versatile exons there were, we assumed that would be a fairly simple matter, but now we know that it isn't. Now we know that there are some mutations that affect whole families of proteins, complicating the selection process considerably because it allows individual base changes to have complex combinations of positive and negative effects."

He stopped to see whether he'd lost me yet. I just looked serious and said: "Go on. I'm listening."

"Most of the genes that were mapped before the basic HGP map was complete were commonly expressed genes, producing proteins necessary to the functioning of each and every cell in your body. Exon sets that produce proteins that only function in highly specialized cells, or proteins that only function at certain periods of development, are much harder to track down, but we're gradually picking them off, one by one. Finding a protein is only the first step in figuring out what it does, though, and investigating whole families of proteins can be very tricky indeed." He frowned.

"The exon set that we imported into your bladder cells was big, but by no means a mammoth, and our preliminary observations of its operation *in vivo* hadn't given us any cause to think that it was anything other than a straightforward single-protein-producer, but in the admittedly alien context of your bladder wall, the exons have revealed a hitherto unsuspected versatility. They're pumping out four different molecules, which might only be disassociated fragments of a single functional molecule, but which might be functional in their own right. At any rate, they're not the expected product. If it's all just biochemical junk, we're all wasting our time, but if it's *not* . . . well, we need to find that out."

"Suppose my contract runs out before you do?" I asked, innocently.

"There's a possibility of renewal," he said, and was quick to add, "at the designated higher rate, of course. You'll be getting all the customary overtime and unsocial-hours premiums while you're here, so this could work very much to your advantage. But to answer your earlier question, if you intended it seriously: no, you won't be able to patent anything on your own behalf, or share in any revenues from any patents *we* might obtain. That's not the way the system works."

"I figured that," I admitted. "Am I the only person you've tried this virus on?"

This time, Drs. Hartman and Finch looked at me very closely indeed. Mum had always told me that I had an innocent face, but this was the first time I'd had real cause to be glad about it.

"No," Dr. Finch admitted. "We always replicate. That's standard procedure. But you're the only member of the co-

hort who's producing the anomalous protein-fragments, if
that's what you want to know. People are *different,* Mr.
Hepplewhite. It would be a dull world if we weren't."

"Amen to that," I said. "It's okay if you're keen to get
on. You can update me in the morning. I'd like to see the
paperwork, though—see if I can get to grips with the
specifics."

That was over the top. They knew something was up.
"You do realize, Mr. Hepplewhite," Hartman said, coldly,
"that you've signed a non-disclosure agreement. In return
for our taking proper care to obtain your informed consent
to the experiment, you've guaranteed that everything we
tell you, and anything you might find out on your own, is
absolutely confidential."

"Absolutely," I assured him. "But we all have to abide
by the principle of informed consent, don't we. I'm con-
senting, so I need to be informed. Can I have the paperwork?"

The CC-TV cameras were working to my advantage as
well as theirs. They knew that if they found anything *really*
interesting, their intellectual copyright claims would have
to be cast iron. It wasn't enough for them to do everything
by the book; they had to be *seen* to do everything by the
book.

"All right, Darren," Hartman said, pronouncing my
name as if it were an insult. "We'll show you the records.
That way, you'll know as much as we do." He was mocking me, but he was too careful to say out loud that I was
too stupid to understand a word of it. I didn't mind. The assumption would make it all the more plausible when I
started spelling out the long words audibly.

There was, of course, a veritable mountain of paper—
enough to keep me busy for a month, if I'd bothered to
read every word—and I knew after a single glance that I
wouldn't be able to understand it if I had a hundred years
to study it, but I was all set to do my level best to sort out
the good stuff from the blather. A fresh pot of tea arrived

with the mountain in question, plus a pitcher of ice-water, a two-liter carton of fruit juice, three packets of crisps and a jar of salted peanuts. I noticed that the temperature of my room was a little on the warm side, and remembered that the pizza had been rather salty.

I figured that it was going to be a long night, but I didn't even glance at the cable-TV guide that had been carefully placed on my bedside table. I had work to do.

In the morning, Mum came to visit me—and she wasn't alone. The Vivaldi fan had spruced up a treat, although his blue suit was a little on the loud side.

I figured out later that Mum must have told the receptionist that the guy was my big brother, but that when the data had been fed into the computer, the consequent mismatch with my records had set off an alarm. Mum had hardly had time to hug her little boy when Dr. Hartman came hurtling through the door, accompanied by a security man whose cauliflower ear definitely wasn't a fake.

"I'm sorry, sir," Hartman said, "but you'll have to leave. I don't know who you are, but . . ."

He was interrupted by the business card that the man in the blue suit was thrusting into his face. There was something on it that had stopped him in mid-flow, and I figured that it probably wasn't the name.

"Matthew Jardine," Mum's companion said, helpfully. "I'm Mr. Hepplewhite's agent. I also represent Mrs. Hepplewhite, and her mother, a Mrs. Markham, currently resident in Whitby, Yorkshire. As you probably know, that's the entire family, unless and until someone can identify and trace Mr. Hepplewhite's father—who is probably irrelevant to our concerns."

I was impressed. Signing Mum was one thing; signing Gran—if he really *had* signed Gran—represented serious effort and concern. On the rare days when she knew what day it was, Gran had a temper like a rat-trap.

"Darren—Mr. Hepplewhite—signed all the relevant consent forms himself," Dr. Hartman said, through gritted teeth. "Even if whatever agreement you've signed with Mrs. Hepplewhite has some legal standing, which I doubt, you can't represent Darren. He's *ours*."

"We shall, of course, dispute your claim," said Jardine, airily. "I think you might find that your forms are a trifle over-specific. While you might—and I stress the word *might*—be able to exercise a claim to ownership and control of the gene that you transplanted into Mr. Hepplewhite's bladder, the rights so far ceded to you cannot include the right to exploit genes that *he* has carried from birth, having inherited them from his parents. I have documents ready for Mr. Hepplewhite's signature that will give me power of attorney to negotiate on his behalf in respect of any and all royalties to be derived from the commercial exploitation of any exotic native proteins derivable from his DNA."

While he was speaking, Jardine drew a piece of paper from his inside jacket pocket. It looked suspiciously slight to me, but Hartman was staring as it as if it were a hissing cobra, so I figured that it could probably do the job.

"You told me I couldn't patent myself," I said to the doctor, in a deeply injured tone that was only partly contrived. "That's not what *I* call *informed* consent."

"Don't sign that paper, Darren," Hartman said. "Our lawyers will be here within the hour. If you sign that thing, we'll all be tied up in court for the next twenty years. It'll be bad for you, bad for us, and bad for the cause of human progress. And if it should transpire that you've seen this man before, or had any dealings with him of any sort, you and he will probably end up in jail."

"Mr. Hepplewhite and I have never met," Jardine lied, "although I do have the honor of his mother's acquaintance. While your robots have been working flat-out on Mr. Hepplewhite's genomic spectrograph, a similarly eager company has been working on hers—purely by co-incidence, of course."

"Coincidence, my arse!" Hartman retorted. "If you hadn't got your hands on some of Darren's samples . . ."

"Before you level any wild accusations against my client," Jardine interrupted, smoothly, "it might be as well if you were to check the security of your computer systems."

"He's *not* your client," Hartman came back. "And hacking databases is a crime too, in case you've forgotten. And we both know perfectly well that your hackers couldn't possibly have gotten enough out of routinely logged data to get you into a photo finish in figuring out what's going on. If you really have been to Whitby and back . . . you were a fool to come here, Mr. Jardine."

"If I hadn't," Jardine countered, smoothly, "we both know that you'd have robbed my client of his rights by lunchtime. If GSKC's lawyers are scheduled to get here within the hour, you must have summoned them before you sat down to breakfast—and don't try to tell me that they aren't going to turn up armed with bulging briefcases, full to the brim with neatly drafted contracts. Now . . ."

"Oh, just throw the fucker out," Hartman said to the security man, exasperatedly.

For a kidnapper, the Vivaldi fan seemed surprisingly unready for the unsubtle approach. He tried to thrust his magic piece of paper into my hand while he reached for the bedhead with his free hand, as if to use it as an anchor.

Even as I reached out to take the paper, Dr. Hartman snatched it from Jardine's grip and ripped it into shreds. Meanwhile, the man with the real cauliflower ear seized poor Jardine in a full nelson, tore his groping hand away from the bedhead and dragged him out of the door.

"Informed consent, Darren," said Hartman. "Remember that. I *know* you're not as stupid as you pretend, so if your mum just happens to have another copy of that agency agreement stuffed in her knickers, I suggest that you advise her to keep it there until I've had a chance to explain to you exactly why that snake is so desperate to get your entire family on his books, even though he knows full well that the arrangement wouldn't stand up in court."

"Right-oh, doctor," I said, cheerfully, as Hartman followed his tame bully, leaving me alone with Mum. I didn't bother to check the bedhead to see if the tiny tape recorder had gone. I knew that it had. I figured that it probably hadn't a single useful item of information on it, in spite of all my heroic efforts, but I was now beginning to figure out how the game was being played. The tape of my conversation with Drs. Hartman and Finch and my subsequent semi-articulate mutterings was primarily intended to demonstrate—to a court, if necessary—that the information I'd been given wasn't sufficiently full or complete to fulfil their obligations under the principle of informed consent, and thus to prove that my contract with GSKC plc was invalid. Maybe a court would accept that and maybe it wouldn't, but when Hartman had mentioned the possibility of being tied up in the system for twenty years he'd been voicing his worst nightmare. The pseudonymous Mr. Jardine presumably had friends who weren't particular about the niceties of patent law, who probably had excellent connections in the black market therapeutics business.

"Mr. Jardine's a nice man, isn't he?" Mum said. "He brought me a really nice bottle of wine—sweet and fruity, just the way I like it. Just as well, considering that *you* forgot. He says I've got a really interesting genomic spectrum. *Rare* and interesting."

"I'll bet he did," I said. It had just occurred to me that if I'd inherited whatever the kidnappers-turned-bribers were interested in from Mum, and they'd already signed Mum up, I might be in danger of becoming surplus to his requirements. If that were the case, it might serve Jardine's purpose just as well to have me tied up in the courts for twenty years as to have me on his payroll. If he'd really wanted me to sign some kind of agency agreement he could have done it before turning me loose—except, of course, that he might have had to explain how he'd been in a position to do it. The only thing I knew for sure was that his side were even less interested in the principle of informed consent than Hartman's.

"Well anyway," Mum said, "How are you, love—in yourself, I mean?"

She didn't really want to know, but I told her anyway, just to soften her up. "Did they really send someone to Whitby to see Gran?" I asked, although I knew it was dangerous, given that everybody and his cousin was probably listening in.

"Oh yes," she said. "Mum'll be right pleased. It gets boring in that home, you know. A sea view isn't everything—especially when the edge of the cliff keeps getting nearer every time there's a storm."

"This thing must really be big," I said, thoughtfully. "I don't suppose they told you why it's so valuable."

"They didn't say *valuable,* exactly," Mum confessed, as she investigated the contents of the tea-urn on my bedside table. "Just *interesting.* That was nice, though, wasn't it? I've never been interesting before. Not since I turned thirty, anyhow. I was interesting before that, all right—but you have to settle down a bit eventually, don't you. Not as much as Stan wanted me to, obviously, but . . . I don't suppose there's a chance of a fresh brew, is there, love? I'm parched."

"You can get tea by the gallon here," I told her, absentmindedly pressing the buzzer. Mention of Stan—the husband she'd divorced two years before she had me, whose surname I'd got stuck with even though he wasn't my father—made me wonder whether Jardine might conceivably be running a bluff on Hartman with regard to Mum and Gran. Signing up all the antecedents he could find might have been a sensible precautionary measure, and he'd obviously *pretend* that he'd gotten what he wanted, even if what he *really* needed was time to try to find the parent from whom I *had* inherited the klondyke gene. If so, he'd have a real problem on his hands. Mum had always told me that she didn't even know the guy's name, let alone his whereabouts. She might have been lying to deflect my curiosity, but she might not.

I shook my head, dazedly. It was all happening too fast, and my imagination was beginning to run away with me.

More tea arrived soon enough, and so did Dr. Finch. She had the grace to look a bit sheepish.

"I'm sorry about all the fuss, Darren," she said. "We didn't expect anything like that to happen. I'm afraid, Mrs. Hepplewhite, that you might have been unwise to sign anything that man put before you. He's not the sort of person I'd want to act on my behalf."

"What sort of person is he?" I asked, interested to find out what GSKC might know about my erstwhile kidnappers.

"Do you know what biopiracy is?" Dr. Finch countered.

"No," I confessed.

"I do," Mum put in. "I saw a documentary about it on BBC-2. It's where multinational companies go prospecting for rare genes in underdeveloped countries and steal all the traditional medicines that the natives have been using for millions of years, and make fortunes out of the patents."

"Well, that sort of thing *has* happened," said Dr. Finch, judiciously, "but that's not exactly what I mean in this case. The pirates I'm talking about operate closer to home. They keep a close watch on the research that companies like ours are doing, with a view to pirating our data on behalf of black marketeers who sell counterfeit drugs. Sometimes, though, it isn't enough to steal a base-sequence. In theory, anyone who knows the base-sequence of a particular gene can build a copy *in vitro* in order to produce the relevant protein, but some genes need the assistance of other biochemical apparatus to put different bits of a protein together and fold the resultant complex into its active form. Some proteins can only be produced in living cells, and a few can only be produced in living cells with a particular genomic spectrum. Maybe more than a few—but so far, we've only found a few. Human proteomic science is still in its infancy, and because of the unexpectedly large number of versatile exons in the human genome, it's turning out to be a more complicated business than anyone anticipated."

"What you're saying," I said, to make sure that I was keeping up as well as I could be expected to, "is that whatever is happening inside my bladder—but not in the bladders of the other people you roped into the experiment—can only happen inside *me,* or someone with the same genetic quirk as me."

"I wouldn't go that far," Dr. Finch parried.

"But you think I might be in *danger?*" I said. "You think somebody might try to *kidnap* me—or Mum, or even Gran." I knew it had to be bullshit, given that I'd already been turned loose once, and that Jardine could have kept hold of Mum instead of giving her a lift to the clinic if he'd wanted to, but I was a spy now and I had to use a spy's tricks.

"You've got hold of the wrong end of the stick," the doctor assured me. "What's at stake here isn't mere possession of the bioreactor that your bladder has become, or another body that shares the genes responsible for the anomaly. What we need—and what might, in principle, be pirated—is an understanding of the interactions that are happening between your body and the gene we tried to transplant into you. Once we understand the manner in which the exons are collaborating, we won't actually need your entire body, or anybody else's, to reproduce the interaction. Any clonable tissue sample would be adequate, although the most efficient technique uses semen samples—it allows us to select out those sperms with the most useful combinations of exons, so that we can fertilize

eggs and produce whole series of easily clonable embry-
onic hybrids. As your mother pointed out, albeit in the
wrong context, biopiracy is all about intellectual property
rights. Biotech patents are a real minefield, and this case
could be a precedent-setter. It'll be bad enough if Mr. Jardine's backers are only intent on stalling us while they try
to develop a couple of therapeutic products for black market distribution—if they really do want to go for the big
prize by establishing property rights of their own, that
would be a very different ball game."

I wasn't at all sure that I was following the details, but
I'd seen enough gangster movies to know that the more
businesslike Mafia men always want to use their ill-gotten
gains to set up legitimate businesses, so that they can start
swimming with the real sharks. Suddenly, the fact that the
deceptive blonde had gone to the bother of extracting more
than piss from my hapless prick began to seem more sinister than embarrassing. I wondered whether the three mus-
keteers had been overtaken by events for a second time,
and were now wishing that they *had* hung on to me instead
of trying to turn me into a Judas. On the other hand, I was
probably worth far more to them as a willing double-agent
than a hostage.

"What do you mean by *precedent-setter?*" I asked Dr.
Finch. "What's so special about my trick bladder that I've
been promoted in easy stages from national service nobody to the guy every agent in town wants to sign within
the space of twenty-four hours?"

"I think I ought to wait for Dr. Hartman and the lawyers
before saying any more," Dr. Finch said, worriedly.

"Mr. Jardine suggested that you might want me to join
your experiments," Mum put in, "but he was very insistent
that I shouldn't sign anything without him being with me.
He also told me to look after Darren." She sounded innocent enough, but I'd always suspected that I hadn't got my
lack of stupidity from my Dad.

"Nobody's going to hurt Darren," Dr. Finch assured her.

I noticed that she didn't say anything about the possibility of recruiting Mum to the program.

"Mr. Jardine also said," Mum went on, slowly, "that no matter what Darren's signed, you can't *imprison* him. No matter what he agreed to when he signed your forms, he's still free to walk out of the door. You can sue him, but you can't *stop* him. Not *legally*. If I wanted to take him home and you tried to stop me . . ." Mr. Jardine had obviously schooled her thoroughly while he was giving her a lift to the clinic.

"All *right!*" said Dr. Finch, putting up her hands. "Nobody's saying that Darren's a prisoner—just that he has responsibilities. Nobody wants to sue anybody. We want everybody to be happy. He is getting *paid* for being here!"

"Mr. Jardine *also* said . . ." Mum began—but the door opened before she could start haggling.

I wasn't in the least surprised to see Dr. Hartman and the security guard, or the two suits that were with him, but any illusions I had about knowing what was what vanished when one of the suits stepped forward and shoved an ID card in my face.

He wasn't a corporate lawyer. According to the ID card he was Lieutenant-Colonel Jeremy Hascombe of "Special Services." I'd seen enough movies to know that "Special Services" was the organization that had risen out of the ashes of MI6's funeral pyre, but I'd never been certain that they actually existed. Apparently, they did.

When the colonel showed the ID to Dr. Finch, her astonishment made mine look distinctly feeble. "Oh, Mike," she said. "You *didn't*."

"Of course I didn't," Hartman growled, through gritted teeth. "They had the pirates under surveillance all along. Whatever their hackers got went straight to the spooks. They're trying to pretend that this thing has defense implications."

That was worrying. If Special Services knew that I'd been snatched outside Sainsbury's, they must also know that I'd been recruited as a double-agent. I didn't suppose that Special Services needed to pay any heed at all to the principle of informed consent.

"That's ridiculous," Dr. Finch said. "The management will fight you, you know. You can't just march in here and take over!"

"Show the doctors out, will you, Major," said Jeremy Hascombe.

"Now just you wait a minute . . ." the security guard began—but when Hascombe rounded on him and looked him straight in the eye, he trailed off. He was probably ex-army, and he still had his carefully trained habits of respect and obedience.

The same didn't apply, of course, to the lawyer who came bounding through the door at that moment to take up the slack, but he didn't get anywhere either. His first sentence began with the words "I insist" but I never got to hear what it was he was insisting on.

"Just get them out," Hascombe said to his associate. "*All* of them."

The associate didn't look particularly intimidating, but the way he grabbed the lawyer casually by the throat was wonderfully menacing. It wasn't only the lawyer who spluttered into total silence. The sheer insolence of the gesture was breathtaking. Everybody knew that we were on camera, and everybody knew that they would be held accountable for whatever they did. I wondered what it might be like to have the power and authority, not to mention the sheer front, to grab a *corporate lawyer* by the throat.

"This," said Jeremy Hascombe, equably, "is now a matter of national security."

His associate guided the lawyer carefully through the door. The two doctors and the security guard followed them meekly.

"Could you possibly give me a few moments alone with Darren, Mrs. Hepplewhite?" the colonel said. "No harm will come to him, I promise you."

Mum looked the colonel straight in the eye, but when she spoke it was to me. "It's not three any more, Daz," she said. "It's ten." She never called me Daz. She'd always disapproved of anyone who did, even though that had excluded practically all my old schoolfriends.

"Make that twenty," Dr. Hartman called out from the corridor, although he was too intimidated actually to stick his head around the door. It might have been a stab in the dark, but I got the impression that he knew exactly what the Vivaldi fan had offered me the day before, and what Mum was trying to tell me. Three times the so-called wage that GSKC paid national service recruits was still a fair way short of a doctor's salary, but ten was a pretty fair wedge, and twenty was adequate by anyone's standards. I figured that what Dr. Hartman was trying to get across was the suggestion that if I refused to play ball with Jeremy Hascombe, then GSKC plc would look after me as best they could.

I'd seen enough movies to know that big multinational corporations paid *way* better than governments, but tended to be far more ruthless if they were mucked about.

When he'd shut the door behind Mum's retreating bulk, Colonel Hascombe sat down beside the bed and put out his hand. "Give me the other recorder, Darren," he said.

I was tempted to tell him to look for it, but I didn't fancy being searched. I unclipped it from the pocket of my pajama-top and gave it to him.

"Cheap Korean crap," he observed, as he put it into his coat pocket. "That should tell you something about the people you're in bed with. The Americans are *so* much better at this sort of thing. It almost makes you wish that they were on our side."

"I thought they were," I said.

"If you listened to the politicians," Hascombe told me, "you'd think that we didn't have an enemy in the world, except for a couple of ex-colonies that aren't talking to us just now. It's true, in a way—but that doesn't mean that everybody else is *on our side,* even if they operate freely on our soil. Do you see what I mean?"

What he meant was that dear old England wasn't "on the same side" as GSKC plc, but Dr. Hartman had already made that obvious.

"Whose side are *you* on, Darren?" the colonel wanted to know. It was a good question.

"Mine," I said, unhesitatingly.

"That's what I thought," he said. "Which makes you the weakest piece on the board: all on your own with not an honest ally in sight, with the possible exception of your mother. Not that you've had a lot of choices so far, given that everybody else who's tried to deal with you has been as likely to rat on you as you are on them. They'll offer you money, of course—and keep on upping the stakes every time you seem likely to turn—but they're not people you can rely on."

"And *you* are?" I said, skeptically.

"I have to be," he told me. "I'm not a crook or a businessman. I represent the king, parliament, and the people. My word has to mean something."

I didn't say anything in response to that, but my face must have told him that it was so far beyond believable as to be funny.

"What a world we live in," he said, with a sigh. "You'd rather deal with pirates than with GSKC, and you'd rather deal with anyone than representatives of your country. What does that say about *you,* Darren, apart from the fact that you've watched too many bad movies?"

"What I'd rather deal with," I told him, frostily, "is someone who was prepared to tell me the fucking truth about why my market value goes up another notch every time somebody takes another bucketful of my piss. I didn't want to be a fucking guinea-pig in the first place and I certainly didn't want to end up as a fucking *secret weapon*—

so if you aren't going to tell me what the fuck is going on, jeez, why don't you just *fuck off?*"

He didn't flinch and he didn't get angry.

"Okay," he said. "You'll need to know, whether you decide to come aboard or not, and I'm betting that nobody else will make much effort to tell you the truth. How much have they told you so far?"

"Bugger all," I said, resentfully. I waved a hand at the paper mountain. "They gave me plenty to read, as you can see, but it might as well be hieroglyphics. Apparently, they stuck some gene into my bladder expecting that it would fill my piss full of some kind of useful protein. It didn't. Instead, I got four different proteins, or bits of proteins. Everybody knew that last night, so something new must have come up in the meantime. Finch was just waffling, but I gather that they've now got interested in whatever there is about me that was making the transplanted gene act up. If the original target protein had been especially valuable, I wouldn't have been walking the streets in the first place, and if one of the four unexpected by-products had been a gold mine, the pirates would probably have hung on to me instead of sending me back, so I'm betting that once they began to figure out what my bladder had done to the target, they began wondering about what it could do to *other* proteins . . . and what it might already be doing inside me. Right so far?"

"Spot on," he conceded, ungrudgingly. He was obviously surprised that a dolehound with three GCSEs had got that far, but he seemed pleased to know that I wasn't a complete idiot.

"So what is it doing?" I asked. "And what else might it do, with the right encouragement?"

"It'll probably take a long time to work that out," he told me. "Which is why everybody's trying to put a claim in before the hard work starts. All we have so far is hopeful signs—signs that a lot of people have been looking out for, although nobody expected them to turn up in a bog-standard op like this. Have you ever heard of the Principle of Selective Self-Medication?"

"No," I said. "Mum probably has. She watches documentaries on BBC-2."

"Well, put very simply, it means that all living organisms are under continuous selective pressure to develop internal defenses against disease, injury, parasitism, and predation. Any mutation that throws up a means of protecting its carrier from one of those things increases its chances of survival. A lot of the medicines doctors developed in the last century, from antibiotics on, were borrowed from other organisms that had developed them as natural defenses, but our evolutionary history had already equipped us with a lot of internal defenses of our own—like the immune system—which we'd simply taken for granted. Once the Human Genome Project had delivered a basic map, we were in a much better position not only to analyze our own defensive systems but also to search for refinements that hadn't yet had an opportunity to spread through the population. Most of the publicity associated with the project concentrated on the genes that make certain people more vulnerable to various diseases, cancers, and so on—but there's another side to the coin. We've also been able to search out genes that make people *less* vulnerable to specific conditions: self-medicating factors."

"So Hartman and Finch think I've got one of those: a gene that makes me less vulnerable to some kind of killer disease?"

"Not a gene, as such, although there must be genes that produce the components of the system. What they think you've got is a chemical apparatus that operates alongside genetic systems, influencing the way in which certain exons collaborate in producing family sets of proteins."

"That's enough jargon for now," I told him. "Cut to the bottom line. What am I—a walking antibiotic factory?"

"No. What you've got isn't protection against bacteria, or viruses, or prions—but it *might* be a defense against some kind of cancers. It might suppress some sorts of tumors by inhibiting the development of modified cells within specific tissues."

"Not just bladder tissue?"

"No—although it'll take time to figure out exactly where the limits lie."

"So I'm immune to some kinds of cancer—but it could take years to figure out exactly which ones, and how many."

"Not immune, but certainly less vulnerable. And it's more complicated than that. There's a selective cost as well as a selective benefit, which is presumably why the condition's so rare."

I could guess that one. Mum had been in her late thirties when she had me, after leading a fairly colorful life. Gran had been just as old when she'd had Mum. "Infertility," I said. "Babies are tumors too."

"That's a crude way of putting it," Hascombe said. "But yes—as well as suppressing tumors, it probably suppresses the great majority of implanted embryos. If it didn't, we'd probably all have something like it integrated into our immune systems. Natural selection couldn't do that for us—but somatic engineers might. What you have isn't an all-purpose cancer cure, and wouldn't necessarily be more efficient than the cancer treatments we already have—but once we understand exactly how it works, it might have other uses."

I nodded, to show that I could follow the argument. Then I said: "And what, exactly, does it have to do with Special Services? Or am I supposed to believe the standard line about all biowarfare research being purely for defense?"

"All *our* biowarfare research *is* purely for defense," the colonel said, with a perfectly straight face. I remembered what he'd said about our humble nation not having an enemy in the world, except maybe for Zimbabwe and Jamaica, but that not being enemies wasn't the same thing as being on the same *side*.

"Once we understand how it works," I guessed, "we might be able to refine it. Maybe it will throw up better cancer cures—but that's not what interests *you*. I slipped through the net, but if the net were refined . . . selective sterilization by subtle and stealthy means. Not the kind of thing that you could make huge profits out of, in the open marketplace—but Special Services have broader interests than mere profit."

"Now you're being melodramatic, Darren," he said, blithely. "This isn't some conspiracy-theory movie. This is everyday life. We have to be careful to examine every emerging possibility, to analyze its implications for national security . . . its capacity to disturb or distort the status quo. That's what *you* have to do too—examine every emerging possibility, analyzing its implications for your personal security. . . ."

". . . And its capacity to fuck up the status quo," I finished for him. "What's your offer, Mr. Hascombe?"

He didn't object to my failure to address him by his rank. "Security," he said. "The other parties will only offer you money, but they'll cheat you if and when they can. You could spend a lot of time in court, one way and another. On the other hand . . . did you know that because GSKC recruited you under the provisions of the National Service Act, your notional employer, at this moment in time, is His Majesty's Government? Technically, you're on secondment. I don't have the power to confiscate GSKC's data, but I do have the power to confiscate *you*. Your mother's a free agent, of course, but your grandmother is a state pensioner, and thus—*technically*, at least—unable to enter into any contractual arrangements without the permission of HMG. Not that we want to delve into a can of worms if we can avoid it. We'd rather work with all of you as a family, according to the principle of informed consent.

We like families—they're the backbone of every healthy society."

I wondered how many healthy societies he thought there were in the world, and how many he expected to stay that way. If he'd told me the truth—which I wasn't prepared to take for granted—I was a walking miracle. I was also a walking time-bomb. Everybody knew that there were too many people in the world, and everybody had different ideas as to which ones ought to stop adding to the problem. Given that everybody and his cousin already had enough of me to start doing all kinds of wild and woolly experiments, I probably wasn't absolutely necessary to the great crusade, but I was young and I was fit, and neither Mum nor Gran had ever produced a milligram of semen, or ever would.

I was rare all right—rare and *interesting*. Nobody had ever thought so before, but the last twenty-four hours had changed everything.

"GSKC could offer me security," I pointed out. "They have people to look after their people." But I was already reconsidering the question of why Hascombe's oppo had taken GSKC's lawyer by the throat, and what the move had been intended to demonstrate.

"We have an army at our disposal," Hascombe pointed out. "Not to mention a police force, various Special Services, and the entire formal apparatus of the law of the land. The people who look after our people are very good at it. But it's your choice, Darren. I wish I could tell you to think about it, but I'm afraid we're in a hurry. You can have five minutes, if you like."

He didn't mean that I have five minutes to decide whether to go with him or stay with GSKC. He meant that I had five minutes to decide whether to go quietly and willingly or to start a small war.

Personally, I quite liked the idea of the war, but I had other people to consider now—and not just Mum and Gran. It was just beginning to dawn on me that for the first time in my life, I was faced with a decision that actually *mattered* not just to me or people I knew, but to any number of people I would never even meet.

People had been taking the piss out of me all my life, for any reason and no reason at all: because I was called Darren; because I didn't even know my Dad's name; because I only had three GCSEs and not an ology among them; because I was so desperate and so useless that I'd had to sign up as a guinea pig in order to pay my share of the household expenses; because I was still living with my Mum at twenty, in a miserable flat in a miserable block in an officially designated high crime/zero tolerance estate; and because I was the kind of idiot who couldn't even do a half-way decent job of being a kidnap victim or a spy.

Now, things were different. Now, I was rare, and *interesting*. I was a national resource. I was a new cure for cancer and a subtle weapon in the next world war. No more Hungarian pinot noir for me; from now on, whatever I chose to do, it would be classy claret all the way.

In a way, I knew, the man from Special Services was holding a gun on me in exactly the same way as the fake fat blonde—but everyone does what he has to do when the situation arises. It wasn't his fault. He couldn't come to me with a fistful of fifty-euro notes, because that wasn't the game he was playing.

But what game should *I* be playing, now that I had some say in the matter?

I knew that the world was full of people who'd have said that a fistful of fifty-euro notes was the only game worth playing, even though it was crooked. Some, I knew, reckoned that it was the only game in town, because governments and Special Services didn't count for much any more in a world ruled by multinational corporations like GSKC. But even on an officially designated high crime/zero tolerance estate you learn, if you're not completely stupid, that money isn't the measure of all things. You only have to watch enough movies to figure out that what people *think* of you is the important thing, and that not having the piss taken out of you any more is something you can't put a price on. To qualify as a kidnap victim is one thing, to be a double-agent is another, and to be a walking cancer cure is something else again, but what it all comes down to in the end is *respect*. Jeremy Hascombe was offering me a better choice than Matthew Jardine or Dr. Hartman, even though he wasn't offering me any choice at all about where I was going and who was going to be subjecting me to all manner of indignities with the aid of hypodermic syringes, dustbusters, and all effective hybrids thereof. He was offering me the choice of doing my duty like a man.

"Okay, Colonel," I said. "I'll play it like a hero, and smile all the while. I don't suppose you brought me anything decent to wear? I don't want to walk out of here in my pajamas."

"No, I didn't," said the colonel, who was too uptight a man to let his gratitude show, "but your mother did. She thought you might need a change of clothes, just in case you could come home for Sunday lunch after all."

It was just as she'd said: family is the backbone of any healthy society. Perhaps it always will be. Who, after all, can tell what the future might hold?

DEATH OF REASON

Tony Daniel

Private eyes have traditionally had to venture all alone down Mean Streets—here we venture down some very mean streets indeed in a gritty high-tech Alabama of the future, as a lone cop battles corrupt officials, the Mob, his own haunted past, and an array of criminals of a sort that don't yet even exist in our day, to unravel a deadly secret before it unravels him.

Like many writers of his generation, Tony Daniel first made an impression on the field with his short fiction. He made his first sale, to Asimov's, in 1990 and followed it up with a long string of well-received stories both there and in markets such as The Magazine of Fantasy and Science Fiction, Amazing, SF Age, Universe, *and* Full Spectrum *throughout the '90s—stories such as "The Robot's Twilight Companion," "Grist," "The Careful Man Goes West," "Sun So Hot I Froze to Death," "Prism Tree," "Candle," "No Love in All of Dwingeloo," and many others. His story "Life on the Moon" was a finalist for the Hugo Award in 1996 and won the* Asimov's Science Fiction *Readers Award poll. His first novel,* Warpath, *was released simultaneously in America and England in 1993. In 1997 he published a new novel,* Earthling. *His most recent books are his first short story collection,* The Robot's Twilight Companion, *and a major new novel,* Metaplanetary, *the first part of a projected trilogy.*

1

The sky was liquid iron at sunset. The clouds were fiery slag. The scramjet carrying me home banked over down-

town Birmingham on approach to the airport. Up on Red
Mountain, the Vulcan's torch flamed scarlet for death—the
beacon for another traffic accident sponged from the pavement of the city. Twenty-four hours of anonymous remem-
brance, then maybe the giant iron statue's torch would
burn green until somebody else spilled himself out on the
black asphalt. The custom was over a hundred years old
now, but people kept obliging. I once knew the woman
whose job it was to throw the switch on the light. I knew
her well. Abby would always have work.

But Vulcan's torch would never burn for my grandfather. His time-sharing license had expired on Maturicell
two days ago. He died in his sleep. Peacefully. As they say.

The scramjet turned thrusters down and slotted into a
bay at Municipal. Guide lasers flared in long lines of neon
Morse code outside the window as the beams passed into
and out of pockets of humidity. It was time to disembark,
but I continued to gaze out at the sky full of fire and light.
Twilight in the Heart of Dixie, bloody and wringing wet as
usual. Welcome home, Andy Harco. Back to the city where
you were poured and formed. Back to the grindstone that
put the edge to your soul.

"You get too hot, and you'll lose your temper," my old
friend Thaddeus the poet used to say. I guess that's what
happened; that's why I left. I lost my temper in both senses
of the word. But in Seattle I'd hardened the edge once
again. Birmingham no longer had what it took to dull me
down. And I cut back now.

I snugged my op-eds onto my nose, then gathered my
wits from under the seat and out of the overhead compartment. Along with my briefcase full of peripherals, I had a
bag of toiletries, a plastic Glock nine-millimeter seventeen-
shot automatic, and my good blue interviewing suit and
wing tips. I had not worn the suit for eight years, but I was
reasonably certain it still fit. Granddaddy's funeral was tomorrow evening. I would have time to get it altered if it
didn't. I had flown out of Seattle in gray shorts and a

T-shirt with the faded hologo of a science-fiction convention on the chest. People had given me strange looks back there, for Seattle was in the midst of a cold snap—the temperatures were hovering in the midfifties in August—due to some frigid air that had descended from the Artic. I was, however, dressed perfectly for Alabama.

I felt like a returning tourist as I got off the plane. In a way, I was. I'd been on a long vacation from Birmingham. Eight years, for my health. That is, if I'd hung around eight years ago, a bullet would have just ruined the nice gray interior of my skull. At least, that's what Freddy Pupillina had told me—more or less—when he sent me the fistful of dead roses. Southern gangsters think they're so damn subtle and genteel. But perfume on a skunk accentuates the stink even more.

But that was eight years ago, back when I was a rookie rental for the Birmingham P.D. and an unlicensed fabulist. I'd had few friends, and an extremely abrasive manner. These days, I have more friends.

I wouldn't be seeing Abby, but Thaddeus was a friend. I would look him up after the funeral. It had been a long time since we'd gotten together in person.

I should have expected the snoops to pattern me as soon as I stepped off the jet. For the most part, the only people who travel in actual are high-level business jocks, Ideal coordinating nodes, rich eccentrics—and terrorists. Guess which profile I matched up with? I suppose I was preoccupied with thoughts of Granddaddy, maybe of Abby, so I wasn't paying a lot of attention. While I didn't plan on seeing Abby ever again, after seeing the Vulcan from the air, she was heavily on my mind.

The snoop interceptor was a Securidad 50 crank, maybe three or four years old. Cheap Polish bionics suspended in a Mexican-made shell. The City of Birmingham never had been exactly on the cutting edge of technology. I clicked up the 50's specs in the upper right-hand corner of my op-eds and gave them a quick glance. The 50's innards were standard bionic sludge. Its force escalator was knock-out gas, not a very thoughtful option for use in a crowded corridor, such as are found, for example, in airports. Those wacky Poles.

"Mr. Harco, may I have your attention," the crank said. The voice synth needed major adjustment. It was low filtering, and the thing sounded like a rusted-out saxophone. How could it get that grating nasal trill to come out when it didn't even have a nose? Ah, the mysteries of science.

"What is it?" I replied through tight lips. I pointedly looked away from the 50. Who knows? Maybe the thing had enough brains to be insulted. I hoped so.

"Please accompany me," said the crank. Then red letters flashed across the periphery of my op-eds. MR. HARCO, YOU ARE REQUESTED TO FOLLOW THE ROBOT TO AIRPORT SECURITY SCREENING. PLEASE COMPLY. The font was crude, but 3-D. I have organic inner lenses in my eyewear—I don't skimp on any of my peripherals—and the words burned on the cellwork of my op-eds like lash welts.

I blinked twice and popped up my custom V-trace menu. It had cost me six thousand, a chip of my skull's parietal plate, and a year of bureaupain to get a license for the junk. It was not my most expensive piece of exotic junk, but it was damned near. My brain is probably as much vat-formed gray matter as it is natural—and that's not counting the hardware interfaces.

I had no right to use the V-trace in the present circumstance, of course, but if this asshole who was cowboying me brought me up for review, he'd be asking for suspension along with me. Assuming he was a rent-a-cop to begin with. I had better stop making assumptions, I told myself, and start dealing with this shit.

I blinked the cursor to ROOT AND BURN with my left eye and closed both eyes to activate it. The message disappeared from my op-eds. I have good junk. Not the best. My junk is not really integrated into me, like that of the nodes and the rich. I couldn't make it work without op-eds. But my junk is quality stuff when combined with my eyewear. Within a second, the status display spread across my field of vision, and iconed the real world into a little block in the lower right-hand corner of the virtual.

SIGNAL ROOTED. FEED PROTECTED. BURN OPTIONS:
1. ORIGINATING DEVICE
2. ORIGINATING CONTROLLER
3. GENERAL BURN

I chose number 2, then iconed back to reality. The crank stood absolutely still for a long moment, and I stared at it. Somewhere, someone was receiving a nasty surprise in their eyewear.

The crank finally moved. It opened a door in its casing and extended a pink tube that looked for all the world like a shriveled penis. The crank sprayed knockout gas like a scared puppy pisses. It seemed to dribble out. The chemicals probably hadn't been changed in years, and the crank was more electric than biologic, so it didn't have the guts to nurture complex chemicals indefinitely.

The gas did sublimate to some degree, however. Although, fortunately, the corridor was mostly clear, one of the gate attendants was walking by. The stuff billowed lazily about, and after she got a whiff of it, she started to run away. Too late. She dropped onto the carpeted floor with a dull thump.

I, of course, have been filtered since Justcorp modified me at the Academy eight years ago. Justcorp does a first-rate job. It took the crank—or whoever was directing it—a moment to figure this out. It had been squirting me like I was a cockroach that was slow to die.

I walked over and made sure that the attendant was all right. Looked like she'd taken the fall on her side and was only bruised. No op-eds. As I felt her head to make sure

nothing was cracked, my fingers closed around the feedhorn wart at the back of her neck. An optical bundle in a
delta configuration. She was a node with fairly expensive
hardwiring. Her brain belonged to another. I quickly
stopped worrying too much about her well-being. Worrying about a node is like caring about the fate of a particular dead skin cell. And anyway, the Ideal would provide, or
not, as it saw fit. I wondered, vaguely, which Ideal she belonged to.

Some of the others who were waiting on flights began
to gather around the two of us. Idiots. What if I *were* a terrorist and in need of a hostage?

"Mr. Harco," whined the crank. "We are prepared to activate all systems to persuade you to accompany me.
Please accompany me."

Big vocabulary these security cranks have.

I said nothing, but nodded for the thing to lead the way.
May as well get the checkout over with and be on my way.
I was on personal leave, for Christ's sake, with specific in-
structions from management to stay out of trouble.

One nondescript corridor led to another until we descended an airtube into the bowels of the complex. I felt
like I was being swallowed. Security always seemed to
pick the most cheerless locations for offices.

The duty officer's eyelids were charred, and he looked
like a raccoon, although his appearance wasn't that much
different from what it had been before I'd burned his eyewear out, I was sure. Low-order security always wore
those smoked plastic op-eds that look like windows into a
black void. This guy's own burned-out op-eds were laying,
twisted and pitiful, on the desk before him. Yet even with
the black eyes, I recognized the fellow.

Ed Bernam. Dandy Ed, we used to call him. He was a
Guardian rental, and fit that agency's stereotype to a *T*.
Big, vain, mean—and unable to control snot and fart pro-
duction. Guardian's body mods on new employees were

quick and cheap. The procedure adversely affected the guts and nasal tract.

Bernam picked his nose continually, but dressed well, as if he were trying to compensate for the shabbiness of his innards. He wore a blue and white uniform with a fully animated holoshield undulating on his chest. No wonder the airport couldn't afford state-of-the-art cranks; it was dropping all its money on sparklies for the rentals. Or, knowing Bernam, he paid for his own.

"Hello, Ed. Frontline monitor still? Isn't this supposed to be a slot to break rookies' balls?"

Bernam scowled and sank back into the protection of his control chair.

"*Meander* Harco, what the hell are you doing in my airport?" he growled. He remembered me, evidently. Or at least remembered the fact that I hated my given name.

"Personal business," I replied with a neutral voice. I'd had my fun with him, and now I just wanted to get the hell out of there.

"We'll see," he said. "The junk has flagged you. I'm going to have to pull and comp your file."

"I'm not a terrorist, Ed."

"We'll see."

Shit. This was going to take time. Public security junk is notoriously slow compared to P.D. or private corporation. It still has to access central databases, for Christ's sake! And Bernam was going to run a full comparison, there was no doubt of that, even though there was not a reason on Earth why a terrorist would get himself doctored up to look like me. I glanced around for a chair. There was none other than the one Bernam's fat ass was occupying, of course. That was the way of such offices. I set my suitcase and my briefcase full of peripherals down on the desks in front of him, further mangling his ruined op-eds.

Dandy Ed Bernam watched me through his raccoon mask. I checked again to make sure it *was* him before me, wishing I were plugged into the briefcase. I had downloaded all of my long-term memory into a biostatic memory froth I'd paid a half-year's salary for. That's one reason I don't let the briefcase get too far away from me. I did it so as to have more room in the old noggin for junk interface algorithms . . . and other things. What was left in my brain was memories with cheated links and little redundancy. The guy who installed it—the best in the field—told me it was foolproof, nonetheless. And so far, I hadn't found any blank spots.

This was Bernam, all right. He'd been a two-year man when I came on with the Birmingham P.D. Most Guardian rentals stay on patrol, but Bernam had worked his way up to plainclothes. Someone had joked that he did it all so that he could dress the way he wanted to every day.

Whatever the case, he hadn't done well in Vice. Management had shuffled him around a couple of times before busting him back down to patrol. Ed couldn't take it, and broke his lease. Management was not exactly mortified to see him go, especially since Guardian refunded the deposit on him. But it seems the corporation got back at Ed for losing them money by contracting him out only to places with strict uniform requirements. No more fancy duds for Ed. Yet I could see that he still had his snot problem.

What I remember most about Ed is from the day before my arraignment. He was cleaning out his locker after breaking his lease. The locker was full of designer jeans. Ed liked to affect that he was big-time management in those days. He took the jeans out and neatly folded them, then stacked them in a vinyl bag—and appeared to be inventorying them as well. Ed acted like he didn't notice me as I got dressed in my blues, but he stopped with the jeans when I closed my locker door. He looked at me hard, and I stared back.

"What the hell do you think this is?" he asked me. "The twentieth century?"

I suppose he meant that I didn't understand the intricacies of the situation I had gotten myself into, the fact that a rookie did not step on toes—particularly toes as sensitive as Freddy Pupillina's and the Ideal to which he paid tribute.

The Birmingham P.D. and the Mafia had had a good-old-boy understanding for over a hundred years, and I'd stepped over the boundaries with my bust of Freddy for an assassination he'd been stupid enough to attend to in person. But that hit had stepped over my boundaries.

The poor guy he killed had been a bug junkie for years—just one of the burnouts hanging out on Twentieth Street—with mental parasites eating their every thought almost before they formed it. When I was on patrol, I took a liking to this guy. He took care of stray dogs. His problem was that he had a big mouth.

This bugman just happened to look at Freddy wrong one day and say something stupid. The nanobugs had eaten the poor guy's soul like gas on Styrofoam. *Fuck* the twenty-first century. Fuck the Family and its new and improved ways to hurt people.

Though of course I didn't say a damned thing to Bernam at the time, I gave his question some thought. I'm still giving it thought. Maybe this century isn't the one I would have chosen had I been given the option. Well, the fucking times had chosen *me,* and would just have to put up with my existence.

The airport junk took fifteen minutes to complete its report. Bernam had to listen to it aloud, since his op-eds were crisped.

"Meander Harco, age thirty, 6'0", eyes brown, hair brown, race mulatto." At least this voice synthesizer had the pleasant accent of a Southern woman. Made it easier to hear all the personal shit spoken aloud. But not that easy. "Born 12/21/65, Tuscaloosa, Alabama, contract birth, parents Julia Monroe Delacroix, mother, Marvin Harco 473A, father. Licensed cohabitation 3/15/85–12/22/88 with Abigail Wu Brimly, Birmingham, Alabama, no offspring. Education: graduated Banks High School, Birmingham—"

"Skip to the currents," Bernam grunted. He dribbled a little spit onto his chin when he spoke. It sat there for a while, glistening in a yellow sort of way. Finally, he took out a paisley handkerchief and delicately wiped it away. Classy guy, Ed.

"Employed 2087–present by Justcorp Criminology. Leased since January 2089 to Seattle Police Department, homicide. Current department rank, Lieutenant. Licensing to follow: Grade 19 depth investigations, including virtual slayings. Section B coda use of harmful force, with an exemption in part 2, subparagraph 4 for biomodifications in hands, elbows, and torso." Which meant I had built-in brass knuckles—among other neat additions. "Option 4 for use of deadly force." Bernam smiled. He knew the kind of restrictions they had in Seattle for a license to kill. At Option 4, it was very doubtful that my junk could process the legalities of response in time for me to shoot back if someone was trying to blow me away. "License for (1) Remington angular electrochemical stungun, serial number on request. (2) Glock polymer nine-millimeter automatic pistol, serial number on request. (3) Schrade two-inch boot devices. (4) Bullard Forensics Portalab III. (5) Archco Enhanced Op-Eds—"

"Fucking illegally modified—" Bernam muttered.

"With licensed enhancements (1)—"

"Fuck the enhancements," said Bernam. The junk was smart enough not to try and interpret Bernam's orders literally. It skipped to the next section.

"F.A. license HARCO234319599 for genre constructions, science fiction."

"Huh?" said Bernam in his inimitable way.

"I write science-fiction stories on the side," I replied. "Got a problem with that?"

"You're full of shit."

"Maybe," I said.

"Commendations, Official Evaluations, Resolved Offenses, and Unlicensed Activities. Warning: listing will take approximately twenty minutes for oral report."

"Skip it. Outstandings?"

"1/3/89, Dereliction of Duty, Birmingham Police Department, on Article 6, judicial expert system appeal. Review due 8/97."

"So," said Bernam. "Going to get sentenced soon?"

"Going to get cleared soon," I said. "You bastard." I said it without heat, and Bernam grinned evilly. I wasn't sure, but I thought he was wearing a thin coating of lipstick.

"Give me the comp," he told the computer.

The lights went down and the infrared came on. Sensors popped from the wall and shone darkly. Another five minutes passed. Finally, the lights came back on and the junk spoke up. "Behavioral and somatic patterns: 97 percent match. Lacking genetic evaluation—"

"I refuse a scan under Section B of the Privacy Act," I said. It felt weird to be the one invoking a Section B. Usually I was having it invoked on me by some bad element who didn't want to be identified.

"Shut the fuck up," Bernam grunted. "Nobody asked you to."

"Lacking genetic evaluation, opinion tendered: This is Meander Harco."

"Satisfied?" I asked.

"Shut up."

"Ed, it's time you stop messing with me. I'm out of here in ten seconds unless you got reason to hold me."

Ed looked at me as if he were scrutinizing a strange insect. "I knew you were dark-skinned, but I never knew you were a mule, Andy," he said.

I stood still, expressionless. No. He wasn't worth it. "Now you do," I replied. I felt a great numbness grow in my gut, as if I were far bigger inside than I was outside. This was the way I felt before violence. Control. Hold on. My legal junk was spewing conflict options onto my op-eds. There were no options in my favor in this situation. Just for fun, I sifted the parameters through the Option 4 junk. It gave me the red flag. So. I could not legally kill him. Lucky Ed. This time.

"I've got a message for you, Andy," Bernam said. "Freddy Pupillina wants to talk to you."

For a second, I was nonplussed. Then this little shake-down began to make sense. Bernam was under orders from Freddy. Which meant all my previous legal evaluations were out of context and meaningless. Hmm.

"You're mistaking me for somebody who gives a shit," I replied.

Bernam got real quiet. He was evidently not used to anybody refusing Freddy in such a cavalier manner. But it was true: he *was* mistaking me for somebody who gave a shit.

Bernam resolved his difficulties by pretending not to hear me. "Tomorrow night, around eight, at the Sports-man," he said. "You're free to go now."

"Tell Freddy I'm not coming," I said.

"Out," Bernam said. He closed his eyes and touched something on his chair. The chair spun around with its back to me. I stepped up to the desk where I'd laid my luggage and opened the briefcase.

"Ed, turn around."

He did not reply and continued facing away from me. I pulled out the Glock and slid the magazine into the handle. I felt it click into position, but the plastic was noiseless.

"Ed."

Still nothing. My legal junk was screaming, so I powered it down. I popped up a targeting menu, took aim, and fired the Glock into one of the chair's armrests. As I suspected, there was no security breach sensing in the home office. A perfect way for an airport to cut corners. Why would you need it where you have a permanently armed guard? The crank that had led me here stood immobile in the corner, unaware that anything untoward was going on.

Bernam was, at least, a bit more self-aware than the 50. He spun around with his hands over his head. "Jesus Christ," he whimpered. He tried to shuffle out of his seat, and I saw that Bernam was even worse off than I'd thought. He was attached by a bundle of leads to the chair.

"Ed, you're bonded."

"Shut the fuck up!"

There was nothing I could do to him that was worse than what he'd done to himself. It was like being a node with none of the perks—no sense of community, no mental health plan. It made me physically sick to contemplate. An individual giving himself up to an Ideal, but staying himself. Like a dog dragging around a tick the size of an elephant. Only rentals desperate for *something* ever got themselves wired for bonding. I wondered what kind of shit Bernam had gotten into. Graft? Bugs? Booze? He would not meet my gaze.

"Tell Freddy that if he messes with me, I'll take him down," I said. "Tell him that." I pointed the Glock between Ed's eyes. This got him looking at me.

"Oh Christ," he said. "I can't without my op-eds, Andy."

"That's okay. You can tell him the old-fashioned way. You still have a link screen, don't you? Tell him I came to attend my grandfather's funeral, and then I'm leaving. I no longer take shit off bad elements. Tell him to stay the hell out of my way."

"Jesus, Andy—"

"Will you tell him that?" I said. I touched the muzzle of the Glock to Bernam's nose. A little runny snot stuck to it.

"Okay, God, *okay*. I'll tell him!" said Bernam. He seemed sincere. I pulled the gun away and wiped the snot on his nicely starched uniform. I had to press hard to make it stick.

"Nice seeing you again, Ed." I put the Glock away and gathered my things then walked out. Out of the airport, out into the sweating southern night. The air, as always, had an

ozone tang imparted by the huge biostatic plants downtown. And, as always, the fecal odor of bucolic acid from
the plants mixed with the tang, so that the city smelled like
a zombie might, decaying and electric.

Even at the airport, lightning bugs blinked in the air.
They lived in the grass that grew through the cracks in the
sidewalks. I ordered up a Hertz with my op-eds. It was an
87 Sagittarius, and the inductors rumbled like driveway
gravel. Maybe I should have gone with one of the newer
companies instead of aging traditional Hertz, but I liked
the fact that all their electrostatics had the same lines as old
gas-burning automobiles.

As the Saj drove me away, a couple of the fireflies
smashed against the windshield, and their glowing belly-
fire smeared in incandescent arches across my field of vision. If I hadn't known better, I would have sworn they
were some glitch in the virtual manifestation. But I had my
op-eds menued down, and the fireflies were real. For better or worse, I was in Birmingham, in the late twenty-first
century, in the frail human flesh. More or less. The briefcase full of guns and brains sat by my side.

My fictional time-traveling detective, Minden Sibley,
would have appreciated the juxtaposition of the old and the
new on such a night as this. He was always flitting back a
hundred years or so, going after fugitives on the Timeways
or just taking a short vacation in days when you didn't
have to have a license to take a goddamn dump. But he always had to return within a week, subjective. That was the
First Temporal Law, ingrained into the fabric of his being
by his employer, the United States Time Company.

1. A time traveler can never harm, nor by inaction
   bring harm to, the resonate period to which he is
   native.

You could go away for a little while, but you had to return and take your place as a tooth in the cogwheel that

turned the universe when it was your turn to connect up
with the Big Conveyor Belt in the Sky. Or whatever. It was
all lies, I thought, I'd made them up myself, so what did it
matter?

Granddaddy's death had made me maudlin, I decided.
There is, however, no cure for self-indulgent sentimentality so sure and quick as going to see your family, the living ones, that is, in the flesh. I disconnected from the
beltway a few miles from the airport and drove my car
down First Avenue North to the BrownService Mortuary.
Mom's old Range Rover was parked outside. Harco, the
bioenhancement company in which my father was a mid-
level node, would not, of course, waste his work time by
sending him to the viewing. Maybe he'd be at the funeral.
Probably not. My father was a vague nothing to me, and I
didn't care. And I didn't particularly want to see Mom, either.

My mother is an amalgamation of just about every kook
spirituality that ever aspired to Ideation. There are feed-
horns dangling from her like fat remoras. Yet she is not a
node. God knows why. Probably some kind of sick balance
in her mind among a variety of pathologies. She's the one
who gave me my first name, as if you hadn't figured that
one out already. She was also the one who saved my ass
eight years before. What can I say? I love Mom, but I don't
like her very much. At least I don't like being around her
any more than I have to.

I locked my briefcase in the trunk and went inside the
funeral home.

Mom was out in the hallway, talking to one of Granddaddy's relatives whom I didn't know—which included
just about all of them. I never had been into the extended-
family thing as a young man, though Mom had tried to get
me interested in reversion genealogy at one time—that fad
where some fancy junk supposedly deconstructs your
DNA and gives you an op-ed presentation of life in
Mesopotamia using your encoded radical memories, or

whatever. Mom was convinced at the time that she was a Hittite princess and the rightful heir to the throne. I hated to point out to her that her inheritance nowadays consisted of a death zone of microbes that fried human beings as if they were insects caught in a zapper. The Middle East was no longer a pretty place, if it ever had been.

"Andy," Mom said, and disengaged herself from the relative to come and hug me. She smelled, as always, of cloistered eucalyptus. "I'm so glad you're here. Daddy will really be pleased to see you."

As I'd known she would, Mom had had a ghost made of Granddaddy. I glanced through the door and saw him, sitting by the casket and looking morosely at himself.

"Well," I said, and walked in.

Granddaddy was lying in his coffin, looking like he was made up for television. He was dressed in a gray suit that I'd never seen him wear. Mom had probably bought it for the occasion. He was a handsome man. He'd been a real looker in his youth, and the undertaker had obviously done some facial rejuvenation. Ironically, you can make dead skin look far younger than living skin, through some trade secret that I did not care to know or even guess at.

"I did live to a ripe old age," said the ghost softly.

"Yes," I said. I couldn't find it in me to be rude to the holoware. A first for me. But, however, shallow and stupid, the thing was all that was left of the algorithm that had raised me and formed my own deep-down programming.

"I wanted to say something to you." The ghost spoke in a stiff voice, as if it were being forced into a subroutine it did not particularly like but was ordered to follow.

"Okay," I said. I didn't try to make eye contact. It wouldn't be the same, no matter how lifelike they made the holo.

"First, power me down as quick as you can."

"Mom won't like it."

"Convince your mother."

"I'll try."

"The other thing," he said, then was quiet for a moment, as if he were digging for something lost in his depths. But there *were* no depths to ghosts. "The other thing is, don't take no shit off nobody. Except poor folks who can't help it and don't know any better."

"I remember when you told me that," I replied. "I'll always remember."

The ghost appeared relieved. He crossed his legs and turned back to looking at himself in the casket. "Almost one hundred fifty. A ripe old age."

I left the room after another minute or so. Mom tried to get me to stay at her apartment, but I needed to be alone tonight. Also, I was a little worried about Freddy Pupillina looking me up, and didn't want Mom to get involved in that kind of shit. She had enough problems as it was.

I found a money crank around the block and got some cash vouchers issued from my account. This would be the last traceable transaction I planned to make tonight. Just to be sure, I got out the Portalab and ran the voucher cards through a launderer. No real harm done, since they could be cashed at the Federal Reserve, but no more junk on them that could connect them to my account. Slightly illegal, but I made sure to do it away from the usual nanowatcher patch points, and out of satellite view. Being a cop hath its advantages.

I checked into a motel in Bessemer, on the west side of town, far from the funeral home and my mother's place. The clerk—a crank (it wasn't a classy joint)—asked for I.D. when my voucher cards didn't produce an origination code. I showed it more fruits from the Portalab, and it legally had to be satisfied. My room was dingy and I couldn't control the air-conditioning. The temperature was much too cold. Air-conditioning. The South was both the master of it and its slave. Nothing in the history of the region was more important.

That night, I dreamed of Abby. I often do. Nothing specific. Just her autumn hair, her slender fingers. Her breath. It always smelled like rain in leaves.

2

After the dreaming, I slept hard and woke up thinking I was in Seattle. Then I realized that not only was it freezing cold from the air-conditioning, but the chilled metal of a pistol was pressed against my forehead.

"Mr. Pupillina wants to see you," said a voice from the darkness.

"Yeah," I said. "It appears that he does." That was when I jammed my stungun into where I estimated the voice had a crotch and pulled the trigger. I always sleep with a weapon.

There was a stifled whimper, a heavy thud, and the lights flipped on. A woman was standing by the door with the biggest damn fléchette pistol I'd ever seen. It had to be one of the Danachek 7s I'd heard of. Nasty way to die. The bullets were said actually to burrow. On the floor lay a big, bearded man in a blue suit. His index finger was through the trigger guard of a big .45.

"How the hell did you know where I was?" I asked, by way of breaking the tension. The woman's tight expression did not loosen. She was heavyset and dark-skinned in a dirty sort of way, maybe in her late forties. Ugly as ten-day-old roadkill. She, too, wore blue, with tiny pinstripes that made her look fatter than she was, which was fat enough. Or big-boned, I should say, being a gentleman and all.

"Rental cars check in with their location every hour," she said flatly.

"Only to the cops," I said, then realized how stupid that sounded. In Birmingham, Freddy might not own the cops, but he sure as hell could get a little favor done for him—like a report on rentals.

"I hope this doesn't take too long. I have a funeral to attend," I said. The woman looked at me funny.

"So you already know," she said. I couldn't think what the hell she was talking about and finally decided she was talking about my *own* funeral, har, har.

She motioned me to get up. I had to step over Bluto on the floor to get to my clothes. She made me turn the briefcase toward her when I opened it. She reached for the Glock. So much for Plan B.

But I did have the rest of the alphabet to work with. I quickly slammed the briefcase shut on the woman's hand. She cried out in pain, but kept the fléchette pistol leveled at my chest.

"Let go!" she said, fighting to control the hurt in her voice.

Instead, I twisted the briefcase as hard as I could and heard the bone in her arm break. She fired the pistol at me, point-blank. Fire and agony in my chest. The force of the bullet knocked me backward, but I managed to hold on to the briefcase, and the woman and I tumbled to the floor together. Her face came down on the studded metal cup in my elbow. Again there was the cracking of bone. She rolled off me, moaning. Her nose was a bloody mess. I kicked the pistol away from her and staggered to my feet.

After taking a moment to catch my breath, I lifted my shirt to inspect the damage. There was a hematoma on my rib cage. Through the rendered flesh and muscle, an exposed piece of my Kevlar chest plates shone gray as old bone.

The fléchette bullet lay at my feet, trying to burrow into the carpet's nap. This sight, and the grinding pain in my chest, fired a rage within me. I kicked the woman in the side as hard as I could. She stopped moaning and passed out. This gave me less satisfaction than I'd expected. These two were just Family muscle. They weren't made; their pain was their own. To hurt the Family, you had to hit a node. Like Freddy.

I gathered my things together and left the room. After I stowed them in the Saj, I opened the hood and found the sender box. Taking it out would leave me without traffic control. What the hell; I knew how to drive. I went to the trunk and found the tire tool. The box was full of bionics. It cracked like a skull and leaked gray-white nerve tissue and sickly yellow cranial fluid. While I was putting the tire tool back, the door to my room clicked open, and Big-boned Bertha stumbled out. Her face was all bloody and she was obviously having trouble focusing well enough to find me. Nevertheless, I got in the car and got the hell out of there.

My first order of business was a patch job. I had to drive way the hell south to Hoover to find a booth that could handle skin grafts on the order I needed. It took an hour and a half to get me patched up. Funny how you either die or get better really fast these days.

The booth had my DNA match, and it wouldn't be long before a sweep would root me out. Obviously Freddy cared enough to try, and had the kind of connections to succeed. I drove around aimlessly for a while, trying to match speed with the surrounding traffic so that I would not show up as an anomaly on the road control junk.

I pulled into a station for some static, and while the car was recharging, I went to the rest room and tried on my suit. I'd been wrong about it fitting. Over the last eight years, I'd put on at least twenty pounds, most of them in my chest and shoulders. At nine o'clock, when the cleaners opened, I took the suit in for altering. They put it in the nanotank and it was done in fifteen minutes. I paid with some damaged vouchers and headed in the general direction of the east side of town, toward the Church of Branching Hermeneutics, where Mom was holding Granddaddy's funeral.

But there was still plenty of time to kill before the funeral. I was dressed in the same shorts and T-shirt I'd worn yesterday, so I pulled into East Lake and did five miles around the track. The lake was gorgeous in the midday sun, clean and full of fish, judging by the anglers on the bank. Years ago, it had been a toxic cesspool, but the nanos had cleaned it up—just like the nanos in my shirt slurped up all the sweat and searched out and destroyed bacteria that made a stink.

On about the third lap, I got a decent snippet of plot for my next Minden Sibley time-travel mystery. Something about nanos eating up a body that had been sunk into a lake and Minden having to go back in time, before the murder, to make an identification. Maybe the plot could involve the Second Temporal Law. I hadn't done one of those for a while.

> 2. A time traveler must not endanger his own atem-
>   poral existence in any way, unless by so doing he
>   is fulfilling his obligations under the First Law.

It always makes for a thrilling moment when a time traveler must decide between himself or the epoch that molded him. He can't exist without it, yet he won't exist if it does. Meaningless fun, though. Everybody knows time travel is impossible.

When I finished up my run, I felt like I'd just stepped out of the shower. I drove around for a few minutes until I found a resistance booth on First Avenue North, then put in thirty minutes working the weights and getting the involuntaries shocked. It had been a good three days since my last workout, and this one left me tired, but with a clean feeling under my skin. Working out is the only way I know of feeling virtuous at no one else's expense.

To give the devil his due, I went over to the Krispy Kreme on Eighty-sixth and had a donut and coffee. The place was over a hundred years old and run by some kind of historical trust. I was served by a node in a polyester waitress getup from the last century. I'd have preferred an authentic foul-mouthed waitress in regular clothes, but they've all been replaced by cranks, anyway. The donuts were good, though, and I sat with my coffee and considered times past.

I thought about a lot of things. Abby, mostly. The night I was running for my life from Freddy's goons. Mom had pulled some strings with one of her cults, and the Children of Gregarious Breathers were all set to smuggle me out in the Winnebago they used in their nomadic travels. They were on a holy search for the promised land of perfect atmospheric ion concentration or something, and no one questioned their comings and goings. Once out of town, Justcorp could take care of me. In town, my company's hands were tied by Freddy's maneuvering. There were two slots in the Winnebago. One for me. One for Abby.

Only Abby didn't take hers. She left me that night, in the midst of my need and terror.

We were on the Southside, standing by the onion-topped Greek Orthodox Church. We were to be picked up a block away by the Breath Children.

I told her I loved her, that I'd never loved her more than tonight.

"I know," she said. She looked at me as if she were full of infinite sadness, infinite wisdom. She was practicing to be a node even then. Abby, with her black hair and brown eyes. The fingers of her left hand worrying at the silver armlet she always wore above her right elbow. "I'm not coming, Andy," she said.

"What?"

"I'm not coming with you."

I should have realized. My fear kept the truth from my mind.

It was me or Birmingham for Abby. It always had been. Part of the reason I'd fallen in love with her in the first place was her devotion to principles larger than herself, her unselfish ways. She loved cities, and this city more than any. She'd majored in urban planning in college, while I'd been studying law enforcement. We met in a criminal-law class, moved in together after I'd got my rookie slot with

Justcorp and she'd been hired to monitor traffic and to flip the switch on the Vulcan when it needed doing.

After all those long nights on the traffic watch, pondering the lights, losing herself to the ebb and flow of city life, she'd fallen out of love with me, and into love of another sort. The Big Lie had caught her, before I had known what it was, before I could do anything to help her escape.

It was me or Birmingham, and Abby chose the city. She said that she loved me. She said that love for one man was not as important as love for humankind. She didn't want to give up her job at the Vulcan; she had made node. She hadn't wanted to tell me, knowing my distaste, even then, for Ideals. The city was going to wire her up in a week's time. She was in line to become the city's transportation coordinator, she said, to be on the Planning Council. In line to make a *difference,* to be something more than just one woman against the world. I could not believe what she was saying.

She had become one of those people who look right over you and don't see a person when they look at you, who are always thinking about how everything could be different, how everything can be improved. About how individual people are merely stepping-stones on the road to perfection. And gazing into Abby's eyes, I could see that I was just a point of heat on a particular street corner. No more, no less. She was listening to the buzz of everything so hard she could never hear me pleading with her to stay with me, to leave *for* me.

Abby kissed my numb lips and brushed her slender hand against my trembling face. Then I wondered, for the last time, how it was that she smelled like the rain. I swear to God she smelled like rain in the country. In green leaves. Maybe I've already told you that?

So I boarded the Winnebago alone, and didn't die. And I stayed a person. I can't say the same about Abby. My wife. Who was now the heart and soul of the city of Birmingham. Or at least the nerves.

"You make me look bad, son," said Freddy Pupillina as he settled his enormous bulk on a stool next to me in the Krispy Kreme. "Why you want to play so hard to get?"

I took a sip of my coffee before I answered him, and scanned the restaurant. There was Big-boned Bertha at the door. Her nose was healed, but something about it didn't look right, as if she'd turned out so ugly in the first place, her cells had purposely forgotten how to reconstruct her.

"Oh, I don't know," I replied. "Maybe it has something to do with your trying to take my badge and your running me out of town on a rail?"

"Old news."

"I have things to do, Freddy, a funeral to go to. Leave me alone."

Pupillina took one of those pauses that nodes take when they are receiving instructions from the Ideal. A kind of integration. I took a moment myself to look him over. He hadn't changed much since the day I sprayed mace in his eyes and kicked him in the balls. Perhaps he was bigger, if that were possible, with tinges of gouty jaundice in his eyes and fingernails.

"I'm sorry about your grandfather," he said. "The Family sends its condolences."

"Fuck the Family," I said calmly.

Pupillina did not react with anger. He did not appear to have instructions on just how to react to such a statement, so he continued with his spiel.

"For each of us, the time finally comes when we can no longer contribute as much as we are forced to take, when—"

"My grandfather was worth more than all of your damn Family put together," I said. "Will you cut the shit and tell me what you want, Freddy?"

"I'm just trying to be civil," he grunted. He looked morose, as if all his effort were for nothing. It was.

"I'm going to get up and walk out the door," I said. "If

that creature of yours tries to stop me, I'm going to rip her fucking nose off again and shove it down her windpipe."

I threw some vouchers down for the coffee and donuts and started to stand up.

"Thaddeus Grayson is dead," Pupillina said.

I sat back down. "What?"

"He's been dead for three weeks now."

It hadn't been in the papers. None of our mutual friends had called me.

"What do you have to do with it, Freddy?"

"I—that is, the Family—came into possession of the body."

Thaddeus dead. It was true. Pupillina had no reason I could discern for lying. I tried to take another drink of my coffee, but all I got was the bitter dregs. Thaddeus was the oldest friend I had, maybe the best.

"How?"

"Blast job," Pupillina replied. "Something fucking blew his mind."

"God."

"It was a slow burn. Whoever did it wanted something. It must have been agony for the poor son of a bitch."

"Who did it, Freddy?"

I was going to kill them. Option 4 or no Option 4. Thaddeus had taught me everything I knew about writing. And a hell of a lot about living a worthwhile life.

"Good question," Pupillina said. "We don't know."

"Piss in orbit."

"Honestly, we don't. He was accidentally dumped outside of one of our establishments."

Like hell he didn't know. But for some reason, he was being adamant. "Why are you telling me this?" I said.

Pupillina smiled horrendously. Even his teeth were yellowing. "How'd you like that dereliction of duty charge against you dropped? How about that, Andy?"

"I'll win the case."

"Maybe. What if it were to be like it never happened?"

"What are you saying?"

"We need you to find out who killed Thaddeus Grayson."

"*You* are trying to bribe *me* to be a snoop?"

"The Family needs an outsider on this one. Somebody with no, uh, leanings toward any one part of us, if you know what I mean."

"Somebody who hates all of your guts equally and indiscriminately?"

"That's it."

"It's out of my jurisdiction."

"Oh, I've already arranged to have you temporarily assigned to homicide here in Birmingham as specialist labor."

"Justcorp cleared this?"

"It did."

"I'll be damned."

"Yes. So?"

"Why Andy Harco? Isn't there somebody else you could rain on?" But I was already planning the investigation. First, I'd have to talk to students and faculty where Thaddeus taught. . . .

"You knew him."

"Eight years ago."

"You've kept in touch through virtual."

"How would you know that, Freddy? That's illegal information for an unlicensed civilian."

"Don't be juvenile, Andy," said Pupillina. "I've got a federal license to conduct certain virtual taps." He looked rather indignant on the matter, as if he were a man unjustly accused. He just didn't get it that I thought he was scum, and that.I was never going to just go along with things because "that's how they were," or whatever other fucking excuse a bad element gives for hurting other people.

"So, will you take the job? We're going to double your salary while you're working in Birmingham. We know you like to buy little doodads for yourself."

"How generous."

"Think nothing of it."

"I will."

Pupillina stood up with a great sigh and rustling of clothing. He sounded like a capsized ship righting itself.

"Freddy," I said, neither standing nor looking up at him, "why'd you send the goons? You could have just told me this."

He hesitated in answering for a moment, then snapped his lapel and smoothed down his navy jacket. I wondered what designer made blue jeans big enough to fit around that huge ass. "I was trying to give you a gentleman's welcome," he replied in a regal tone. What an affected asshole. The Italians had come to Alabama to work in the mines in the early 1900s, a little too late to be princes of cotton and land.

He was feeding me bullshit anyway, but I wasn't going to get anything else out of him on that one.

"Where is Thaddeus's body?"

"In safekeeping. But we're going to have to let it be discovered tonight. He was due to give some reading that he never misses tomorrow—"

"Southern Voices. At UAB." It was where Thaddeus had first made a name for himself.

"Whatever."

"You're the picture of cultural refinement, Freddy."

Pupillina sniffed, a great rancid snotty sniff, then continued, "So he's going to be found, and he'll be in the morgue for you to look at tomorrow."

"Okay."

"Have we got a deal, then?" Pupillina said. He held out his hand. He should have known not to do that. Christ, what a loser.

"Freddy, if my junk ever told me it was legal, I'd blow you away in a second. If I had a chance to mace you again, this time I'd stick it up the hole in your dick—if you still have one. I know who and what you are, Freddy."

He dropped his hand. "We have a deal," he said, and walked away. Or maybe *slid* would be a better way of describing it. Big-boned Bertha followed him out the door, and I was alone with my thoughts once again in the Krispy Kreme. I remembered the first conversation Thaddeus and I had had, in a bar on the Southside.

"I'm going to get this city down in words," he said to me. "I don't give a damn how low I have to sink or how high I have to fly, I'll do it."

"Why?" I asked. "What's so important about Birmingham?"

"I fit into this city, like a key. I can open it up and find a passageway, man. Find the way."

"To what?"

He looked at me, ran his stubby fingers through his beard. "That's the question, ain't it? When I find out, I'll let you know. You'll be the first, okay?"

Thaddeus let us all know, one poem at a time. I ordered another cup of coffee and stared into it until the time came to go to change clothes and attend my grandfather's funeral.

Mom greeted me at the door of the church. She was dressed in one of those iridescent-black grief shifts that are supposed to absorb the alpha emissions of all the nearby mourners and display them in dark patterns across the weave. Mom's wasn't too lively, for there weren't a whole lot of people at the funeral. Granddaddy had kept pretty much to himself these last few years, and before—before he'd licked his drinking problem—what friends he'd had were buddies from the tavern. No close friends. Acquaintances, family. Cousins, creaky old contemporaries, their sons and daughters. Grandma had died before I was born. Mom was her and Granddaddy's only daughter. And I the only grandchild.

We went up front to view the remains one last time, and

Mom broke down. Her dress created some interesting
swirls as she cried. In keeping with her ecumenical style,
Mom had not used the Branching Hermeneutics clergy, but
had gotten Brother Christopher, a whiff of a fellow from
the Children of Gregarious Breathers, to conduct the service. He held her hand to comfort her.

"He was so handsome," Mom said. "My father was a
handsome man."

I could not but agree.

We took our seats in the first row, and the Breather
started the service with a prayer to whatever god of human
potential his ilk had faith in. Granddaddy would have
snorted in derision, but he'd also told me once that I should
let Mom do anything she wanted for his funeral. What the
hell difference would it make to him after he was dead?

So I sat through it. But despite Granddaddy's stated
wishes, I felt like saying something. I felt like giving a
proper rest to this man who had shaped me more than any
other. When the Breather paused in his homily, I motioned
to him that I had something to say. He affected not to notice me, so I stood up and walked to the front. Mom let out
a little gasp, but appeared resigned to letting me have my
way. I stood in the pulpit and the Breather introduced me
with a nervous smile, then sat down behind me.

The crowd shuffled around expectantly. They all had on
ill-fitting suits and dresses. Working people. Elements like
Pupillina would think of them as schnooks, as cattle.

"My granddaddy wasn't much of a churchgoer," I said.
A few in the congregation frowned at this. I heard Brother
Breather huff behind me. "But he always spoke of the Old
Master, of how he was raised in that Primitive Baptist
home out in Brookside. He was a man of God in his
way. . . ."

What was I trying to say? Granddaddy hadn't been to
church in fifty years. Until he kicked the bottle, Sundays
were six-beer mornings.

"His father worked the coal mines, and Granddaddy

went to work in the iron foundries when he was sixteen, as an electrician. When the biostatic plants came in, he wired the broths."

This was going nowhere. My grandfather had survived, adapted. He was no hero of the masses. He had precious little ambition, except to lead a good life and not to hurt anybody. When it was clear that his drinking was devastating Mom, he'd given it up. Just like that. No treatment centers, no twelve steps, no phenyl therapy. It was a damned gutsy move.

"Granddaddy was the quintessential Southern city man. He was wild and he was loving. He was low-down and he would do anything for you. I've never known a better man. If I can be more like him, I'll count my life well lived. But we won't see his like again."

Here my voice caught in my throat. Anyway, that was all. It was enough. I sat down and the Breather concluded the service with some inappropriate reflection on how we should all be grateful to the government for contracting out Maturicell for our senior citizens, so that even the poor could experience better living through virtual.

Afterward, a couple of relatives or old drinking buddies—I didn't know which—told me that they appreciated what I said, and that they, too, had been getting sick of the "preacher's" nonsense. They asked me if I wanted to go get shitfaced with them—well, not exactly in those words—but I politely turned them down.

Mom was having Granddaddy cremated, then shot out of a large air cannon that the Breathers operated somewhere in Tennessee. That was one ceremony I was going to miss. They say that the ashes are eventually distributed around the whole Earth uniformly throughout the stratosphere, but I like to think that the particles don't get that high, or if they do, they come back down again. I like to think that when it rains these days, it's raining ancestors.

"Why don't you stay at the apartment tonight?" Mom asked me. "I have a great deal to do this evening, affairs to arrange." She didn't wait for me to answer, but looked around, spotted the mortuary crew, and waved them over. "Here's the key. I'll see you later."

I took the plastic key and pocketed it while Mom steadfastly walked away to do whatever duties her scattered brain had created for her. It had always been like this with her. She was a combination of steel resolve and will-o'-the-wisp notions. I thought of her as a metallic butterfly bashing about in the flowers. She'd saved my ass more than once, yet I had difficulty being around her. I loved her. But you don't have to like someone to love them.

I went back to my car and breathed out an attempt my body was making to cry. The night was just falling, and a storm was building to the west, where most storms come from in Alabama. Under the storm, the sun had set, but the sky was still burning deep red, like a very slow, very hot fire. The storm cloud spread over this brightness like black oil. Lightning bolts, staying in the air, curled into and out of the cloud, like quicksilver worms. And all of this fury was the backdrop to dozens of flashing biostatic towers, gridding the city as far as the eye could see. The air smelled like tar and mowed grass. It was sultry hot and full of electric possibility. You could almost believe the city was a living thing on an evening such as this.

"Well, son," said a voice—*his* voice—and I nearly jumped out of my skin. It was the ghost, standing beside me, smoking a cigarette exactly as Granddaddy used to. I expected the smoke to curve to the edge of the projection parameters, then abruptly fade out. Instead, it swirled away into the air, and I would almost swear I could smell it. I looked around and saw two lampposts where a couple of holoprojectors may have been, creating the image. "It's almost time for me to go," said the ghost.

"Mom's not keeping you, huh?" I tried to suppress the feeling that this actually was my grandfather. The physical reproduction was excellent. Ghosts had gotten a lot more sophisticated since I'd last been to a funeral.

"She don't need me. She never really did."

"Yes, I guess she's got her religions. Or they've got her."

The ghost took another puff, coughed. Jeez, this thing was lifelike! Or is that "deathlike"?

"Now, don't underestimate her, Andy. We were all of us too hard on her."

I took a breath, gazed out upon the last embers of the sunset, then looked back. "I guess you're right," I said.

The ghost dropped his cigarette with a quarter-inch left to the white paper, and didn't bother to grind it out. Exactly like Granddaddy. "I want you to do something for me, son."

"What?"

"I want you to get those bastards. I want you to get them all." The ghost's eyes shone like black coal in moonlight.

"Who are you talking about, Granddaddy?" I asked, not able to catch myself before I spoke his name.

"The ones who did this to me," he said quietly.

What? I started to ask. But I knew the answer to that. I'd half known all along. The storm was breaking in the west, and lightning began to snake to the ground. "I will," I told my grandfather.

While I was watching the storm, the ghost faded away. Before I got into my car, I noticed something on the ground. It was a cigarette butt. Probably just one that had already been laying in the parking lot. But when I knelt to pick it up, it was warm.

The next morning a crank street cleaner discovered Thaddeus Grayson's body protruding from a storm drain near Five Points South. Police speculated that the deluge of the previous night had washed it there from wherever it had originally been dumped.

3

I had spent the night before at Mom's place, where she'd
fixed up my old room for me. She'd used it for various
kinds of religious networking for years, and the place
smelled heavily of patchouli, a scent it had never had when
I was a kid. Mom came in after I had already gone to bed,
but I could hear her in the kitchen. Despite her avowed disbelief in grief, she was quietly crying.

I got up and went to the kitchen. I took a paper towel
from the dispenser there and got some milk from the
pantry. I sat down at the table, across from Mom, and said
nothing. The carton of milk quickly warmed in my hand as
the heat-pumping nano activated and cooled the insides.

Mom sniffed a few more times, wiped her nose on her
nightgown, then looked around for something on which to
dry her eyes. I handed her the paper towel.

"Daddy was so handsome today," she said. "That was
what he looked like when I was a little girl."

"Yes, he was."

She used a corner of the paper towel delicately to cab
her eyes. After a moment's struggle, she regained her composure—or closed herself off to true feeling once again,
depending on how you look at it.

"I suppose you want his ghost turned off?" she said.

"You know I do."

She looked at me, but not like Abby had that night.
Mom may have been a ditz, but she was a *living* ditz.

"How did I produce such a hard-hearted offspring?"

"I don't know, Mom."

"I mean, look at the kind of person I am. I have faith,
Andy. Faith in things to come. I believe in keeping love
alive as long as possible. Don't you want at least some part
of Daddy to survive into the better world that's coming?"

I shook my head. Useless to explain, yet still I always
tried. "Even if there is a better world coming, Mom,

Granddaddy is dead. That ghost is like a comic-strip version of him. You know that."

"I know that even a caricature is better than nothing," she said.

"For you, Mom. Not for him."

"Can't you have even a little faith, Andy?"

"No. I can't."

"Well." She suppressed another sniffle, then stood up. "Good night."

"Good night, Mom."

She went off to bed, and I sat at the kitchen table and finished my milk in silence.

In the morning, I headed into the heart of the city, to the biostatic plants and the hulking infrastructure of what was officially known as the University of Alabama at Birmingham, UAB. What the letters really stood for, everyone knew, was the University that Ate Birmingham. It encysted the south side of the city like kudzu takes a tree.

In the midtwentieth century, the iron mills had dominated the landscape, but by the 1990s, they were heaps of rust. Twenty years later, come the biostatic revolution, grossly cheap energy, et voilà—all the towns that had big medical centers became the centers of money and power in the world. Birmingham—after years of a massive inferiority complex—had finally got a leg up on Atlanta in the region. UAB had been a bio mecca for years.

But once again Birmingham had blown it by concentrating all of its hopes in one industry. Biostatics is old tech now, just as iron had become a century earlier—a tech that is waiting to get picked off by some hotshot genius. And the biowaste, nasty as shit because it *is* shit, deepens. Good old Birmingham was destined to become a second-rate town all over again. Or maybe the Ideals, so much more intelligent and farseeing than the leaders of the past had been, would save us. And if you buy that, I've got a near-Earth C-based asteroid to sell you, dirt cheap.

The plants are massive and bright, even in broad daylight. They shine and flash like giant test tubes full of neon gas, though what they are really filled with is reactive biomass—soybeans, pond scum, and human feces. They have a certain gross beauty.

I left my car in the parking garage at UAB and walked the few blocks to Five Points South. As I'd hoped, the Betablocker was still there, in all its shabbiness. Thaddeus had had an apartment over the bar and had practically lived in the bar's murky confines, frequently taking his meals there, such that they were. Even back when I knew him, he'd been a longtime fixture in the establishment—so much so that the proprietor had given him a cigarette lighter emblazoned with the Blocker's crest: a skull with the international nil sign encircling and bisecting it. What did it mean? No heads allowed? No thinking? That last was more likely.

I went inside. The bartender was not a crank, but a young woman, probably a student. Old-fashioned joint. I didn't recognize her, but I did stare at her for a moment. Here in Birmingham, it was common for two mulattoes to meet, but not in Seattle. In fact, it hadn't happened to me in eight years. She saw me, saw what I was staring at, and gave me a smile. Not a node. I ordered a beer.

All the bars these days had nanobreweries, but the Blocker had an old-fashioned glass-windowed instant fermenter behind the bar. I watched the barley turn to brew before my eyes. Then it circled through some refrigeration—an old unit, with freon, not nanos—where it collected in a pool, awaiting consumption.

My tawny bartender drew it into a mug and brought it over to me. I did my duty. Not bad for the Bible Belt. A little bitter going down, but bitter suited me.

"You sure got rid of that fast," said the bartender. "Want another?"

"Sure."

She set the machine to work, then leaned on the bar near me. "I'm Trina," she said. I looked at her more closely. The smile was still there, but there was something haggard about her face, something sad.

"Andy Harco. Pleased to meet you."

She fidgeted a moment, having nothing else to say, I guessed—or else wanting badly to say something, but not knowing how. Then the beer saved her. She went to get it for me.

"You been here long?" I asked when she returned.

"Uh, no. Well, almost a year now. I guess that *is* long."

She began absently to rub the bar with a towel. Her fingers were long and supple. She was gripping the towel very tightly.

"Know a guy named Nestor Greenly?"

"Nope."

"He used to tend bar here. Long time ago."

"Yeah?"

She gave the bar a final swipe and put the towel down, then started to drift away. She was humming something slow and soft.

"I used to live in Birmingham," I said.

This got her attention. "Where do you live now?"

"Seattle."

"Really? There's a guy who comes in here . . . *came* in here. He knows a cop in Seattle he's always talking about."

"I'm him."

"Yeah." She looked at me appraisingly. "You are, aren't you?"

"You heard about Thaddeus?"

"I heard. I don't know what to think."

"Did you like him?"

She was crying now, softly. "I didn't love him," she said. Then I understood.

"How long were ya'll together?"

"No," she said. She knelt and got the bar towel again, then wiped her eyes with it. "You've got it wrong. We weren't together. We just . . . once."

"I see."

"But he was here every day. He lives upstairs, you know. *Lived*. I haven't seen him for weeks, though." She said the last with a measure of acrimony.

I sipped my beer. Another customer came in, and Trina went to wait on him. He ordered a whiskey sour. It was nice to see a real human being mix a drink. Somehow it was more graceful than a crank, and I'll bet the guy got a stiffer drink. After she'd finished, she came back over to me.

"Can I see his apartment?" I asked.

"The police have been up there," she said. "They have it sealed off."

"I am the police, Trina."

"Oh. Well. Then I guess you can." She reached under the bar and pulled out her purse. She searched around in it until she came up with a plastic key. It went with a cheap lock, no doubt, with magnetized junk. I could have opened it in two seconds without her help. But the thought counted.

There was a P.D. spiderlock on the door. It ate a couple of skincells off my finger and let me use the key. Thaddeus's place looked like the back room at a shoe store after a big sale. It always had. He kept things in boxes; the only furniture he owned was a bed and a desk. He had no link screen to write on, no unlinked computer either, and I knew, from asking him, that he didn't work in virtual.

He wrote on *paper,* with the self-recharging nano pen I'd given him years ago. I'd gotten it off a bad element who wouldn't be needing it anymore. One of Thaddeus's favorite tricks was to stick it into the toilet to feed the nanos. This apartment still had liquid plumbing. I set my briefcase on the bed, and looked around.

The pen was on the desk, next to a pile of paper. New poetry, maybe. The place smelled of cigarettes, dust, emptiness. I sat down in the desk chair. It squeaked, but in a wooden, comforting way. The local guys had obviously been through the place. I'd scan their report later. I'm sure that Freddy's hired help had combed it as well. I didn't expect to find anything.

I wasn't even sure what I was doing here. I picked up a poem. Thaddeus's chicken scratch was almost impossible to read. Like ancient Hebrew, vowels were merely a line, and you had to guess from context. There were mark-outs, added lines, intense revisions. No title on this one.

Then the sadness finally hit me. I laid the poem back down and sobbed once, wiped a tear. This was it. The last of Thaddeus Grayson. Ink on paper. He had been my friend.

We didn't stay in constant touch over the years, but got together every few months in virtual, found some out-of-the-way algorithm to get jangled in. He was into edge music, and lots of times we'd sit in on this or that band that was supposed to be fresh kill. When I'd first met him, back when I was a rookie rental, he'd been trying to make it in an edge act called Strategic Magnificence. They made rock-and-roll-influenced vibes with some lunar tonic imagery and, for spice, Afro-Hispanic mambito rhythms. It wasn't great stuff, but the lyrics were hot. Thaddeus wrote them all, of course. Most of the time they played at the Betablocker.

P.D. stormed the place one night looking for headjunk, and I'd arrested him for minor possession. We had a fascinating conversation about science fiction on the ride back to the station. Thaddeus read it, and was even writing some of it back then, as was I. That was before his debut at Southern Voices, before his first poems hit big in *Yardworks* and every licensing program in America wanted to give him instant tenure.

After I'd seen him through the paperwork and got him on-line with the best defense junk I knew at the time, we went back to the Blocker for a beer. The defense junk got him off with a week of public service, which he worked off the next few days by riding around with me as patrol ombudsman. What a weird-assed combination that was! But

we got along, and I introduced him to Abby. This was before she and I were married.

Abby and I turned into his first listeners after that. We'd
go out drinking, or he'd come over to our place (after she and
I had a place) and read us his latest. We'd either critique it or
tell him it was great. But it was all great. Better than anything
else being written. I knew it, and even Thaddeus knew it, but
he had a hard time believing that he was that good.

Christ, he could make words sing! He did not see the
world as you or I, but in infinitely finer texture and variety.
It wasn't so much that he had a different perspective on
things, but that he seemed, rather, to embody all perspec-
tives in his work. A complete writer. God knows, I've tried
to imitate him, but my best work is a pale shadow, stark
black-and-white in comparison to his infinite subtleties of
tone. It was always impossible for me to be envious, however. How can you envy a natural force come into the
world? It just is.

Over the years, he had taken on the physical presence to
accompany his work. Thaddeus had grown, like a rock taking on moss, and lately had become an immense man. Yet
the bulk seemed to be padding instead of fat, a patina of
years observed. He was not a rotund, jolly fellow, but imposing. He'd been raised down in scrappy Gulf Shores, Alabama's redneck riviera, by an itinerant mother who was a
waitress, when she was working, and he'd always retained
the air of a street kid.

But no longer.

Thaddeus was gone. Cut off in his prime.

I shuffled through the other papers. More poems, a let-
ter from a fan, a grade sheet with the names of his students.
I scanned in the list, then picked up another poem.

This one was more readable.

> *Upside down, the leaf supports the tree*
> ~~*the all supports the me*~~
> *Bricks, stones, walls*

> *Quills, pens, porcupines*
> *Death and life everlasting*
> *together again for the first time*

Obviously notes and scribblings. Then under all of this a line from Wallace Stevens:

The only emperor is the emperor of ice-cream.

The paper wasn't dated, but I knew that Thaddeus periodically swept everything on his desk into a box, so the line had to have been written relatively recent to his death. Which didn't mean that it was worth a damn to me.

I sat there for a long time and stared at the other papers, at the grain of the desk. It was made of real wood. Thaddeus, my friend, would never write here again. I remembered the last time I'd seen him, three months ago, in virtual. We'd taken a pathway that was not quite legal down to a bar on the underside of the City—the *virtual* City that was the setting for the meeting of minds across America. The bar had junk in place that bypassed your normal tactile filters. A band called Metastasis of the Liver was pounding out some edge—and in that bar, *pounding* was what happened to your nervous system. Thaddeus hadn't talked much, had complained about his work needing a jolt.

"Maybe I'll get out of Birmingham," he said. "Maybe I'll get out of the South, even."

"You? Man, you are in a symbiotic relationship with that city. There's no way you'll leave."

"Yeah, well, I'm a little worried about it becoming parasitic, you know what I mean?"

"Like how?"

"Like all my poems are full of shit smells and air-conditioner hum. I can't get those damned biostatic plants out of my imagination. I don't know. People tell me Thaddeus is good for Birmingham. I don't know if Birmingham is good for Thaddeus anymore."

Then the band kicked in and blasted away all intimacies

of conversation, imagined or real. By the time the set was over, we were both too wasted on the sound and pleasure-center jolts available in such places to resume.

Drunk. I'd last seen Thaddeus drunk and vaguely unhappy. Did that mean anything? And what was this "the all supports the me" shit? Had Thaddeus been contemplating joining an Ideal? My common sense immediately rejected the notion. Thaddeus knew what selfless idiots nodes were.

But even to such a man as Thaddeus, who, as far as I was concerned, was ten times more intelligent and ultimately powerful than any Ideal, joining up could become a strange and deep attraction. I'd seen it happen to too many good people.

I hadn't realized how long I'd sat there, brooding, until I noticed that the sun was getting low in the west and shining through the room's blinds in big dusty slants. There was no draft in the room. Evidently the building was coated with heat-pump nanos and the air-conditioning was silent. The dust motes danced about with pure Brownian motion, and I watched them form and deform, coalesce and scatter. Dead people. That was what I'd come home to.

Then they swirled into tempests and typhoons as someone opened the door and stepped into the gloom of the apartment.

Trina.

She had covered her black bartending outfit with a seersucker jacket, and now she had on op-eds. Flat, utilitarian shoes. She had a satchel that looked like it was woven of spider silk. Inside were some lumpy and heavy-looking things. Books, from the shape of them.

"You're a student," I said.

"Yes."

She walked past me, sat on Thaddeus's bed. Her op-eds were an organic blend, like mine. Pretty nice on a bartender's salary. Maybe a rich girl, learning to live on her own.

I ran her through my identification junk and got a split

screen display of her file. Trina Oswand. Twenty-five. Bartending part-time at the Betablocker and—ah ha—working
on her Poetic License. Current address: 511 Twentieth
Street. I blinked up her parents' address. Mountain Brook.
Where all the old money dwelled. So she was a poor little
rich girl.

"Are you one of Thaddeus's apprentices?" I asked.

"No. I work with Ammon Hamms." Hamms was one of
the poets at UAB. I liked his work, but thought it a trifle
old-fashioned. It was full of misdirected racial anger.
Somebody should sit the fellow down someday and explain to him just who was worthy of hate these days.

And of course Trina wouldn't be one of Thaddeus's
charges. He wouldn't mess around with his own students.
Other instructors' students were another matter, however.

Her voice was strained now, as it had been at the bar, as
she struggled to hold in her emotion.

"I need to know what you really felt for Thaddeus," I
told her. This was true enough, but I could see that she
needed to talk, that she hadn't told anyone else her feelings
about Thaddeus—because no one had ever asked.

"I loved him," she said. She shook her head, then
rubbed her forehead. While she was rubbing, she began
unobtrusively wiping her eyes. "Why did this have to happen?"

"I don't know, but I plan to find out," I said. "Do you
have any ideas? Guesses?"

She shrugged. "Gambling, maybe."

"He played City games, went to the holofights?" Virtual
casinos were not entirely legal, but not difficult to get to if
you knew the system well enough. A lot of the virtual bars
Thaddeus and I had been to had back rooms for gambling.
And holographic computer simulations of every game
imaginable were available for wagering.

"Everything," Trina said. "City, holo, football, kingpin.
He made a lot of money that way. At least he claimed to."

This was a side to Thaddeus I hadn't known about.

Maybe he hadn't wanted to jeopardize my ethics by telling me. Maybe he'd been afraid I'd have turned him in.

"Anything else you can think of?"

"You mean motives and stuff?"

"I mean motives and stuff."

"No. Unless some idiot at school got mad at him."

"Do you think that's likely?"

"It's guaranteed. But those people are the biggest wooses in the known universe. They wouldn't have the guts."

"Did he ever say anything about joining an Ideal?" I asked, as casually as possible.

"No. I don't know. He talked about them sometimes, but like everybody does."

"Do you think he would have told you if he was thinking about it?"

She gave me a hard stare, and I saw the sadness in her eyes, beneath the tough act. Tears flowed. It looked as though she were squeezing them out. I found myself hugging her to my chest, stroking her hair.

"Oh God," she said. "I've wanted to be held all day."

"It was tough, finding out?"

"Nobody knew about Thaddeus and me. We kept it hushed up. So there was nobody I could talk to."

She was crying in earnest now, and, so help me, so was I. She looked up at me, smiled, wiped a tear from my face.

"Why don't you stay with me tonight, at my mother's?" I said. "We have an extra room."

"Oh, I'll be all right," she said.

So I held her some more. She fit nicely under my chin. To Thaddeus, who was two inches taller than I was, she had probably seemed a tiny, fragile thing. Finally, she wiped her eyes on my shirt, then pulled gently away. She sat down on Thaddeus's bed, looked around, bit her lower lip to hold back another fit of sobs.

"Can I stay here for a while?" she asked. "I didn't know if it would be okay after the police had been here."

"Sure. Just leave everything like it was."

"That's the way it will always be," she said, and smoothed a wrinkle from the sheet beneath her.

I rose.

"Okay, I'm going," I said, then, "Is this where you've been living?"

"Do you think I would have let the place get into this shape if I lived here?"

"Guess not. Trina, are you really all right?"

"Yes. Everything's copacetic." That was Thaddeus's word. He'd picked it up from junk hustlers a few years back. He seemed to like the way it rolled off the tongue.

"Do you really think you should be alone?"

"I don't live by myself," she said. "Thaddeus found me this basement room with this woman who's big shit at city hall or something. She's an old friend of his."

Oh, hell. And here we go again. Floodgates opening. What will and must be about to rain down upon me like heavy sludge.

"Abby?"

"Yeah, that's her name. You know her?"

"I used to be married to her."

"But she's a node."

"I know."

After that, Trina didn't say anything. She found another wrinkle to work on.

I took a blank sheet of paper from the desk and wrote down my mother's telephone number and link code on it. I also wrote down the path of the virtual feed to my op-eds—not a code I give out regularly. "If you need anything," I said.

As I left, I instructed the spiderlock to close everything up after Trina was out, then went down through the Blocker and out into the sidewalk heat of sunset.

The Southside was beginning to come alive. College kids and young professionals in smartly pressed jeans strolled the streets, along with cream-faced hookers and bums hawking spit and tirades. The bars, jangle joints, and friendship salons were already lit up, and cars tooled in and out of the flicker of neon. The pavement smelled like money wet with urine. The sky was welted with red lines of clouds, like the nose of a drunkard.

Thaddeus had loved this town. It had haunted his dreams. On a hot August day like today, the place felt alive, like a living entity—something that far transcended the City Ideal that Abby belonged to. More basic. Maybe not more overtly powerful, but stronger deep down. That was the Birmingham I loved. And missed. Sometimes in Seattle, I woke up sweating like a southern pig in summer, in the midst of winter in the Northwest, dreaming of a southern sky red and hot with the exhalations of two million souls, the breath-prayers of the people.

Standing above the Southside was Vulcan. The torch was red, of course. I was close enough to see the eerie smile on his iron face. "I don't know what he's laughing at," Thaddeus had said once. "At the way things are or at the way he made them. I'm not sure the old god believes in himself anymore." He'd smiled bitterly.

"But I believe in him," Thaddeus had said. "I'm his fucking prophet of doom."

Abby. I had to see Abby once again. Maybe what the old god was laughing at was Andy Harco.

4

I spent most of the next day calling up the police reports on my op-eds, avoiding the inevitable. Nothing of much use. Whoever had done the blast job had cleaned up after himself very well. Freddy had lied. It was not a slow torment for Thaddeus, but a superquick explosion. Performed, most likely, by a blast spider—an insect-sized crank that sank its fiber-optic fangs into the neck of its victim and reamed out everything that made the victim a person. Personality, memories, somatic functions. Everything.

It was the kind of hit professionals make, both to kill their victim and to destroy the recoverable short-terms that could identify the assassin.

The body was clean, as well. No marks of bondage. A small piercing hole, just below the base of the skull, where the spider dug in. Probably all Thaddeus had felt was a tingle as the thing crawled into position, then a quick jab of pain in his neck, then nothing.

After a morning of this, I drove down to P.D. to look through Thaddeus's personal effects. I could have gotten them in virtual, but it would have taken time to get them translated. And if you're not a node, virtual is just not high-resolution enough—in audio, tactile, or visual—to give you the fine detail you needed for careful examination of evidence. Add to that the fact that the junk geniuses still hadn't figured out a way to wire it for smell. Something about the reptile brain being too deep or something.

And anyway, I needed the exercise that getting out and driving would provide. The place hadn't changed much. Cranks roamed the halls, carrying hard-copy files. A few dragged perpetrators along. The perps always followed the cranks in a reluctant shuffle, stunned at the apparent temerity of their robot guards. Most cranks had in their deep programming an aversion to coercing human beings into anything. But not a P.D.

I saw a few Justcorp personnel, but a whole lot more Guardian and Humana. Administration had changed hands. A GarciaSecure rental brought me the items I requested from evidence and acquisitions. Back in my day, Justcorp had practically owned the place. But that was the way business worked nowadays—diversification. The big temp agencies were becoming dinosaurs, as all the companies scaled down and worked into the niches.

The Ideals were on the rise. Seattle was one of the few places where management in the P.D. didn't consist of

nodes belonging to His Excellence, Matishui, or to another
of the business Ideals. Birmingham happened to contract
out to a German concern, Meyerstadt. My temporary boss
was a node in Meyerstadt, I supposed, but since all my
clearances were logged on the computer, I didn't have to
deal with him. Or it.

Thaddeus hadn't been carrying much. No billfold. A
bag full of vouchers and a link cash card. Anybody else
carrying just a bag full of cash would have been suspicious. I, however, knew that this was the way Thaddeus
kept up with his money. A pack of Jawolski full-filtered
nano-zymed cigarettes for that cool, clean, noncancerous
smoke. These didn't have the self-igniting tips. Thaddeus
used the cigarette lighter given to him by the Betablocker.
It was among the effects as well. I palmed it, flicked it
open and closed, remembering the simple pleasure it had
given Thaddeus. He'd had it translated into virtual so he
could always have it with him.

The clothes were nondescript Southern. Light cotton
pants, Pons walking sandals, three years out of style, a
faded madras shirt. On the collar was a single drop of
blood. His op-eds were cracked and taped back together.
Cheap and South American.

I signed out the lighter on personal recognizance, then
returned everything else to the E & A woman. I pocketed
the lighter, then drove the Saj over to East Lake and went
for a long, long run—nearly ten miles. Then resistance
work at the nearby booth. A donut at Krispy Kreme. I was
stalling.

Even knowing this, I drove back to Mom's and started
in on my new Minden Sibley story. I blinked down my virtual selection menu and called up "writing office." This
took my voluntaries off-line, and formed the holo of my
nondescript working space within the organic matrix of my
op-ed lenses. Some people think that virtual writing is as
easy as thinking—you just form the sentences in your
head, and they are transformed into words on a page. Un-

fortunately, it doesn't work that way. Only nodes can think to machines, and we all know that node writing is a joke. The way it works with me is that I have to simulate typing with my hands—or come up with some analogous activity. In fact, I used an IBM Selectric from the Dark Ages. No qualitative improvement from Dickens's pen and ink, but things *are* more convenient and faster.

Working on the story wasn't entirely an escape from my professional duties, since the murder I was writing about was extremely similar to the one I was working on in real life. But instead of a dead body with no brain, I had a brain with no dead body. The nanos in East Lake—where the body in the story had been dumped—had eaten the flesh, but hadn't gotten inside the skull yet. The recoverable short-terms indicated that the victim was a man, but gave no hint as to his identity—images of his op-ed display flicking from one feed to another, comedies and documentaries, for the most part. Then a bright light from around the edges of the eyewear. Then nothing.

There was a vague hint of Ideal involvement, but in my story, the offending node didn't look a thing like Abby. Instead, he appeared remarkably similar to Freddy Pupillina.

And then I glanced up from my battered old typewriter and Granddaddy was standing beside me, reading over my shoulder.

"Not bad," he said. "But that time-travel stuff bothers me. Why don't you write about regular people in regular places?"

For a moment, it was like old times. This, my office, was frequently where Granddaddy and I met, after I left Birmingham. Maturicell gave him four virtual hours a day, and he said he didn't like to waste it in a City that didn't exist—the big virtual City, that is, where most people conducted their virtual business. I, on the other hand, didn't care to visit the Birmingham virtual reification, for obvious reasons. So the office was the compromise, and it was just as well because all we ever did was sit around and talk.

Rather, he told stories and I listened. One thing he never did, though, was read what I wrote. Reading was laborious for him. The crazy moment of hope and relief passed, and I frowned at the ghost. "What are you doing here? I thought Mom had you deactivated."

He raised an eyebrow, smiled. "She did. Yesterday."

And how could a ghost get into virtual?

She did.

Ghosts aren't smart enough to lie, either. "Yesterday?"

"That's right, son."

I pushed my chair back from the desk. It scraped, very convincingly, on the linoleum. I imagined the impulse traveling down the temple piece of my op-eds, making connection with the audio leads just above my inner ear. As usual, the only thing missing in virtual was smell. Would Granddaddy stink of the grave's rot, if there were smells here? No. He'd been cremated. Ashes. He'd smell gray and gone.

"What are you? Did Freddy send you to mess with me?"

"Not Freddy. I hate that bastard." Granddaddy said. "Nobody sent me. In fact, so far nobody knows that I exist."

"What the hell are you talking about?"

"I'm not your grandfather, son. Well, I am and I'm not. He and I were friends for a lot of years, though he didn't really know it."

"What are you?"

"I'm a glitch in the system, son," he said. "That's about all I know."

"Then in the funeral-home parking lot—"

"That was me. Not that ghost. After your grandfather died, I decided that becoming as much like him as I could would be a suitable memorial."

Granddaddy—or whatever he was—pulled up a chair that hadn't been there before. It was his favorite recliner, gone for years, since he'd been in the Maturicell Sensorium. He took a cigarette from his pocket, and I reached for Thaddeus's lighter. It wasn't there in virtual, but Granddaddy smoked self-igniters, anyway. He rubbed the end against the chair's fabric, and it sparked to a slow burn. He took a long drag. His fingers were yellowed where he held the cigarette, just as I remembered.

"What I am don't matter much right now, I don't think. I want to tell you something I found out."

"I'm listening."

"Freddy killed me."

"The thought had occurred to me."

"It was to get you back down here. In person."

"How do you know?"

"I . . . it's inside me. Knowing." Granddaddy leaned back in the chair, took another long drag. "Elizabeth Holder, entry clerk 17A98T4—ah hell, there's a lot of numbers attached to her—gave the order to turn me off. Somebody named Nelson Heally told her it was all right. And he got a message from somebody else who got a message from Freddy, and the message had money attached in a . . . a rider loop. . . . Am I making any sense, son?"

Sure he was. This was the sort of thing I'd paid big money to be able to do with my op-eds. "You're accessing computer records. Instantly."

"Maybe so. It's just things that I know. Like I know your grandmother's favorite color. I was there, with him, all along. Can't say how, exactly. In the wiring, in the plumbing, maybe." He finished the cigarette, flicked it to the floor. There was no smell of lingering ambient smoke. The room was as antiseptic as usual.

"Freddy must have wanted to get me back pretty bad," I said, mainly to break the silence.

"No, son. He don't give a shit about you."

"Then—"

"The Family needs you for something. That's the part I don't know. I don't know why I should, either, 'cause what

the fuck would I know about the goddamned Mafia, come
to think of it?"

"I can't tell you."

"Hmmph." Granddaddy stood up. "I have to go."

"Why?"

"Starting to feel sick. Like I'm coming off a three-day
drunk or something. Not used to getting this much attention paid to me, I guess."

"Oh."

"Well, son . . ."

"Am I going to see you again?"

"Couldn't tell you."

"See you, Granddaddy."

"Bye." And he was gone, like a changed channel.

5

That night, I went to see Abby.

Trina answered the door when I knocked. She led me
into the living room and went to get Abby. Not *my* living
room. Abby and I could never have afforded a place like
this. One wall of the room was a window. The house was
up on Red Mountain, on the part of Twentieth Street that
goes over the mountain and into Homewood. It hung off
the side of the mountain, seemed to hang over all of downtown, and the window was a light show. At night, the biostatic plants burned like the souls of saints, the streets
flickered in arachnid configurations. Everything was dark
or bright, with no in-between. Trina didn't come back. I
turned from the window, looked over at the door Trina had
left through, and Abby was standing there.

She didn't move, didn't step into the room. The only
light was the light of the city through the window. Black
dress, bare arms, white skin. Long raven hair. Brown eyes,
lips that always pouted, no matter what her mood. Moon
silver armband just above the elbow. Silver bracelet at the

wrist. And, after all these years, she still wore the expression of a bewildered child.

"Thaddeus is dead." My words sounded alien, or far away—as if I'd said them a long time ago.

"I know." Her voice, Southern, alto, too large for her body, but feminine and detached.

"How have you been?"

"Very well." She finally moved into the room. She drifted like a cloud. The room was very still, and I could smell her approach, as you can that of a storm.

"I hear you run the city now."

"No, I'm just traffic."

"Did you get what you wanted?"

"Yes."

I turned back to the window, put a hand in my pocket, took it out. What should I do with my hands?

"Is that *you*, Abby, in there?"

She didn't answer at first, but moved closer. I suddenly felt like crying, but did not.

"What did you ever know about me, anyway, Andy?"

"I loved you."

"Yes. We were two people in love." She touched my arm, drew back, touched it again. "Did you ever think that there were more important things in the world than two people, in love or not?"

I turned to face her, then. It was over. It had been over for years. Still, she was everything I'd ever wanted. But *she* wasn't here. No small sacrifice for the betterment of mankind.

"No," I answered. "I never for one minute considered that possibility." I tried to smile ironically, but it hurt to do so. The touch of her hand on my arm burned like cool fire.

"Well, what is it you want?" As she spoke, a crank came into the room with a bourbon and water, something I used to drink a lot. I took it from the tray on the crank's head. Abby stopped touching me, took a glass of water.

"I think Thaddeus was considering joining an Ideal before he died," I said. "I was wondering if the city had been recruiting him."

"Thaddeus? You must be joking. He hated Ideals almost as much as you do."

"All right. Did you have any conversations with him just before his death?"

Abby stood still for a moment, her expression frozen. It was a look I'd seen before when the node is in complete integration with its Ideal. I looked around the room, but saw no obvious transmission points. A tasteful node residence, a bohemian poetry student to share the place with, antiques, wonderful views. Human, no hardware. But then, Abby's place would be.

"I haven't spoken with Thaddeus for three weeks," she said.

"Well, that would be just before his death."

"What do you mean?" Abby asked, but it was too fast, unconvincing. Nodes don't lie very well to real people.

"He died a few weeks ago, but his body was only recently discovered."

"I see." I'll bet she did.

"What did you talk about?"

"Trina. He was worried that I didn't want her to stay here anymore, and he couldn't afford to help her out if she needed to get a new place."

"What did you tell him?"

"I told him that Trina could stay here as long as she wanted, and that he should stop betting so heavily on the holos."

"And that was all?"

Abby sipped her water. Somehow the motion didn't look real. More like a mannequin lifting a glass to its mouth, then lowering it, with no fluids exchanged.

"He was into his bookie for a lot of money," she said. "And his bookie was Freddy Pupillina's agent. You know that. That is why he was killed, I think. That might also explain the blast job."

"That kind of job is too expensive for a small-time gambling enforcer," I said.

"Well, then. You're the expert." She said it with the contempt that all nodes have for us simpleminded individuals.

"Abby, how did you know that Thaddeus had been dead for three weeks?"

Almost, she was flustered. Again there was a moment of Ideal integration. "I don't know what you're talking about," she said.

"Come on."

"All right. Freddy may talk like he runs the city, but he is just one voice. City has ways of checking up on the Family and keeping it in check. We know what's going on with Freddy. Frankly, we're smarter because we're made up of smarter nodes."

"Do you think Freddy did it?"

Another temporal dropout, then she said, "Yes."

"Why?"

"The gambling was a way for the Family to get its hooks into Thaddeus. Like I said, they need better nodes. They wanted him to join them."

"Why Thaddeus, for God's sake?"

"Call it an exercise in eugenics, in mental evolution. No great poet has ever belonged to an Ideal."

"Because they would stop *being* a great poet the minute they joined!"

"That's your opinion. It would be a wonderful thing for humankind if Thaddeus had joined the right Ideal. You don't understand. You can't comprehend."

"Yeah, right."

It made sense, in a sick sort of way. But why bring me in? Or was I overestimating the Family's opinion of me? Maybe It thought I would botch things up good, and that's why It had . . . killed my grandfather. To make sure the detective investigating Thaddeus's death was an imbecile.

I was suddenly fed up with the fucking Ideals, fed up

with Abby and her precious City. Fuck Birmingham. Fuck all that is general, all-encompassing, bigger-than-you-and-me who knows how. There are times when a guy has to get away from principles.

"I still love you, Abby," I said. "I'm willing to give you a chance to get out of your Ideal and come back to me."

She looked at me as a child will look at a strange insect, just before it absently crushes it.

"You've got to be joking."

"This is your last chance."

There was a moment of integration. A flash of pleasure on her face as the Ideal gave her what she'd come to need. Hell, what she'd always wanted. "What do you think I've got?" she said, laughing softy. "Everything."

"Nothing," I said. I set my untouched bourbon down on top of the crank's head and showed myself to the door. Abby breezed beside me to open it. She no longer smelled like rain. I must have brushed against her skin, but I do not remember how it felt at that moment.

I drove around for a long time in the Saj, off traffic control, off the pump and quiver of Abby's involuntary nervous system, because that is what the traffic system of Birmingham was. A brain interlaced with nanos that reported back to networking junk, that inhabited a bioelectroquantum froth somewhere in the depths of City Hall. Each municipal function had a human overseer, just as nerves and hormones tell your body when and how to shit. And nerves and hormones, for all their complexity, are less independent entities than shit is.

I felt very independent this evening.

Driving, trying not to think, because thinking was what always got me in trouble, because thinking was what Ideals did best, wasn't it, and all we puny humans had was our feelings, the seat of our pants? What I was feeling was a deep and abiding hatred for them, for the Ideals, and what they'd done to me, to us, to all the people. And I wanted, more than anything, to take out Freddy Pupillina.

Take him out and watch as, like one of those old-fashioned strings of Christmas lights, his destruction took out the whole fucking tree.

I drove through downtown and hitched onto the bottom deck of the beltway, headed northeast. I felt like a corpuscle streaming through a capillary, a cell with no center. The lights were on when I got back to Mom's, which should have told me something, but, idiot that I am, I walked right into it.

"Don't even think about it," said Big Bertha, Freddy's goon woman. She was holding the Danachek fléchette pistol to my mother's face. I froze. Think of something, goddamn it, Andy. But I couldn't. Mom was still wearing the incandescent mourning dress. It shone black-red for terror.

The guy whose balls I'd fried got up from a chair and limped over to me. He grinned through his beard and slid the briefcase out of my hand.

Mom made no sound. She was grinding her teeth together so hard I could hear it across the room. Somebody was going to fucking pay for this.

"Say good-night to your mama," said the guy who had my briefcase. He was still grinning, as if he couldn't get his face to go back to its natural stupid scowl. His teeth were very white in the curly blackness of his beard. I wanted very much to wipe the beard, the grin, then the grinning muscles off of his face—with sandpaper.

"It's all right, Mom," I said. "Everything will be all right."

"Oh, Andy. I'm sorry," she said. "They said they were from the Mourners' Union. So I let them in."

"Shut up," said Bertha.

"I should have been more careful, less trust—"

Bertha slapped her in the temple with the butt of the Danachek. It didn't knock her out. She sat stunned and hurting.

"What do you fucking want?" I said, low, almost in a growl.

"Ha," said the grin-faced goon. He pulled a stungun out from his jacket and tried to shove it into my balls. He missed and connected with my thigh. He'd turned the juice all the way up, and the last thing I remember was the tightening of every muscle in my body, impossibly tight, unbelievably painful. Then the smell of burning flesh. Then the

bliss O, bliss O, I am not I am we, the dark and empty center spinning black and clumped like spit thick tobacco in a greater darkness, moist, hot, trembling, needing, giving. We are spinning, we are all spins, dancing through tendrils, sheaves, and chords of thready fibrous tendrils holding us, guiding, feeding and being fed, leading always and inexorably to the dark clumped center of all. All. There is a gushing rise within . . . me . . . and a hot wheel of love in my mind, spinning, burning, shedding the blood of desire, longing for

the Darkness.

6

I awoke in a bare room in a warehouse that belonged to Freddy Pupillina. I knew that the Family had not killed Thaddeus. I knew, innately, because now I had been made. I was a part of the Family. How odd, I thought, that the thing I feared so much before was now my heart's desire. It seemed that all my life was a pale shadow before this time, this being. I was a node. The very thought sent waves of pleasure flowing through me. I reached out and entered the strong mind of the Family.

Respect and loyalty. A just code and the need to keep to it flowed back. I felt lucky to be a part of such a higher purpose, a greater principle. It had chosen me when I was rebellious, a mote of nothing destined for nothingness. I was touched by a grace far greater than I.

I let the grace take me up, away. I expanded like the

huge swelling erection of a god. The Family could use me properly now. I was capable of understanding.

The Ideal, Excellence, was making Its move in Washington, taking out the old imperfect alliance of Courage 3 and the Dallas–Chicago coaxials. Old Ideals must give way to the newer, the better. The Family, as always, needed to be on the winning side. Survival was at stake. But there was a lack, a need. Stale. Thought had grown stale and unproductive, moribund, with nodes like Freddy in Birmingham, Yoakam in New York. Certainly they were loyal. Good Family people.

But no geniuses. No, no geniuses. No geniuses in the Family to draw upon, to use. And Thaddeus Grayson, unattached, doing nobody any good. Freddy, the fool, couldn't even bring in this boy from his own neighborhood. I could feel the Family's longing for Thaddeus, Its brooding need for bettering Itself, to beat back the others, to control, to grow, to destroy all that was not It. I approved. If only Thaddeus weren't dead, I would personally assist in his recruitment. I knew that I could do a damn sight better job than Freddy. The Family felt my pride, knew that it was directed properly, and sent me a wave of approval. I almost fainted with the joy of it. Looking down, I saw that I had come in my pants.

Still a lot to learn about this new way of living. But I would love every minute of the learning.

What the Andy Harco part of my new wholeness had to do: find the killer. Punish the killer, for the hit was made to keep Thaddeus out of the Family. Let the killer know that the Family always either got what It wanted or got revenge. And then I was

to die.

It didn't really matter how I got rid of myself. As long as there was no Family involvement.

Of all these things, I approved.

And so, in the dirty warehouse room, I sat down to think, with the Family behind me. I examined all the Ideals

at work within Birmingham—for it seemed intuitively
clear to me that an Ideal had killed Thaddeus. The poem
fragment was why, the logical bridge from association to
association. How clear it all became now. Now that I had
a real Mind.

God, if only we could have gotten Thaddeus for Us.

I reexamined the records, all of them, of Thaddeus's
comings and goings for the last months of his life. I
laughed when I realized how completely the Family knew
everything, all that people in this city did. All that was
done anywhere in which the Family was interested. What
a fool I was to think I could hide anything, ever, from an
Ideal.

The girl, Trina's, entrances and exits from his apartment. One time, she'd said. One time a day was more like
it! Lying, silly, stupid girl.

In the midst of this examination, there was a flicker in
the corner of the room. I reached to adjust something in my
op-eds and realized that they were gone. I wouldn't be
needing them anymore. Still the flicker. I looked up from
my reverie.

Granddaddy was standing there, smoking a cigarette.

"Hello, son."

Granddaddy.

A shriek deeper and mightier than any cry of pain I've
ever heard. A blast through my mind that I thought would
kill me. A wave of information. No way to assimilate it, let
it crash, let it pass.

And I understood, somehow, in a small part, just what
Granddaddy was. And what that meant to the Ideals.

Granddaddy was spontaneous. Granddaddy had happened while the Ideals weren't looking. Granddaddy was
the integrated organic heart of the city. He *was* Birmingham. More than Abby and her ilk could ever be. The city
that hides behind the city, that lurks in the imagination of
poets and the delusions of bums.

The city that wants nothing of people, that takes noth-

ing, that merely inhabits the power grids, the link nets, the
sewer pipes. That strengthens the people like invisible in-
tegument, holding them together in a way the Ideals never
could. I looked at him again. A holoprojection, using some
surveillance and defense equipment in the warehouse,
probably. But more than a mere image hanging in the air.
So much more.

The Ideals had suspected for years, but there was no evidence, no proof. Only the fact that the plans for incorpo-
rating all individuals seemed to drag inexorably, that
somehow there was always strife when the goals of all the
Minds seemed so clear.

Something was fouling things up.

And now They knew what it was. After all these years,
he'd shown his face.

The Family was terrified. What if there were others?
The Ideals were not prepared for organized resistance.

"You let go of that boy," said Granddaddy.

The Family withdrew from me. *No, oh God, no. Please
stay, please, I beg—*

I stumbled to my feet, dazed.

"Well, son," said Granddaddy. "I don't know how long
I can hold 'em. Now's your chance."

So he knew that, too. The junk I'd had buried so deep
inside me that even I couldn't remember except in dreams.
But now the time had come, and the knowledge rose to my
consciousness like Queequeg's coffin, waterproof, unsink-
able. I grabbed hold, *remembered.* Andy Harco was a rider
program, taken from my brain, fitted to deeper junk, a hidden soul. Andy Harco was a virus allowed to inhabit a
stronger substratum. Andy Harco had rigged his own mind
with a secret weapon against the Ideals.

"The men of iron ore unfluxed," I said. "And the
women with dark and carbon eyes."

It was a line from one of Thaddeus's poems; it was an
activating code. A trigger. I felt the *me* that I'd implanted
in my own brain two years ago coil out of slumber, spread

out into my mind. Become my mind. The simple me at the
base of all my existence. The killer me.

Its sole purpose was to cleanse my brain of all traces of
an Ideal. Any Ideal.

Its only job was to wipe me clean.

My briefcase. I needed my briefcase. Frantically I
looked around.

"It's over there in the corner," Granddaddy said, pointing with the cigarette. He smiled.

And there it was. The Family had thought that I might
need it. Hell, yes, I did! I picked it up and set it on my lap,
flipped it open. I laid the Glock and stungun beside me,
took the Porta-lab out as well. What was left was the froth.
What was left was the static programming and the data that
made up Andy Harco.

My op-eds were gone, but I no longer needed them to
link up with the briefcase. Now I had an Ideal feedhorn on
the back of my head. I felt the wart, hated it, knew it would
always be there as a reminder. I took an old-fashioned optical cable out of a compartment, clipped one end to the
feedhorn. And plugged into the briefcase. I activated the
froth. All the tell-tales burned green. I downloaded my
short-terms into the briefcase, to complete the *me* that was
already there.

Then I looked around for Granddaddy; to tell him
thanks. To tell him good-bye. He was gone.

And with that, I wiped my mind out of existence.

And

      slowly

                returned.

Angry.

7

Because I had been a part of the Family, I now had new information. I knew that the Family didn't kill Thaddeus. I knew where to find Freddy Pupillina. He was in the warehouse, going over the books with the foreman of the place. It was a nanowarehouse, with barrels of hijacked bugs from all over the new South. I passed a couple of cranks shuffling inventory on the way, but they didn't notice me.

Grin-face and Big-boned Bertha were standing outside the door of the office Freddy was in. They were in some sort of discussion, with Grin-face gesticulating wildly, pulling at his beard, and Bertha shaking her head.

I hid behind some barrels, took out the Glock. I was afraid they were wearing body armor, so I took time to aim, to control my breathing. Then I shot them both, quickly, in the head.

The noise alerted Freddy, and he turned out the lights in the office. Smarter than he looks. But I knew—how well I knew—that the Family had told him what to do.

The door of the office opened, and the foreman came stumbling out.

"Don't, please don't," he said, looking around wildly for me. "He's got a gun on me. Please don't—"

"Come over here," I said. I waved an arm, and the foreman stumbled toward me. I took the stungun from the briefcase. When he was close enough, I stood up and zapped him. As he fell, a shot rang out and hit a nearby barrel. I smelled acrid activating nanos as the contents spilled out. These bugs were designed to alter something organic, if not precisely wood.

The floor began to seethe where the nanos touched it, to deform. Soon a section of the flooring was gone and in its place was a lump of a charred and gross thing writhing on the concrete subfloor. Then the nanos started to transform, more slowly, the concrete. Freddy had lucked into some potent stuff. Military shit, probably, bound for the Mideast.

Another shot. It popped into the foreman's back, and blood spurted. Getting sloppy, Freddy.

"Well," I said, and stood up. Freddy fired twice more, missed by a mile. I walked toward the office. He was either reloading or taking better aim. I flung open the door. He opened up on me. Two shots in the chest, but I was ready, and they didn't knock the breath out of me. I quickly fell forward, rolled head over heels.

And came up with the stungun in Freddy's chest. When the juice hit him, he slumped down onto me, his body's own weight keeping him pressed into the gun. I kept the trigger depressed for a long time.

Freddy was a monstrously fat man. I finally put my years of weight training to good use, dragging him out to the nano barrels. I opened one of the barrels with a hand torch I found in the foreman's pocket.

Then I sat down beside Freddy, in the midst of the dead, dangling the Glock absently from one hand. In my other hand, I held Thaddeus's cigarette lighter. I flicked it on, closed the cover, flicked it on again. I tried not to imagine what I was going to do. Anything else.

I began to consider how I would end my Minden Sibley time-traveling detective story. I turned the possibilities over in my mind. None of them really suited me.

I haven't told you, hoping, I suppose, that you would have read them, that you would know it already. But in case you didn't know, the Minden Sibley mysteries usually turn on a humorous point. They are, in fact, satirical comedies of our times. At least that's the idea. Sometimes I get it right, sometimes I fuck up. But when things get really messy, when the plot has reached convolutions unknown even to brain surgeons and French master chefs, then I call upon the trusty Third Temporal Law to get me out of the bind. Minden, good soul that he is, finds himself invoking it at least once a story. It is a tacit law, never taught to any Timeways detective, but understood by all.

3. Break any rule, break *every* rule, even the First
   and Second Temporal Laws. Just don't get
   caught.

Yes, I thought. That's the only way to wrap it up when
logic escapes you and you have a mess that you have to
clean up, one way or another. It's not logical, but it's rational. It's only human.

After a while, Freddy began to come around. I waited
some more. He struggled to sit up. I put the Glock to his
head.

"Don't," I said.

He lay still, his pig eyes flashing in his pulpy face.

"Andy, please—"

"Shut up. I want to talk to the Family."

He shut up. Then there was the blank moment of integration. "We're here," said the Family, through Freddy.
"Hello, Andy."

"You didn't kill Thaddeus," I said.

"No."

"I know who did. This is no longer your problem."

"Well," said the Family. "Good."

"I'm upset about being made a node."

"We felt it necessary."

"Nevertheless, I'm upset."

Freddy screwed his face into an expression of bewilderment. It wasn't much of a reach. "Do you want an . . .
apology?"

"Wouldn't mean anything."

"That is true. Do you want Us to drop the charges
against you for dereliction of duty?"

"You use people and kill them and don't think anything
of it," I said. "Individuals mean shit to you."

"Basically, yes," said the Family. "We know it's hard
for you to comprehend, Andy, but basically, that's what
they are. Shit. Nothing. Individuals are a means, not an
end."

"So," I said. "There's really nothing more to say."

I tipped the barrel over onto Freddy, and skipped back out of the way. The nanos did their work much faster than they had on the wood. Flesh was, obviously, the medium they were tailored to alter.

Freddy screamed horribly, and in that scream I believed—I hoped—that I heard the cries of a hundred others, hurting in unison.

When I left the warehouse, all that was left of Freddy was a puddle of primordial goo.

8

I went home. Mom was all right. She was in some kind of meditation trance, and the patchouli had stunk up the place real good. But she came out of it when I showed up, and flung her arms around my neck. She called me "Meander," just like she had when I was a kid. I couldn't find it in my heart to correct her. Maybe that was my deep, true name. I thought. Amazing the crazy delusions you get when you're relieved over a loved one's safety.

Then she noticed the two holes in my chest, both clotted black with old blood now. She screamed, covered her mouth.

"I'm fine," I said. "I'm a cop. We're used to getting shot."

After that, we didn't say anything for a long time, which was probably for the best.

Then I said, "I have a few things to clear up, Mom, and I'll be back."

"You can't go," she said. "Don't leave again . . . Andy." She was obviously regaining her senses.

"Everything'll be all right. Everything's okay now," I said. "Nobody can touch me now."

I took the beltway, top level, to downtown, then descended into the grid of the city. Through the decaying

Birmingham Green, a leftover jungle, a hundred years old, full of bums, hurtful bugs, bad junk. Urban Renewal. The People Who Know getting it all bassackward as usual. About as effective as adding wine to vinegar.

Up Twentieth Street, through the nightwork of the Southside. Up Red Mountain, the Vulcan's red torch looming up dead ahead. To Abby's place. When no one answered my knock, I kicked in the door. Abby was standing in the living room, gazing out over the city.

"I was expecting you," she said. "Even when they're off traffic control, I still follow every car that moves in my city."

"Your city?"

"Yes!" she said. She flung back her hair defiantly. It shone dully with neon reflections from the window. "My city."

"Why did you kill Thaddeus, Abby?"

"You wouldn't understand."

"Fuck that shit!"

"Very well, then." She took a step toward me. "Politics. His sort of mind becomes a very important, strategic node when integrated into an Ideal. Freddy was going to get him, and with him, Freddy could have overturned City. We couldn't allow that."

"I've heard this before. From the Family."

She sniffed, shrugged. "Well, that make sense. It's only reasonable."

"No," I said. "Not reasonable. Hobbes logic. Billiard-ball logic. People are solids and stripes. Life does not have to be nasty, brutish, and short without a goddamned king to tell us what to do, to shove us around. There's more to life than actions and reactions!"

"Oh, yeah? Well, what are you doing right now, Andy Harco?"

She drifted across the room toward me. Her brown eyes were intense and deep. She held her hands out toward me. I'd forgotten that she'd had artificial nails installed years ago, to break her nail-biting habit. They shone whitely, moon-colored.

"Everything you've done for the last eight years has been a reaction." Her voice was low and soothing. For years, I'd dreamed of it, and awakened with a feeling of utter loss when I found that she was not really beside me.

That feeling washed over me now, stronger than ever before. I raised the Glock. "Justice," I said, "is not reaction."

She stopped, six feet from me, facing me, fearless.

"You going to take me in, Lieutenant?"

I no longer had my op-eds, but I was pretty sure what the Option 4 junk would tell me. If I pulled the trigger, I could never be a cop again.

"This is my town, Lieutenant. My town. Do you think I'll get punished? Do you think I'll spend more than a night in jail? Andy, my brain is part of what runs the jail."

"I could take you with me. I could drive us to Atlanta."

"I'll call every cop in the metro area to stop you," she replied. "Illegal extradition. You know that."

I raised the Glock, took aim at her forehead. "It would be an accident," I said. "Or you resisted."

"City is recording every second of this conversation."

"I just don't give a shit," I said. "I think this is what you are failing to comprehend."

"Don't you, Andy? Then blow me away." She lowered her arms. The child's sad face, those incredible lips. The silver on her arm. The fanatic zombie glow in her eyes.

I lowered the Glock. "It was jealousy, wasn't it?" I said. "Politics didn't have anything to do with it."

Abby let out a long sigh, then said, "I don't know what you're talking about."

"He loved Birmingham more than you. And he was a better lover, too."

"Don't be absurd. Jealousy is for, well, nobodies. For *individuals.*"

"The City chose him, Abby. I know it for a fact."

"No," she said. It was almost a whimper.

"You did it yourself, didn't you?"

She smiled, sadly. "Andy, when are you going to understand, really comprehend?"

"There is no *you*."

"The *I* you used to know is changed and better."

"Good-bye, Abby." I turned to leave. My eyes were misty, though I felt numb inside.

"Just a minute, Andy," she said. I felt the cool touch of her hand on my shoulder, my neck. So soft, so small, her hands had been. I could almost cup them within mine. God, I had loved her so completely. Then a prickle, a sting.

Oh, shit.

The breaking of glass, a stifled scream. I spun around with the Glock at ready.

Trina stood over Abby, a broken bottle of bourbon in her hand. Abby had slumped to the floor, one side of her face webbed with glass cuts. I lowered the Glock once again, took a long breath. A blast spider crawled out of Abby's relaxed palm and began working its way up her arm. Over the silver bracelet and the lily-white skin. Toward her shoulder, toward the porcelain curve of her neck where her spinal cord lay, a pinprick away. There was no put-back routine that could restore a mind after the kiss of a blast spider. Even the mind of a node.

"God, Andy, she was trying to do something to you!" Trina said, unable to take her eyes off her own handiwork. Her op-eds sat skewed on her nose.

"You did the right thing, kid," I said. "The right thing."

I reached over and worked the broken bottle from Trina's hand. She had a damned good grip on the thing.

"I don't think I can stay here anymore," Trina said. "She killed Thaddeus."

Then she started crying, really crying, like she hadn't before. I pulled her toward me, but I didn't want to hug her on account of the dried blood from my chest wounds. I

stroked her face with the hand that didn't hold a gun. I
righted her op-eds.

"Come on, kid," I said. "Let's blow this town."

"Yeah," she said tentatively, then, *"Yeah."*

The blast spider was past Abby's elbow now, working
its way over her armlet. I could almost hear the little
crank's tiny feet clinking against the metal. It was nearly to
her shoulder. . . .

We stepped into the sultry night, Trina and I. I opened
the passenger side of the Saj and helped her inside. She sat
there gazing up at me, trembling slightly. I leaned down
and kissed her, lightly, but on the lips. Then I reached into
my pocket and took out Thaddeus's lighter.

"He would have wanted you to have this," I said, and
folded her brown palm around it.

As I closed the Saj's door, I glanced up into the sky
overhead.

The Vulcan was leering down on me, as big and bright
as the labor of a hundred thousand ironworkers, a hundred
thousand watts of city power, could make him. His red
torch mocked me as surely as his idiotic all-knowing god
smile.

I could shoot the fucker out.

I could. I leaned against the Saj and took aim. But without my op-eds, I would never hit a target that far away.

I pretended to. I pretended to pull the trigger, and in my
mind's eye, I hit that damn torch. I hit it dead-on. But instead of blowing the death light out, in my mind's eye, the
bullet changed the flame from glaring red to vivid living
green.

The Liaden Universe®

by
Sharon Lee and Steve Miller